She spotted the dark, daring demon once again. Dressed in black, he almost blended into the night. Confident and handsome, he uncrossed his booted foot and his arms and turned to face her.

His black jeans, snug on his lean hungry hips, made her suck in her bottom lip. The man was hot. She was going to burn. Maybe get more involved than she wanted. But at the moment she didn't care. Her feet kept stride with the thrumming music.

The honed muscles of his arms beneath the sleeves of his black shirt flexed, giving away his anticipation. She arched her brow. A hint of a smile touched her lips, and her high-heeled steps quickened.

When she was in front of him, face to face, the music stopped, and her surroundings faded away. No one else in the standing-room-only club and nothing else along the bustling river existed, just her and him. Her heart hammered, her knees went weak. But she stood her ground and looked into his eyes. They weren't black, but dark, dark brown. Liquid almost. She could drown in them.

His mouth was full, firm, sinful. And waiting.

"I'll bet you're one of the original sins," she said, sure that he was.

He cracked a devilish smile. "Babe, I'm all of them."

D1608165

Reviews

DEVIL IN COWBOY BOOTS

4 1/2 from Two Lip Review—"...a very hot, sexy read that will draw you in from the first page to the last. The heat between Mercy and Spence is so instantaneous and combustible, you'll be grabbing for some ice. The characters are very believable and well developed and blending in secondary characters and a secondary plot makes this story all the more delicious. This is the first book I've ever read by Sylvie Kaye, but it certainly won't be the last. She has a way of combining humor, intrigue and sensual delights to keep the reader entertained from start to finish! I'm positive you won't be disappointed at any time!"

5 Angels from Fallen Angel Reviews—"Sylvie Kaye packs many sexual experiences, romance, deception, friendship, and wraps it all up within the last few chapters brilliantly. Sylvie's characters have substance and the story flows so well, entangling all of the many elements very seamlessly. DEVIL IN COWBOY BOOTS is a well rounded read with a beautiful end. I'm a sucker for happy endings. If you are, too, do not miss Sylvie Kaye's DEVIL IN COWBOY BOOTS." ~ Tracey

Devil In Cowboy Boots

by

Sylvie Kaye

This is a work of fiction. Names, characters, places, and incidents are either the product of the author's imagination or are used fictitiously, and any resemblance to actual persons living or dead, business establishments, events, or locales, is entirely coincidental.

Devil In Cowboy Boots

COPYRIGHT © 2007 by Sylvie Kaye

All rights reserved. No part of this book may be used or reproduced in any manner whatsoever without written permission of the author or The Wild Rose Press except in the case of brief quotations embodied in critical articles or reviews.

Contact Information: info@thewildrosepress.com

Cover Art by *Angela Anderson*

The Wild Rose Press
PO Box 708
Adams Basin, NY 14410-0706

Visit us at www.thewilderroses.com

Publishing History
First Scarlet Rose Edition, August 2008
Print ISBN 1-60154-393-X

Published in the United States of America

Chapter One

"I've just seen the devil, and Sister Frances Doria was dead wrong." Cindy swooned, pointing toward the mist on the other side of the San Antonio Riverwalk.

"And you're only figuring this out twelve years after graduation." Mercy shook her head before squinting across to the *Starry Night Club*, where fake fog in a hellish shade of green swirled to the sound of live music.

"She didn't tell us he was handsome," Cindy gasped. "She only mentioned the evil part." She turned away. "Don't look. We run the risk of turning into pillars of salt."

"Don't look where?" Mercy stared across the water, but a party boat decked with colorful flowers and small white lights sailed by, blocking her view. The passengers waved, shouting to the landlocked crowds along the walkways.

Mercy waved back, half-hearted, and just as the lounge band at the club on the other side struck up a loud rock beat, the green mist parted to reveal a shadowy masculine figure.

And all hell broke loose within her. The rhythm drummed through her brain, urging her to indeed go out in a "Blaze of Glory," while her breath halted and the close, humid night wrapped itself around her in a hot hug. She stood spellbound by the man's captivating appearance.

Tall, lean, with smoldering eyes that grabbed hold of her insides and made them clench with want.

Mercy had to force her tongue between her lips to speak. "If he's the devil, why is he wearing cowboy

1

boots?"

"Sister Frances Doria never mentioned that part either." Cindy shook her head, apparently at the oversight.

"It's about time we crossed over to my uncle's club." Mercy's breath came in wisps, as if the man drew the air from her lungs and throat and pulled it across the river to him. All the while his dark eyes seared into her soul.

"Let's wait until later," Cindy said. "I doubt he's the type for what you have in mind."

"He's not a type." Mercy sighed. "That man invented hot and steamy." The black, smoky depths of his stare dared her to come to him.

Fluid, sexy, and relaxed, he leaned his provocative body against the wall of the brick balcony and crossed one booted foot over the other. The fake green fog lingered at his heels.

Mercy's pulse picked up speed. "I'd bet my next life he's the one."

Cindy studied him and scowled. "How can you tell?"

"I can feel it between my thighs...oh, never mind exactly where, but trust me, I know he's the man of my fantasies."

"I've had fantasies fulfilled by men that didn't look like they've been to hell and back. I think you should wait. You've only been in town two days."

"If I stay uninvolved emotionally, he's perfect for me. While you live here now, I don't. In two weeks when my vacation's over, it's back to Pennsylvania and my bland existence for who knows how long."

"Promise you won't do anything hasty."

"I'll look but not touch." She yanked Cindy by the arm and elbowed her way through the people milling the crafty gift shops, fragrant flower stands, and savory sidewalk restaurants.

When she glanced back, he hadn't moved.

Impatience pulsed through her veins and her pussy as he continued to stand in the fading green haze as if waiting for her.

"I wish you'd hold out for a man who looks capable of more than a one night stand." Cindy hopped on one foot to adjust the strap of her platform shoe. "No, I take that back. Two. Just to make the point that he can do you again at will."

"I'm aiming for a dozen one-nighters," Mercy said, the pounding beat of the music ever driving her forward. "Enough hot, unforgettable sex to see me through the endless boredom of my medical transcription job in Lily Pond, where the baddest boy in town thinks a G-spot is somewhere on the golf course."

They climbed the stone steps that led to the bridge and to the fulfillment of the uncontrollable need she somehow knew he could satisfy. Once on the other side, she let go of Cindy. They shouldered through the people, single file, until they reached the blue-canopied entrance to the club.

"I can't watch this. I'm getting a cold drink. Something *not* called Sex on the Beach." Cindy headed for the bar, and Mercy followed the music out onto the balcony where the green fog had dissipated.

She spotted the dark, daring demon once again. Dressed in black, he almost blended into the night. Confident and handsome, he uncrossed his booted foot and his arms and turned to face her.

His black jeans, snug on his lean hungry hips, made her suck in her bottom lip. The man was hot. She was going to burn. Maybe get more involved than she wanted. But at the moment she didn't care. Her feet kept stride with the thrumming music.

The honed muscles of his arms beneath the sleeves of his black shirt flexed, giving away his anticipation. She arched her brow. A hint of a smile touched her lips, and her high-heeled steps quickened.

When she was in front of him, face to face, the music stopped, and her surroundings faded away. No one else in the standing-room-only club and nothing else along the bustling river existed, just her and him. Her heart hammered, her knees went weak. But she stood her ground and looked into his eyes. They weren't black, but dark, dark brown. Liquid almost. She could drown in them.

His mouth was full, firm, sinful. And waiting.

"I'll bet you're one of the original sins," she said, sure that he was.

He cracked a devilish smile. "Babe, I'm all of them."

She tried to remember all seven but she could only recall pride. He had a right to be proud. His body was to die for. He looked like he could take her to all the erotic places she wanted to go.

Her fingers twitched with the temptation to run them through his slightly longish, thick, black hair. But that was only for starters. Where on his sleek body wouldn't she like to touch? She inhaled deeply, only to fill her lungs with his manly scent, which brought another sin to mind, lust.

"Recounting all your sins?" he asked, his voice low and soul searching.

Not only was the devil a mind reader, but the sound of his lulling voice erased any embarrassment she might have felt at getting caught checking out his sinful assets. Nothing she did or said around him seemed to make her flush with anything other than an aching need deep in her core.

She shook her head, wishfully.

"Denial." He reached out to touch her jaw, and she thought about stepping back, her no-touching promise to Cindy flashing briefly through her mind.

But, technically, she wasn't laying a hand on the

man.

Spence stroked a finger along her jawline. The movement slow. The moment endless. Her skin felt tender and warm to his touch.

His nerve endings sizzled. He hadn't meant for her to scorch him. From the second he'd spotted her on the other side of the river, all blonde and honeyed, he'd played with her to pass the time. She wasn't his type. Too wholesome. Too innocent. Hell, there wasn't an inch of spandex or leather anywhere on her body.

Yet his finger lingered on the soft, delicate skin along her jaw, wanting to trail down the curve of her slender neck into the sloping vee-neckline of her body-hugging, ivory dress. But he checked himself, pulled away. She was so fresh-faced beautiful.

She'd cause him trouble. Her kind wanted more than he was able to give. He should leave, walk away.

"My name's Mercy," she said, when the last thing he wanted to know was her name.

Her voice sounded husky and desirable, hitting him in the lower gut. His cock strained inside his jeans.

"Mercy's an appropriate name for picking up sinners." He crooked a half smile, wondering if he could scare her off. Save himself the trouble of turning tail and leaving.

She smiled fully, rosy-lipped. Sexy. Tantalizing. Mercy. He'd need a lot of that for what he'd like to do with her mouth.

Starting with shoving his tongue halfway down her throat until she moaned his name and ending with her swallowing his cum to prove she was his and his alone. But nice girls didn't do those things, and the women who did he avoided exchanging first names or body fluids with. That's what nicknames and Trojans were for.

5

Mercy hadn't asked his name, and he hadn't decided yet if he would give it to her if she did. Although he damn well knew he shouldn't even be considering the notion.

"Do you have a name, sinner?" Her eyes shone blue and innocent like salvation and he found that way too tempting.

Spence made his decision.

"Sinner will do." For now, a part of him thought. When all of him should've vowed forever. Revealing his name might make her more permanent than right-now. He was treading into a dangerous area. Nothing was as seductive as her goodness.

He waited for her to bolt. But the sweet thing stood there, gloriously ready to take him on, her body oozing with feminine sexuality. Everything from her fingers to her legs was long and slender, made for loving. Licking.

Could he take advantage of her? His swelling dick shouted yes. Somewhere in the back of his brain another voice whispered no, not unless he wanted to remain lost for all time.

For now, he dwelled with his own kind. The hopeless. Lost souls who buried their problems in each other's bodies for a night and moved on. Streetwise people.

She smiled and nodded, her pretty halo of blonde hair bobbing with the movement. "Interesting name. Do you dance, Sinner?"

The band had returned from their short break to strike up the chords to some song. He knew he was going to give in to her for tonight. Probably condemn his soul further by doing the dirty with the clean, young thing. But he wasn't going to go down easy.

"I don't dance to anyone's tune but my own," he dared.

Her smile widened, her lips moist and pink and beckoning. "Then this is your song."

He listened, chuckled. The band played a Texas two-step and the lead singer was crooning, "She's got the devil in her eyes."

Chapter Two

Once on the saw-dusted dance floor, Sinner danced to his own music all right, a much slower rhythm than the band played. He held her so close Mercy could barely breathe. Her breasts pressed against his broad chest in a soft crush.

Her nipples ached and swelled, and she'd only known the man a few minutes. Regardless of what Cindy thought, he was definitely the one—the man to help her reach sexual Utopia. Something she couldn't achieve in the staid, small community back home where everyone knew everyone's comings and goings.

And this was all about coming.

"Careful," he murmured.

If he'd been reading her mind again, his warning came way too late. Between his husky voice and his warm breath near her ear, thrills spiraled to her hot, wet pussy where she craved his attention the most. Any thought of caution seeped from her body.

Only when his strong arm wrapped around her waist to right her balance did she realize his advice was directed at her dance missteps.

Mercy tried once again to concentrate on her feet. *Slide, slide, step, step, step.* But sliding with Sinner across the floor wasn't something she could keep her mind on for long. His taut muscles, stretching sensuously from his thighs to his lean hips, incited a fascinating distraction. While his legs moved in time with hers, his groin clashed against hers.

And another muscle, which he made no attempt to hide, flexed against her belly, foretelling of a dance that needed no music and she was sure would have a much wilder rhythm.

Sinner felt hard and hot—and huge. Mercy sucked in a moan.

Her head spun with hazy plans. Her first vacation away from home in years was the ideal time and place to let her hormones run wild. Who knew when she'd get another opportunity? Her breathing was labored, she snuggled closer. The fantasies she'd read about, dreamed about, wondered about, were as close as this man's body heat.

Through half-lowered lids, she gazed up at him. Tall, sleek-muscled, sexy. His cocksure jaw shouted out his confidence. He'd probably given lots of women lots of fantastic orgasms. She exhaled, long and slow, uncertain of her next move.

Maybe she should edge away, play a *little* hard-to-get, but with him holding her so near...actually, he was barely touching her with those marvelous, strong hands of his. One rested lightly at her hip, the other at her shoulder.

While she clung to him like her favorite dream.

How in the devil had he managed that?

Feeling wanton, she didn't pull away from his steamy body and the promise of things to come. And she planned to come. Sinner didn't look like the kind of man to leave a woman hanging.

In need of a shave, Sinner's rough chin rested against her forehead, its scratchy tingle arousing and sensual. She sighed, catching a hint of his masculine scent, a woodsy aftershave mingled with whiskey.

His breathing was even and steady, and she wondered if she could make him gasp and groan. Mercy certainly intended to try.

9

Shutting her eyes, she let herself experience his heartbeat. The thud sounded faint and faraway, as if a wall were built up around his heart. Suddenly, she wanted to break down all his barriers.

Quite a feat for a two-week vacation, if she even stood a chance. So far, he hadn't offered anything. Not even this dance.

She'd asked him.

Mercy looked up into his eyes, so dark her own were reflected there. He'd been watching her. His intense gaze melted her pussy, and a gratifying heat pooled between the folds. A good sign. Her desire was running hot and high. A climax in the making, she hoped, along with a few other fantasies she'd like him to bring about. She swallowed dry air, and then licked her lips to moisten them before smiling up at him. He didn't smile back. His mouth remained stern, firm, and so temptingly near.

"So what do you do, Sinner, besides sin?"

"Ranch."

He certainly didn't give much away.

She nodded. "Do you have a ranch?"

"Spread."

Now? How wide?

Her eyes rounded, she missed another beat, another step.

His serious mouth cracked a smile as if he'd once again read her thoughts.

"I have a small spread and ranch house."

Oh. She nodded again. "Aren't you going to ask me what I do?"

"Nope."

Her smile faded for a second. But then in a quick, white-hot fantasy, like the one she was after with Sinner, if it even lasted the length of her vacation, she imagined a whole lot of information wasn't necessary.

She stroked her hand over his taut shoulder.

10

Radiating heat scorched her palm. Slowly, she trailed down his soft, cotton T-shirt and over his hard biceps, which flexed beneath her fingers. The man's body was made for exploration and she hoped to make a full expedition of it. She sucked in her bottom lip and stared up at him.

"I take it we're through dancing." His words were silky and slow, but struck between her thighs with the quickness of a heat flash before a summer storm.

"The music hasn't stopped yet," she said, coyly, enjoying the hunger she saw in his eyes. Making him groan for Mercy was starting to look like a possibility.

"For us it has." He dropped his arms from her body and stepped back.

He stood in front of her in the middle of the dance floor while the other couples circled them. Her only contact with him came from the exquisite steam their bodies gave off and the intensity of their eyes, each searching the other's for what they wanted, needed, demanded.

Spence hadn't realized Mercy would have a demanding streak. But she was so damn hot. She had him by the stones. He couldn't walk away now. Not without having her at least once.

"It's time we talk about my spread," she said, teasingly, slipping her small soft hand into his large rough one. His blood pumped hot, firing all his pistons so hard and fast he couldn't turn her down now if he wanted.

"When such provocative things come out of your mouth, I have to wonder if you can live up to them."

Inwardly, he smiled at her guts. It both surprised and weakened him each time her innocent-looking pink mouth talked trashy.

She tugged on his hand to move him along. He dropped hers. Bad enough her sweet sensuality had sucker-punched him, but he wasn't handholding some first date here. He was only looking to get laid.

He draped his arm over her bare, slender shoulder, running his knuckles along her smooth jaw as he walked her away from the stifling, stale air of the dance floor toward the steps leading off the balcony and the hint of a fresh river breeze below.

She stared up at him. Her eyes large, blue, and trusting.

"Where to?" he asked, stopping before their descent, giving her a last chance to back down.

He wasn't sure why. His cock wanted her anyway he could take her, while something inside him remembered how a man desired a cherished woman, for all time, for life, love, and marriage. Crazy. He ran his fingers through his hair as if to wipe out the warring notions.

"I'm not sure where." She sounded uncertain but brave.

By her technique so far tonight, he could tell she wasn't used to making bold advances. A cold spot near his heart warmed and the hot spot near his fly cooled.

"Let's just take a walk." He peered down into bottomless blue eyes that did things to him that were more intimate than sexy.

"Wait." A female voice screeched from somewhere behind him as they stepped forward.

The sound cringed his nerve endings, but he glanced over his shoulder anyway. It came from that woman who'd been with Mercy when he first saw her on the other side of the river.

"Wait. We have to talk." The woman with the floppy hair and floppy mouth was hotfooting in their direction. Her short brown hair flying, helter-skelter, along with her yellow-flowered wedged shoes.

He clenched his back teeth but waited. What had he gotten himself into here? He wasn't into threesomes...at least he hadn't been in a while.

"I'll only be a moment." Mercy darted out from under his arm toward her friend.

While the two women chattered with their heads together, he scanned the nightclub. For a few distracted minutes with Mercy, he'd let her suck him into her sexy, carefree space, almost causing him to forget why he was here.

He jammed his fingers through his hair again. This had to be the first time in two years Parker hadn't consumed his thoughts. And, since he'd hit town several weeks ago, his ever-searching eyesight. So far, he hadn't been able to hook up with the bastard, missing the man by fleeting opportunities each time.

With no sign of the murdering, lying sonuvabitch, the night had been slow until Mercy came along to relieve his boredom. Once he'd given in to the idea of her relieving a lot more, his balls ached.

Until a moment ago, when her soft blue eyes and sweet scent had clouded his mind. *Let's take a walk.* Had he really said those words? Had he been willing to give up watching for Parker, unsuccessful as tonight's outlook was, to go for a mere walk?

With another glance at her hot ass, he shook off the dumb idea and lust returned with a vengeance. If he kept his needs restricted to below the waist, he'd be better off. He couldn't afford to screw up.

He scanned the place again, slower this time. No Parker. None of his lowlife flunkies either. Or Google, a man who'd search out and sell any information for a price.

He breathed deep and smiled, slowly. He still had Mercy in his sights. The night wasn't totally shot to hell.

****

"Where do you think you're going with the evil

13

one?" Cindy tapped the wedged sole of her platform shoe, smudging a trail through the sawdust scattered from the dance floor.

"We're going for a walk and he's not evil. He's just a sinner," Mercy guaranteed her friend with a pat to her shoulder.

Their parochial school upbringing had made Cindy overly cautious. While all that uptight restraint eventually had caught up to Mercy, urging her to make up for lost time.

Cindy nodded toward a table near the bar where another woman and three men sat. "I hooked up with some friends from work. My coworker, Jay—he's the non-devilish, clean-cut one with the sandy hair and freckles, a man a woman can feel secure with." She paused for effective.

"Yes, yes." Mercy checked if Sinner was still waiting. His dark, lusty eyes rested on her. The moist inner lips of her vagina quivered.

"Jay knows a bartender who knows where your sinner lives if we have to prosecute," Cindy persisted.

Mercy rolled her eyes. "The man's only crime is he's too sexy for his own good." Waving bye to Cindy, she took off toward Sinner.

"Do you have your cell phone?" Cindy called after her.

"In my pocket." She smoothed her hand over the slash of material in her dress where her phone would remain in its off mode so as not to disturb her and Sinner.

Chapter Three

"Ready?" Sinner drawled when Mercy returned to his side.

She nodded. She was more than ready to take the plunge with Sinner. She'd been waiting for a man like him for what seemed like forever.

His hard, confident body and demeanor sent the message he could take her to the edge, show her the precipice, and jump off with her to ride the rush to orgasm.

"I've been in dress rehearsal all my life," she said with an assuring wink.

"We'll see about the dress part later," he murmured near her ear. His hot breath and suggestive tone strummed through her, racing her pulse and puckering her nipples. He must've changed his mind about going for a simple stroll. A shiver of excitement clenched her vaginal walls as she smiled up at the rangy, tall man steering her toward the exit.

They took the spiral metal steps leading from the balcony at a fast pace. Laughter and chatter from the mingling people above and below clashed with music from the competing barrooms along the river, making it hard to hear the clank of the stairs beneath their feet. But she felt each rapid thud through the soft soles of her leather high heels. Urgency became palpable between them.

Once down onto the body-crushing riverwalk, he took her hand in his warm, firm one. Expectation heated her blood and sped up her heartbeat. The idea of sex with Sinner flamed her body with enough fire to cause friction in the satiny crotch of her panties.

Her leg brushed against his as they hurried. His thigh muscles were long, lean, and strong. They held the promise of stamina, the kind of legs to take a woman to orgasm while standing up. She'd read about such muscular balance in one of last month's women's mags, and the fantasy flushed her mind and her body with scalding heat.

"Sure you don't want to change your mind?" he asked when a flower vendor caused a bottleneck in the pathway, stalling their progress.

She'd change her roundtrip ticket home before that happened. But he sounded like the one who wanted to back out.

"If you're having second thoughts..." She shrugged with a nonchalance she didn't feel. Disappointment pooled in her belly. "Just kiss me good-bye." She gazed at his lush mouth. "Otherwise the curiosity will kill me."

"Curiosity?"

"To know if you taste as good as you look."

With a low growl, he took her challenge despite the people sandwiching them from both sides. Lowering his head, he kept his lips teasingly out of reach at first.

Then his hot mouth met hers, melting her bones and pooling fluid in her womb. Her knees went rubbery, but his steadying grip on her waist kept her upright. Her mind swirled with hot, carnal flashes of Sinner's cock sliding deep inside her. She moaned, ready for lavish tongue-on-tongue action when he pulled his potent lips from hers.

"Things are moving again." His dark, bold eyes drilled into hers. His breathing edgy.

She wanted to move, but beneath him. A wistful sigh escaped her lips. "Are we going forward or back?" Or both, along with in-and-out. She waited,

16

standing her ground even as a heavyset man and woman jostled her.

His eyes held hers for a long moment as if deciding something weighty. "Lead the way," he said, not swaying her in either direction.

She tucked her arm into his strong one and headed away from the *Starry Night Club*. Need and the fire low in her belly ignited by his kiss drove her on. If the touch of Sinner's sensational mouth in the midst of a crowd could so easily bring her to the brink of such simmering desire, imagine what a full-blown kiss along a deserted section of the Riverwalk could arouse.

Eventually, they followed the meandering river and the sound of rippling water instead of staying with the crowd. The stone path felt uneven beneath the thin soles of her strappy-heeled sandals. Wooden benches beckoned, but they passed them by. Fragrant white and pink flowers stirred as they brushed past. The air felt thick and warm like a lover's cum.

When they edged through a narrow portion of the pathway, she trailed her fingers over an area of a stone wall, wishing they'd stop and sit and she'd taste more of his kisses. That he'd go deeper and longer this time.

But Sinner pushed ahead, taking her hand and the lead. Soon the walkway widened and they were side by side again. Laughter. Two giggling women hustled in the opposite direction. Whistling. A lone man with his hands in his pockets strolled in the shadows but was soon overtaken by them. Whispers. A couple cuddled on a nearby garden bench.

Mercy and Sinner moved onward into the darkness with only an occasional street lamp to light the path.

When they reached a lonely bend in the waterway, abandoned by even the stragglers they'd encountered, Sinner signaled to an empty bench, then released her hand and sat down.

With his arms sprawled across the slatted back of the bench and his booted ankles crossed, he looked up at her, watching her through slit lids. Slashes of his dark, fluid eyes both challenged and turned her on as she stood in front of him.

"Come, sit." He tossed his head, motioning to one of his outstretched arms and the space next to him on the green-painted bench.

She didn't want to sit next to him. She expected more. Much more from Sinner. Should she dare to follow her brazen instincts?

She breathed in the heavy, humid night air. Had she come this far to chicken out? Returning home to her unsatisfying sex life with nothing more adventuresome than the missionary position to look forward to flashed through her mind. Here was the answer to her lusty dreams, a hunk of masculinity sitting, waiting for her to let go of her restraints and claim him as her prize. She licked her lips.

"That spot looks too hard," she said silkily, sidling a glance at the wooden seat.

Raising her gauzy skirt ever so slightly, she slowly edged the hem higher until the warm breeze chilled her heated thighs. He tilted his head back and narrowed his gaze even more, but she caught the glazed look he tried to hide as she straddled his lap.

Fitting her legs through the open back of the bench, she snuggled her breasts against his wide, muscled chest before wriggling down tightly onto his denim-covered crotch. The slow slide of her naked thighs against the roughness of his jeans caused an exciting tingle to travel upwards and settle in her vagina.

"And maybe this spot will get even harder," he mumbled.

Her thighs gripped his hips. A sigh slipped from her lips. A half-grin stifled his moan of pleasure.

Both her hesitancy and brashness amused Spence. Compared to the women he'd been with, she was as green as the new grass he'd been meaning to plant near the ranch house porch. She brought a freshness and lightness to his heart that he didn't want there but had a difficult time denying himself.

She tangled her long, delicate fingers into his hair and cradled his head. Her nails lightly massaged his scalp, the movements more comforting than sexual. He relaxed into her hands and waited to see what the sweet thing thought would rock his world. Her fearless inexperience was as much a turn on as some of his most erotic fantasies.

And rock she did. She rolled forward and her soft, warm pussy spread and notched itself over his crotch. He could feel the lips of her sex stretch wide through the silkiness of her panties, gliding over the coarse denim of his jeans. His hard-on reacted like a fist, stiffening and gripping in his gut.

He groaned. She smiled, pleased with herself.

Lifting his head, he bit at her bottom lip and tugged her to him. He fought for all he was worth to keep his feet grounded and his hands on the bench when what he desired most was to slip past her panties, grab hold of her hips, and pump for all his worth.

Instead, he sucked her lip into his mouth. She tasted sweet, slick, and warm like he knew the lips of her pussy would. He worked over her mouth, crushing it, wanting to consume and own her if only for this one night.

All thoughts of what he wanted dissolved when she flicked her tongue to his lips. Gentle, wet, and inviting. She traced its velvety tip over his upper lip before slowly moving to his lower one, sending lusty promises down his spine, straight to his rigid and now quivering prick.

"Babe—" he started to say, but she slipped her tongue inside his mouth and in no time the only form of oral communication he cared about was mating with her hot tongue.

His heart pounded in his chest. Even through the fullness of her breasts and her pebbled nipples, he felt her fluttery heartbeats against his powerful ones. His fingers ached to let go of the back of the bench, but if he uncrossed his ankles, his dick would become an unstoppable presence to reckon with.

He barely managed to hold back. His tongue simulated fuck games with hers until he ached from blue balls. She was killing him with pleasure. He was going to die with his boots on and a hard-on to be envied. Yet, he refused to make any moves on her first. He was going out with a clear conscience.

About her anyway.

He tried to push thoughts of Parker and the *Starry Night Club* from his mind for the meantime. But from this vantage point along the river it wasn't easy. He had a clear view of the club. After a quick glimpse to the street above to assure him a gaudy red Caddy wasn't parked in the club's lot, he squeezed his eyes shut and concentrated on her silky tongue, her lush breasts, and the scent of her skin. Fresh. Powdery. Not cloying and heavy like what he was used to. He inhaled her. The sunny fragrance of her hair where blonde wisps tickled his cheek, her honeyed breath panting beneath the pressure of his mouth, and the womanly scent of her dewy skin all smelled delicious. He wanted to lick the flavor of her body, taste her perky nipples, and sample her innermost places.

There were a lot of things he wanted that had been put on hold until after he evened the score with Parker. For his dead friend Mark's sake as well as for his own peace of mind.

But the only *piece* he wanted to think about at this moment was Mercy. He planned on giving her whatever her sultry, hot body desired. But nothing extra. He couldn't afford to get into it, into her, too deeply.

He trailed a kiss down her neck. Nipped at the spot where her throat and shoulder met. She didn't disappoint. She was salty, musky, and mouth watering. Everything a man craved in a woman.

"Sinner," she murmured, and Spence remembered his name. His name for tonight with her. Others called him worse things. Things she was better off not knowing.

"Hmm," he answered.

"Do you want to tell me what you like, and I'll tell you what I'd like?" She leaned back on his lap. Her lips were swollen from his kisses. Her eyes glittered with desire.

She wanted to chat, and as much as he enjoyed when her banter turned dirty, especially in her amateurish style and her ladylike tone, he had no plans to get better acquainted with her. Not verbally anyway.

The look on his face must've told her so because she hastened to add, "For starters, what kind of condoms do you use?"

"Ribbed," he growled. Grasping her vee-neckline in his fingers, where he'd wanted to get his hands from the first, he tugged.

She rocked forward, smiled, and then slid back again. Her eyes turned a darker, glassier blue. She moved again, setting a sensual rhythm. Slow, grinding, mesmerizing.

He slipped his hand into her lacy bra. The material of her flimsy, ivory-colored dress was pale against his skin. Cupping her silken breast, he teased her already puckered nipple. The tip was so stiff and so ready for him. He rolled the nub between his fingers, pinched it lightly, plucked it until she moaned.

All throaty and sexy. A turn on that strained at the fly of his jeans.

In the throes of passion, she tossed back her head, exposing a tender throat, the delicate skin throbbing with her murmurs.

He couldn't take his eyes off her. Every move and sound she made was hypnotic.

Her eyelids fluttered as she sat back again. "Do you have a *ribbed* condom with you?"

His thumb stopped, paralyzed on her nipple. This time her question was less about getting to know him and more to the point.

"Uh-huh." He nodded, closing his eyes for a moment, thanking his lucky star. She was going to fuck him. Although she'd acted like she would, had teased and gone through the motions, he'd figured her to split and run before anything too sweaty or too gritty took place.

With an exhale, he opened his eyes and with a last squeeze wriggled his hand free from her breast to jam it into his pocket. When she widened her thighs to give him pocket-digging room, he instantly missed the heat and contact of her tight body.

Extracting the condom from his jeans, he dangled the foil packet between his fingers, wondering if non-streetwise women knew how to handle rubbers. With a grin, he taunted, "Do you know how to rip and roll?"

Her slender hand stopped short of the packet, and he knew she didn't. Her girlish hesitancy gave him pleasure. Suddenly he wanted to be the first. The first man she sheathed in rubber. *Ribbed* rubber.

She glanced over her satiny shoulder, to the right and then to the left, obviously checking out their state of privacy. But he knew here at the bend in the waterway, they were out of sight enough. If she was daring enough.

"I read a how-to," she said, taking the foil square from his fingers. "If you don't mind being my test subject."

Mind? He couldn't believe his stroke of fortune. "Practice away."

She slid off his lap, bent at the waist, and tugged the metal closure of his fly. Her fingers were cool and gentle against his belly, less than adept at opening his jeans. The corded muscles in his legs and back twitched from having stayed still for so long, but he wasn't about to move and blow things now. Not unless Mercy asked him to.

Hell, who was he kidding? Even if she ordered him to, as far gone as she had him now, he'd obey her.

But she succeeded in loosening the metal button and then went after his zipper.

"Uncross your legs," she said in a whispery soft but matter-of-fact voice.

Spence uncrossed his ankles, giving her the space she needed to unzip him. She slipped to her knees between his thighs and tugged. The metallic teeth began to grind down slowly, exposing an ever-widening vee of dark curls with each inch of denim that gave way. Finally, his erection sprang loose, popping up its head like a one-eyed jack.

"*Mmm,*" she murmured her admiration, and his cock bobbled almost taking a bow. She grinned. "I think a reward's in order."

"For the right reward it might roll over and bark," he said gruffly.

Mercy laughed, slight and throaty, a wet dream come true kneeling between his legs. She tugged on the waist of his jeans to loosen them even further. He arched his spine to assist her.

Interesting, very interesting, all blonde, slender,

and sexually willing.

A pearly drop formed on the tip of his dick. He clenched his jaw and his gut. She'd better hurry before he shot his wad and became worthless to her.

That's when she began reading the condom packet, aloud. "Twist and shout?" She arched her eyebrow and stared up at him.

"There's a twist at the tip. To stimulate both partners. Do you need a sex-ed class before we go on?" He was feeling vulnerable and exposed, and if she asked any more questions, he was going to go soft or go off. And either one was an embarrassment.

At last, she tore the square open and carefully peeled away the foil, holding him spellbound with each graceful but swift motion of her long, nimble fingers.

He gulped. His throat went dry when she placed the rolled condom in her moist, open mouth.

After that, he didn't need any *twisted-pleasure-rubber* to stimulate his nerve endings or heighten his sensitivity. With her mouth open wide and her blonde halo of hair descending over his lap, she made the most erotic picture he'd ever seen. His stomach tightened as his cock twitched. He held his breath, feeling as if his eyes were about to cross.

He moaned out loud as soon as her soft lips touched the end of his penis. He didn't care if she heard him. Bets were off. Games were over. She won, hands down. No hands, really.

When she pressed down on the head of his cock, her tongue hot through the membrane of the rubber, his restraint almost popped. He gritted his teeth until perspiration broke out across his forehead.

As she took him further into her mouth, she kept her firm, moist lips wrapped tight around his shaft. The slow, inching pleasure almost killed him as his heart slammed in his chest.

Gentle pressure and friction from her mouth

enclosed him, sending shudders through his body as her lips and her tongue unrolled the condom onto his shaft. What sweet torture.

"Mercy," he hissed her name or maybe it was a plea.

She looked up at him with a proud smile as she finished unrolling the rubber all the way to the base of his dick with the help of her cool fingers.

Between the delicious heat from her mouth, followed by the chill of her diligent fingers, he'd reached his edge.

He grasped her hair in both his hands. "That was great, baby, but I can't wait any longer."

When she rose, he grabbed onto her hips to help her up onto his lap. Pushing the nylon crotch of her panties aside, he embedded himself into her slick, hot pussy in one quick motion.

He hadn't meant to be so forceful, but he'd lost his head. Both of them. And so quickly. He'd buried himself to the hilt, yet couldn't get close enough, go deep enough.

She moaned, taking in his length before starting a steady, stroking advance-and-withdraw motion that slowly built in momentum.

He grasped her hips and arched his own to mark the rhythm she set. He smothered his face in her neck, hugged her breasts to his chest, losing himself in Mercy, drowning in the scent of her musky sex. The sound of her panting breath. The softness of her giving body.

He gasped for air, lifting his head away from her devouring sexuality and spied a flash of color from the corner of his eye. Parker's Cadillac glittered in the distant neon glow from the *Starry Night Club*.

What to do?

She was still working it; he'd gone still.

Come?

Go?

Come first.

Then go.

Why now?

He groaned. He'd waited for that son-of-a-bitch Parker for weeks.

Aw, hell.

His cock, not to mention Mercy, was going to hate him for this, but he couldn't take the chance of letting Parker slip away.

Not taking her to orgasm wasn't his style, but...

"Sorry." He winced, and with one swift move and a pop of suction-releasing contact, he lifted her from his lap to set her on the bench while he took off on a run after Parker's Caddy.

Mercy shrieked as he sprinted toward the bend in the river. He tossed a brief glance over his shoulder and saw he'd missed his target. She landed on the gravel path in front of the bench on her ass.

While he zipped up his still rubber-encased dick and ran for all he was worth, he heard her. Instead of cursing him, when she had every right to, she was grumbling something nonsensical.

"Sister Doria was right-on about pride going before a fall."

Chapter Four

"Sinner."

Spence heard Mercy call his name, but he kept moving. He couldn't go back. He had to keep his focus on the prize. For Mark as well as for himself.

He had hardly believed the neon-blinking stars shining their garish blue lights on the red Caddy, making it appear purple in the parking lot of the *Starry Night*. Too bad his break had come while he was deep inside Mercy. She was the only sweetness to enter his battered life in the past two years.

While he raced up the pathway, he glanced back one last time and smacked into the flower vendor, nearly toppling the guy. Shoving some money at the sturdy man, he told him what to do with his flowers and stepped up his pace.

Up ahead, he ran into more problems when the crowd thickened and slowed him down yet again. Boldly, he pushed by whatever bodies got in his way. As he closed the distance between himself and the stone overpass leading to the nightclub above, the street became denser with bustling people. His pace snailed with the crossover still yards ahead of him.

He felt bad about Mercy, for leaving her sexually unfulfilled. But he had to get to the *Starry Night*. He had to keep his eye on the prize. On Parker.

He elbowed through a laughing group who threatened to make him wait while they bought ice cream. Damn it, but he'd waited long enough to get his hands on the slimy owner of the club. Two years with little else to think about.

A young woman shrieked an indignant slur as

he rushed by, his shoulder jamming her vanilla cone into her chin. When her young man shoved him back, he grunted an apology to the couple but didn't pause. What the hell was one jab to his ribs compared to the pain Parker had inflicted on him after Mark's death.

He'd been convicted and sent to jail for the manslaughter of his best friend on testimony from the lying son of a bitch.

A renewed surge of determination drove him forward. He remained untouched by the looks of surprise or annoyance on the once-happy faces of those who got in his way. People out to drink, dance, eat, and have a good time. Like he and Mark had that fatal night.

Finally, he broke from the crowd and bolted for the cement steps leading to the streets above. Curses followed his thudding footsteps.

Once on the sidewalk, he raced like an Olympic runner. His arms and legs pumped hard to close the few blocks distance.

No traffic at the intersection. Luck might be his lady for the night.

Then he came upon it. The spot of the incident, where Mark died and his own life changed forever.

He ran even harder, if that was possible. His blood pulsed in his ears, his heart pounded as if it would burst. But his heart had already been ripped apart by the happenings of that hateful night.

Police sirens, ambulances, a jail cell. Recollections flashed as he forced a hard dash and ran past the ditch where his dreams had died.

Up ahead, neon lights swirled out the letters *Starry Night Club* in a twinkle of fake blue stars. He urged his legs to work harder, faster. They ached. His muscles protested, burned. The humidity hugged his skin like a glove. His lungs fought for air as he spurred himself to keep going. For Mark. For himself. For his sanity.

He dodged a man and woman, arm in arm, who were leaving the restaurant next to the club.

Headlights flickered in the parking lot up ahead. The red Caddy's engine roared. He was so near he could smell the exhaust fumes. The glow of taillights glittered like eyes in the night as the car pulled out right in front of him. He gulped for air. A spurt of adrenaline shot him forward. He was near enough to touch the red metallic paint on the rear fender of the sleek car as it slipped through his fingers.

He stood gasping, bent over, wet with perspiration while the car disappeared before his blurry eyes. Sweat mixed with tears. Frustration settled in. He railed at himself. He should've been here.

Instead of seeking solace in Mercy.

****

Mercy had never been dumped by a man in quite this way before.

She brushed gravel from her panties and the back of her dress as she got to her feet.

Just what had been Sinner's problem?

She was certain he hadn't come. And neither had she. At this rate she was never going to reach the illusive big 'O' or fulfill the sexy fantasies she'd read and dreamed about.

She groaned. What did she expect fooling around with a man called Sinner? Orgasmic Nirvana?

Damn. She straightened the ivory skirt of her dress, rubbing at a spot of dirt near the hem. At least her dry cleaner would be in ecstasy when she got another twelve bucks closer to her retirement Mecca in Boca Raton.

Who the hell did Sinner think he was with his strong arms and tantalizing mouth and the promise of an orgasm that had been so close her clit quivered even now? She rubbed her legs together to rid herself of the notion of him inside her, hot and stiff.

Exhaling, she let off some of her anger along with some of her steamy, sexual frustration. She really should look into buying a vibrator. She'd seen an ad in the back of this month's *Women's Way* magazine for The Magic Wand. Came in iridescent colors, too. Hard, shiny, satisfying.

But she did so want her first orgasm to be with a flesh-and-blood male. And Sinner looked to have so much manly experience.

Not to leave out his largest potential, the one he'd tucked into his pants at the last minute before he took off.

Mercy finger-combed her hair while she blocked out all the other firsts she'd wanted to experience with Sinner. At least she'd gotten her condom fantasy out of the way. While meandering a less-than-enthusiastic pathway back toward the *Starry Night Club* and Cindy, she shook her head. Cindy wasn't going to believe how Mercy's seductive evening had ended.

As she passed by the man pushing his fragrant cart, he waggled a handful of colorful, beribboned flowers at her.

"No. No, thank you." She waved him off. Life wasn't so bad that she'd resort to buying her own flowers just yet. Although she could picture it happening after she bought the purple, shiny vibrator.

"The gentleman paid," he explained. "He said to give the *corona* to the blonde lady in the pale dress." The vendor persisted, forcing a headpiece of brightly colored flowers in hot pinks, deep yellows, and vibrant blues into her hand. Satin streamers in matching hues danced on the hot, humid night breeze.

The corona looked like something from a sixties

love-in, and Mercy wasn't feeling too loving at the moment. "That was no gentleman," she mumbled, wanting to rub her butt as a reminder of her fall but refraining.

"The headwear is worn to celebrate fiesta, love, life," he said gaily.

With a polite smile, she accepted the halo of flowers but she'd be damned if she'd wear it.

And why had Sinner bought her flowers after dumping her right after the most erotic sex act she'd ever performed?

She'd been practicing that condom trick with a banana since she'd seen the video on late night pay TV last month.

Her anger sped up her footsteps as she wove in and out of the passersby. Soon she found herself at the base of the steps to the balcony. Looking up, she didn't spy Sinner. Wherever he'd been headed, it wasn't the balcony.

What would she do if she spotted him inside?

She climbed the stairs, her sandaled soles tapping each step. She had no choice, really. Self-respect dictated she *whap* him up alongside his head and the devil with whatever happened afterwards.

As soon as she entered the lounge, she scanned the crowded dance floor before checking out the rest of the room. She didn't see the culprit, only Cindy at the bar. Friendless.

Mercy edged onto the blue leather stool next to her friend. "Where'd your coworkers go?" She glanced up and down the dimly lit bar.

"Obviously Sister Doria knew about junior executives when she said early to bed and early to rise makes a person wealthy and wise," Cindy said.

Mercy nodded. "Did junior-exec-Jay leave, too?"

"Jay included. He didn't offer to walk me home, drive me home, or see my home." She sighed before saying in a gush, "Oh, you missed your uncle by minutes. He said he had to leave town but hoped to see you before you left for home. An emergency. A sick friend." She jangled a set of keys from a leather star initialed with a P. "The key to his place. He insisted, even though I explained you were staying with me."

Mercy tucked the key into the pocket of her dress. Great, now she had to worry about her finances until her uncle showed up and she could talk to him. If he even showed up before her vacation ended. Borrowing money wasn't so impersonal that she wanted to discuss it long-distance over the phone. She heaved a sigh. What else could go wrong?

Flopping her circle of flowers onto the bar, she groaned. "I need a drink."

"Your uncle said to ask Lenny for *anything* we want. He's the good-looking, good-smelling one." She pointed to the buff, auburn-haired bartender, who was busy *whirring* a pastel blender drink and who would've been a hunky prospect if it hadn't been for Sinner.

Despite his despicable behavior toward the end of their romp, Mercy couldn't get Sinner off her mind. Or perhaps because of his behavior.

Cindy nudged her, and Mercy met her friend's eyes in the bottle-cluttered mirror behind the bar. "I see the vendor hit you up for flowers. But you're supposed to wear the posies in your hair not throw them around like a game of ring toss."

"I'm not wearing any halo from a man called Sinner." Mercy waved to get Lenny's attention. The bartender flashed her a toothy smile and signaled he'd get to her next.

"Seems out of character for a man like that to buy flowers." Cindy sipped her wine before choking out, "His name is Sinner?"

Mercy smacked her friend on the back. "I'm surrounded by sin it seems. Sinner and Sin-dy."

32

After another cough, Cindy squeaked, "You can't lay that on me. Jay thought I was named after Cinderella."

"That might explain why Prince Charming didn't take you home. You should've worn your glass slippers instead of the floral wedgies." She looked down at Cindy's feet. "Honestly, I don't know how you can walk in those things."

Cindy wriggled her bare toes as best she could in the six-inch high, platform-soled shoes. "More than likely it had something to do with my coworker, ravishing Rita, also known as the corporate slut. Whatever she whispered in his ear turned his head. And his body followed." She downed the last swallow of wine left in her glass and slid the short-stemmed goblet to the edge of the bar for Lenny to refill when he finished flirting with a redhead who looked more likely to tip over from the weight of her breast implants than any other kind of tip. "So where did your date from Hell go?" Cindy turned to Mercy again.

"We were getting it on," Mercy explained, lowering her voice, "on a park bench and—"

"In plain sight?" Cindy gasped, her eyes widening. "Do you think that's wise?"

"We were nearly in the dark. There was a streetlight, but it and most of the people were on the other side of the bend in the river." She licked her suddenly parched lips as she briefly recalled the rock hardness of Sinner's lap and her rocking ride. "The fantasy of public sex must've really kicked things up a notch for me. I was so close to coming."

With a sigh, she closed her eyes, wishing the sumptuous feeling back. But it failed to materialize. She flicked her eyes open to stare into Cindy's round, brown ones. "I could feel an orgasm stirring when he up and left."

"Mid-coitus?" Shock tinged Cindy's voice.

"More like coitus interruptus."

"In the middle of a compromising position." Cindy's forehead puckered like corrugated paper. "What kind of man does such a thing?"

"Obviously a cowboy." Mercy shrugged.

"Coming from Pennsylvania, we don't know much about cowboys." Cindy's head bobbled like the *Lord of the Ring* Frodo decorating the toilet tank in her apartment.

"Maybe when you're in Texas longer, you'll find out more about the men," Mercy rationalized. "In the meantime, there's always Lenny."

They both stared down the length of the bar, studying the handsome, eye candy. Tight jeans. Tight buns.

"Lenny's probably heard it all," Cindy said. "Everybody blabs to their bartender."

"Soon as he's done hitting on the redhead, let's ask him."

Eventually, Lenny pried himself away from the redhead's cleavage. Behind a dashing smile, he hid any exasperation he might've harbored over having to return to drink-making.

"Lenny, this is Mercy. Parker's niece." Cindy did the introductions.

Lenny's smile widened at the mention of his boss.

"Nice to meet you, Lenny. Give us something strong enough to put an awful evening out of our minds."

"For how long?"

"Forever."

"Didn't score, huh?" Lenny said, nailing their problem on his first try. He winked knowingly. "I've got just the thing." Turning toward the gleaming bottles of colored liquors, he grabbed a few and began mixing like a scientist about to create a cure for the ailments of womankind.

And maybe he was.

When Lenny returned, he held out two frosty glasses of red-and-yellow alcohol like coveted trophies. "I put it on the boss's tab."

Cindy took hers and sipped. "Let's toast my transfer to Texas and the bathroom industry that got me here." She held up her glass. "To the Mesopotamia."

"I take it that's the pink-and-gold marbleized whirlpool-for-two in your condo."

"What a design coup that was." The light in Cindy's eyes flickered then went out. "I didn't realize how bland my life was until now. That product development was the most excitement I've had all year, and I haven't tried out the jets in the tub solo, let alone with anyone."

"Maybe Jay has a kink or two he needs Jacuzzied," Mercy suggested. "He looked pretty uptight."

Cindy frowned.

Mercy picked up her glass. "To Mister Clean and Mister Down-and-Dirty, who both ran off too soon." She swallowed a mouthful, shivering as the sweet and sour tastes assaulted her at the same time. Then she turned to the bartender. "Now, Lenny, what can you tell us about cowboys?"

Chapter Five

The next night, as soon as Spence stepped his booted foot inside the noisy, smoky *Starry Night Club*, there she was.

Though he wasn't eager to see Mercy after the fiasco on the park bench, his dick was. The muscle leaped to attention, eager to take up where they'd left off before he had blown his chance at Parker, catching only the red glow of the man's taillights.

Faced with the prospect of peeling off a dry rubber while explaining to Mercy what was none of her business, he'd decided to call it a night and take his sore cock home. Vaselineing it up, he'd spent the night grieving for the moist slit between the creamy thighs of the soft-eyed beauty when he should've been focusing on finding Parker.

He sucked in a determined breath, but even in the dim lighting, Mercy was hard to miss perched on the barstool. Her luminous blonde hair and ruby red dress drew him to her like a beacon. Her mouth was slashed in red to match her slip of a dress, and the sight hit him low in the gut like a sucker punch.

What in the hell was she doing here?

He rifled his fingers through his hair. He'd never laid eyes on her tight little body before last night, and now what, she'd become a regular?

She was a sad reminder of last night's bad endings. He'd sent her flowers by way of the vendor to apologize for his shortcomings. But nothing could make up for allowing Parker to get away. He had no choice but to ignore her and concentrate solely on watching for the prick.

He sauntered over to his strategic spot on the balcony where he could watch everyone's comings and goings. For an hour or so he succeeded in keeping his eyes away from hers. Her blue ones. He hated that he remembered the color. It made her seem special, and he needed her to be nothing more than a dry hump, ugly as that was.

But her presence in the room haunted him. He swore he could feel her breathe. Hot and heavy. Her lungs expanding, and with each movement, her luscious breasts swelling. Her sensitive nipples willing and stiff, waiting for his touch to make her ache and whimper for him.

He sucked in the warm, dank night air drifting up from the river below. Across the way a couple strolled hand-in-hand, carefree. Something he hadn't felt in too long to remember. Something he craved to feel again.

"After," he swore under his breath. After he cleared his name and put Mark to rest. Once he was sure there was no risk of danger to anyone close to him, he'd seek out a woman like Mercy and let himself feel again.

Her laughter intruded on his thoughts, the sound throaty and sultry. Even with a dance floor of bodies muffling the distance between them, her voice got to him, coaxing him to approach her, touch her silky skin, make her moan. Every second he spent trying not to watch her, he became even more aware of her presence.

He dared a glance her way. Hell, even her shadow on the wall next to the bar where she sat with her willowy long legs crossed was sexy and tempting.

He looked away, searched for a reason for his inexplicable attraction to her. It wasn't like him to obsess over a woman. Not even his steady girlfriend, who'd walked out on him during the trial.

Parker. Stalking the slimy bastard was boring business, and Mercy was just too damn pretty and tasty to overlook. She was ignoring him tonight, and the more she did the worse he felt about not making it right between them.

She had to be aware of him over here in the shadows where he lurked, noticing her every move.

And when had that happened? Damn, but she had a way of making him forget his intentions. Forget about Parker and redeeming himself for full chunks of time.

He crossed his arms, steeled himself against her, refusing to give in to his baser needs.

After several hours, he gave in. If they were both going to spend their evenings in the same place, no matter how smoky or dusky, it was going to be damn hard to pretend she didn't exist. And if not her, then her loud-laughing friend with the whacky shoes and hair.

During the band's rousing drum solo, he figured he'd garble his way through a half-ass explanation for accidentally letting her pretty butt taste the stony walkway. Once he got that off his mind, he was sure he'd be able to concentrate his undivided attention on Parker, where it belonged.

He elbowed his way through a few office types to get next to her at the two-deep bar. When he leaned in, she smelled sweet like flowers and musky like sex all at the same time, and he almost forgot he'd come over to brush her off.

"Hey," he grunted more than said.

"Don't come near me." She gave him a sideways glance, her heart-stopping blue eyes turning cool while her pert nose turned up.

The red dress looked so soft against her tits he had to brace his hands on the mahogany bar to stop from reaching over and finding out. He knew how silky the body underneath was and that had him panting like a thirsty barnyard dog. "Did you like the flowers?"

Her spine stiffened, which thrust her breasts out and made for a brain-splattering distraction. He watched her chest rise and swell as she huffed, "Thanks, I figured them for a sympathy wreath."

So much for saying it with flowers. Giving his excuse a more sincere shot this time, he said, "I'd like to apologize for what happened last night."

"I'd like if you ate dirt." She smiled with her moist pink lips.

"Babe," he said, "I can explain." But he knew damn well he couldn't. He couldn't pull the innocent bystander into a possible street fight regardless of how badly his body craved hers. And he sure as hell couldn't spell any of it out for her.

"Don't make me call the bouncer." She turned her head, tossing her blonde curls enticingly across his nose. His fingers twitched, wanting to grab the herbal-sweetened strands in a bunch, hold her captive, and kiss her until she said all the words he wanted to hear.

Instead, he had no choice but to walk away.

As he made his way onto the open balcony, he tried to drum up some anger at her, but she had every right to be pissed.

He moved back into the shadows. Hardened his heart. He didn't need any woman. Not right now. Not until he forced Parker into confessing his perjury and cleansed himself of the taint of jail and manslaughter.

****

"It was above and beyond the call of duty for Bob to not only give us a ride home last night but to take the afternoon off and show me Sea World. We did everything from high-speed rides to a slow walk through the manicured gardens." Mercy rested her elbows on the bar and tried to look enthused.

"I gather he didn't make your hormones sing?" Cindy raised her eyebrows.

"No. Only Sinner's managed to do that."

"It's just as well. Bob's one of Ravishing Rita's groupies. He's never offered more than a hello before he saw us with that office slut." Cindy waggled her blue-striped, wedge-soled foot.

"I detect resentment, Cindy, and I don't think it's because of Rita and Bob." Mercy eyed her friend. "Has she been hitting on Jay again?"

"Yes, but unsuccessfully this time." Cindy grinned and swiveled around on her barstool. When she came full-circle, she leaned in and whispered, "Don't look, but the sinner is watching you."

"All night I've sensed his eyes on me."

"Lenny can have him bounced if he's weirding you out."

"It's not like that. I don't feel stalked. I feel kind of watched over. It's hard to explain." Mercy certainly didn't suffer any attention deficit when Sinner was around. He made her feel desirable for merely inhabiting the same building as he did, and that was a difficult sensation to deny herself.

Against her better judgment, she gave in to the compelling pull of his blatant male sexuality and sneaked a peek. Immediately, his disarming, dark eyes locked with hers. On contact, a flutter of lust stirred low in her belly, hungry and devouring. Somehow, his sinful, confident stare assured her that he was the only one capable of satisfying her.

She touched her hand to her stomach to still the smoldering desire sending signals to her brain. Erotic, visual ones of his hard, hot body shadowing over hers, bringing her to climax.

He tipped his head questioningly, and she knew she should turn away before she gave in to the carnal sensations flooding through her.

Her pulse pounded in wild beats as she

unhooked her high heels from the rung of the stool. Her feet sought the floor and a path over to the man whose eyes promised sex with a satisfying ending this time.

Suddenly, Cindy blocked her view. "Any plans for tonight that I should know about?"

"No." Mercy sighed, wishing Sinner had been more cooperative the other evening. He could've ended her orgasmic quest and made her vacation a gratifying, memorable one.

"I hate to leave you stranded if I get lucky with Jay." Cindy checked her wristwatch. It was time for her coworkers to show up.

"Not to worry," Mercy said. "I can always ogle Sinner and dream about would-have-beens."

"Don't get all moony-eyed and think about forgiving him. Remember how he treated you."

"That won't work, Cindy. His treatment was pretty darn arousing, up until the last moment."

"Then concentrate on the last second and the gritty landing."

Ignoring her friend's tendency to over dramatize, she said, "I can't help but wonder why he ran off? Do you think it's me and not the men I've dated?"

"No, I remember the men back in Lily Pond." Cindy leaned closer. "Maybe Sinner has erectile dysfunction and can't maintain his, a..."

"Hard-on." Mercy nodded.

"Don't give up on all men, just Sinner. There are plenty of nice men like Jay."

Mercy quirked her nose.

"Okay, so Jay's slow with the moves, but at least he doesn't look as if he has a pact with the devil. Stay indignant, stay determined, and stay away from Sinner." Cindy sighed. "Or else I won't be able to enjoy myself for worrying."

Mercy stuck her chin out, her resolve strong. No

sense in ruining both their evenings. "I won't give up or give in."

****

Minutes before two a.m., while the bartenders hustled last call for drinks, Spence slouched against the wall. It looked as if neither Parker nor Google were showing up tonight.

Feeling low, he looked for Mercy. He thought about asking her to dance in the hopes of indulging in the soothing suppleness of her enticing body.

She stood talking to her friend, whose boyfriend had apparently run out on her, and another woman, a looker with a corporate air about her. He strolled over, but didn't speak. Instead, he tapped Mercy on her bare shoulder just for the enjoyment of touching her skin. When she faced him, he let his hand linger on her warm, fragrant flesh.

"Want to dance?"

"I don't like this song," she said, her delicate chin stiff with resolve.

"You pick the music then." He met her eyes, holding them with his.

Sexual currents crackled. Static, hot and electric. The moment stretched. The music played on.

She had to know asking her to choose was a concession for a man who claimed to dance to his own tune.

"This is the last song," she said at last.

"Come on, Mercy, throw a little my way."

His hand coaxed her naked shoulder. If it wasn't so damn near to closing, he'd have more time to work at breaking down her barriers.

"No, thanks." Her words sounded softer.

He nodded. "Tomorrow night then."

Before she could refuse, he strode away into the misty night.

Chapter Six

Mercy and Cindy sipped sparkling water at the bar the following night while Cindy waited for Jay.

"Don't feel as if you and your coworkers have to come here on my account." Mercy stabbed at her ice chips, feeling down since her mother's phone call, which had focused on her long-term future over her immediate one. Why couldn't Uncle Parker be at the club instead of Sinner?

Cindy shook her head of short hair. "Jay likes it here."

With a quick nod, she griped to her friend, "My first week in Texas is half over and I haven't laid eyes on my mother's favorite brother. She's going to be disappointed if I don't get to see him."

"Before you frown..." Cindy poked her in the ribs. "Make sure there are absolutely no smiles available."

"Sounds like the world according to Sister Doria," Mercy chided.

"You don't get to be a hundred without knowing what words to live by." Cindy crossed herself apparently in memory of the dear, departed nun. "So, why don't you give it a try?"

Mercy gritted a smile and indulged her friend. "I was waiting until after I spoke with my uncle, but I'm retooling and relocating. I've decided to go back to school and move away from Lily Pond."

"It's about time." Cindy crinkled her forehead. "But what does your uncle have to do with it?"

"My credit's kaput. I foolishly invested my savings along with money I borrowed on my credit

43

card in a deal that went bust."

"Oh, no." Cindy gasped and then went speechless, which only proved how terrible Mercy's situation was.

"The investment broker I was dating guaranteed me huge profits. Turns out his advice was as lousy as he was in bed. I had to move back in with Mom so I could keep up the payments on the VW, which I need to get to work."

"Wow, you said you'd had a financial setback, but I didn't know it was so drastic. Maybe I can cosign a loan—"

"No," Mercy said. "I didn't mean for it to sound as if I was hitting you up. Thanks for the offer, but I couldn't repay you for a long while. According to Mom, Uncle Parker can well afford to lend me the money long term and interest free."

Cindy sighed wistfully. "It must be nice to have an uncle, rich or otherwise."

"It would be if I hadn't missed my opportunity to speak to him. Uncle Parker hasn't even phoned since he left the city."

"His sick friend must be pretty sick. Your uncle's obviously a devoted friend."

"Oh, to the extreme. He once mortgaged his home to help out a friend. Mom worries that he's too caring. Although, she does like the fact that he keeps in touch with her."

"Then he'll call soon." Cindy sipped her drink and looked up from her straw. "It must be nice to have family."

"Aw, Cindy. You're like my sister." Mercy pushed aside her own worries. "You'll have a family of your own someday. A husband. Kids."

"I wish someday would hurry and get here."

"The slow moving Jay. Hasn't he kissed you yet?"

"No, but I'm holding up hopes for tonight. He

asked me to meet him here without the group."

"A first date." Mercy pointed to Cindy's dress and then to her feet. "That would explain the basic black dress and the sedate black wedgies."

"I went for classy." Cindy slurped her water through her straw with a sucking noise.

"You pull it off well."

"Thanks." Cindy glanced around the room. "Jay's not here yet, but your devilish, brooding sinner is. As usual, he's looking sullen and watching you."

"Sometimes he smiles," Mercy offered, peeking over her shoulder at the handsome stud who made her pulse sing vibrato. "When he does, it's like an unexpected gift." She looked away, trying not to let her mind stray to his other gifted parts. "Besides a great smile, he has a great mouth," she added, keeping her thoughts well above his belt.

"You shouldn't be thinking about his mouth," Cindy berated all the same. "Think about your bruised butt instead."

"The only bruises were restricted to my ego."

"*Grr,*" Cindy said in frustration, but stopped mid-growl when a male voice from behind them interrupted.

"Dance?"

Cindy squealed, jumping from her stool. "Jay."

"Hi, Mercy," Jay said politely before taking Cindy in his arms and dancing her out onto the floor.

Seemed even corporate cowboys knew the two-step. Mercy watched for a minute, then went back to stabbing her ice chips while contemplating her suffocating life back home in Lily Pond and how she was going to escape without her uncle's financial backing.

Knowing she couldn't do anything until her uncle returned or called, she let her mind drift to her more immediate problem. The first week of her vacation was half over, and she hadn't spiced up her sex life or experienced an orgasm.

"I think this is our song."

Speaking of orgasms, that voice belonged to Sinner. So far he'd been her only chance at one. Her pussy wept with hope, and she had to restrain herself from spinning on her stool and flinging herself into his arms like Cindy had done with Jay.

"Sounds like a medley of love songs to me." She glanced into his gleaming, dark eyes as he eased onto Cindy's vacated barstool. Another thrill of arousal raced through her body when his muscled arm brushed her suddenly sensitive one.

"Slow songs," he corrected.

He was right. Why had she brought up love? Sinner wasn't the type of man a woman fell for. He was the rough-and-ready, made for fun and climaxes kind. When he stuck around long enough to finish.

Which brought to mind that he hadn't. And her pledge to Cindy about remaining unapproachable where he was concerned.

"I'm not in the mood for slow," she said, dismissing him so she wouldn't have to fight the hot, provocative urges he incited in her.

He grinned. "You were in the mood the other night. I can handle hard and fast if that's what you're after."

She licked her lips as the temptation of hard and fast puckered her nipples. Yet she managed to hold out.

"The other night isn't something you should remind me about." She concentrated on sipping her sparkling water, which had lost its sparkle and its ice, probably due to the meltdown surrounding Sinner. He radiated sensual heat and masculine sexuality, and she so wanted to indulge in both.

She braced her spine, trying to be strong. Her pride was more important that giving him another crack at showing her paradise by the lamplight in the park. Wasn't it?

His finger stroked her arm and stoked her fires. Heat poured through her veins, causing moisture to break out on her forehead, her upper lip, and drip onto her panties. The heat and dampness pooling between her thighs made her itch for the thrust of his cock, hand, tongue. Anything he could touch her with would probably do the trick.

"Stop that," she said without conviction.

"What?" He met her gaze with a half-lidded one and a *make-me* look that made her want to make it with him instead of making him stop.

"Stop touching me like that," she murmured.

When he moved his hand away, she missed the fire of arousal he ignited, and all the possibilities of hot, horny sex he'd conjured up.

She let out a breathy exhale and dredged up her indignation. "Ditching me while I—we were in the most vulnerable position a person, persons could be ditched during..."

"It was business. Nothing personal."

Spence watched her blue eyes as they rounded with annoyance. Eyes that looked fantastic in the dim light of the smoky bar. In any light, he imagined. He'd like to see her in the daylight and sunshine.

"Business is no excuse," she protested. "In fact, it makes me feel worse."

"I could make you feel better." He lowered his voice.

"Why should I believe you?"

He felt her falter so he jumped right in. "I owe you one. You know we're good together." The interest shining in her glassy eyes urged him on. He leaned close to her ear. "I'll give you two *screaming* orgasms if you forgive me."

"Screaming," she mouthed. "You can do that?"

He nodded.

"Two?" The warmth of her breath tickled his jaw and sent hot surges to his ever-hardening boner.

"How many times have you come in one night?" He traced the blue vein on her inner wrist.

"Not many," she purred.

"Just as I thought. One. I promise you two, possibly three, but it might take all night." He knew it wouldn't. Every move she made and every word she uttered made him hard. Besides, he didn't have all night. Google had called to meet him later. With rumors circulating that Parker had left the city, he needed the informant's input.

After a pause, Mercy said, "I take it we wouldn't be sleeping on the Riverwalk park bench."

He didn't do sleepovers. Not anymore. Not since before his trial. Now he fucked women instead of sleeping with them. But he didn't bother mentioning that.

Her wrist remained lax on the bar as if paralyzed by his touch. He petted her with the pad of his finger and urged her on with more soft assurances. "I could show you my spread." He crooked a smile. "Or we could go to your place."

Taking her hand in his, he stood while easing her away from the barstool. She was next to him now, and the heat of her body felt exhilarating. He knew how well she fitted him. His muscles twitched at the memory. The one in his jaw and the one in his jeans.

He shifted closer. His pelvis cradled her belly, allowing her to feel the stiffness and weight of his arousal.

She didn't move away or feign indifference. He could almost hear her body moan. She breathed heavier, faster. When he stepped back her breasts heaved slightly, and he could see her nipples peak beneath the washed denim material of her dress. His eyes stroked her body, grazing the tempting brass zipper running from her collar to her knees. He returned his gaze to her face. Her cheeks were hot and flushed, her lips parted.

He gave her time to make her decision.

Patience had come to him the hard way. After waiting out his jail term, he now waited out the man who put him there. Both were much longer waits than Mercy could demand.

After a pause, he leaned in and touched his lips to her ear. His tongue flicked at her lobe before he whispered, "What do you say, babe?"

"I have a roommate."

Chapter Seven

"The ranch isn't too far out of town," Spence said, trying to gauge her reaction in the dim lighting of the bar.

"I couldn't go there," Mercy murmured, looking away.

He knew what she meant. She'd have no means of escape if he turned out to be a crazy, which he wasn't. But she didn't know that.

He let her work it out in her mind but circled his hand around her wrist. He could feel her pulse, rapid and heated beneath his callused fingers as he flicked his thumb in a coaxing, steady rhythm.

After a few moments, she gave in. "Let me check with my roommate about the availability of our place."

He nodded, and she slipped from his grasp, leaving his hand feeling empty and tingly.

As she crossed the hardwood floor her slender hips swayed, and with each movement, her skirt stretched taut across her shapely butt. He sighed his approval and caught a whiff of her light, spicy scent lingering in the air where she'd stood. Floral and citrus. Sweet and tart, just like Mercy.

He watched as, with a nudge, Mercy interrupted her loud, floppy-haired friend, who was dancing with the well-dressed, smooth-talking, corporate crook, Jay. If rumors were true, Jay deserved to be in jail for the white-collar crimes he'd pulled off.

Sinner snorted. While he'd wasted in jail for a crime he hadn't committed.

Shrugging off his irritation, he leaned his back

and elbows against the polished bar. Jay wasn't his concern. And even if he became his business by association with Mercy through her friend, how much damage could the corporate climber inflict on either of the women during their two-week vacation?

Mercy's roomie was waving her hands excitedly and running off at the jaw faster than the speed of a flying fist. She obviously wasn't happy about the prospect of Sinner spending any time in their hotel room. Let alone all night.

Not that he needed all night to fulfill his promises to Mercy. Not that he had all night, but neither woman knew that.

Across the room, Jay intervened. He took Cindy's chin in his hand and squelched her chatter while he contributed God-knows-what to the conversation. Mercy nodded to whatever Jay was saying, which Sinner figured didn't hold out much hope for his cause. Jay's kind didn't help anyone without a self-serving reason. Or a price.

Then suddenly Mercy flashed an I-told-you-so grin at her friend, and Jay nodded his agreement.

It looked as if the corporate flunky was assuring the women that Sinner was housebroken. Go figure.

Mercy returned still smiling. "Our place has suddenly become available. In the wise words of Doria, two's company and four's a crowd, so Jay's going to show Cindy his etchings."

Sinner scratched his head. Who in the heck was Doria?

"Jay swears he really does have etchings," Mercy said with a laugh, misunderstanding his apparent confusion.

****

The condo was in an upscale neighborhood. Contemporary, with lots of sleek marble, slick leather seating, and shiny chrome. He dug his hands into his back pockets. "I was expecting a hotel."

51

"The corporation Cindy works for uses this apartment for entertaining clients." She gestured to the spacious rooms as her words echoed off the walls. "She has use of it as part of her per diem package for moving across country on short notice."

So Cindy wasn't on vacation with Mercy. He nodded, noticing the unpacked boxes piled near the mirrored foyer. She must've arrived shortly before Mercy started her hiatus.

"Kind of bare," he said. Sparse like his jail cell.

"Don't let the minimalist décor fool you. Despite its sterile appearance, it's plush. Wait until you see the bathtub." Her eyes twinkled.

"Can't wait." He raised a brow. *Women*. What in the heck could be so exciting about a tub? He preferred showers. Moving further into the cavernous living room, he said, "My place has more clutter."

After the stark reality of jail, it damn better had.

She tossed her purse onto one of the two chairs flanking a dark blue sofa in the otherwise white, oversized room. "I'm sure yours is homier." Her hint of a smile told him clutter was the last thing on her mind.

"If you call Salvation Army surplus homey." With a grin, he sat down on the sofa. The cushions were so firm he didn't sink in. Crossing his booted foot over his knee, he tapped the buttons on the nearby glass end table, playing them like a kid's piano.

But there was no kid stuff here. In a flash, the overhead chrome lights dimmed, the blinds opened to a glittering display of the lighted city below, and mellow music filtered from the surrounding, four corners of the room. "Quite a setup."

"You should see the bathroom. Heated towel bars, marble tub." She closed the short distance between them with a few steps before kicking off her high heels. "Big enough for two."

Again with the bathtub. He had to admit she had his interest peaked. If he read her tone and the hooded look in her eyes right, she was hinting at trying it out. He cocked his head, waiting for her to come right out with it.

"It's never been used, according to Cindy." She moved nearer, the hem of her skirt brushing his knees.

"A virgin tub." He tossed her a questioning look. "We could see about breaking its cherry."

But he was merely paying her lip service. He didn't have any intention of christening the thing. No fussy bubble baths for him. Although there were a few tricks with a showerhead he could show her if he had time.

For now...he reached up and tugged at the seductive zipper that ran the length of the front of her dress. Inching it down, he exposed her tantalizing fair flesh to his intense gaze in gradual increments. She shivered with expectation. Her nipples puckered and swelled, straining against the flimsy material of her bra. The muscles in her taut belly quivered as the rasp of the metal descended over them. The lace edge of her panties caught, but he managed to loosen the fabric with a few jiggles.

He paused at her mound. Dark blonde curls showed faintly through the sheer material. For a second, his fingers fumbled, until at last her denim dress lay open to his stare from collar to hem, the beauty of her body with it.

All within kissing distance. The light musky scent of her sex invited him in. He stripped the dress away before leaning forward to let his breath dampen and heat her sex lips through the silky crotch of her panties. She trembled, shifted her stance a little wider. He lathed his tongue over the filmy nylon covering her pussy until she was soaked. She tasted provocatively sweet through the thin barrier. Beneath the matted fine curls, her clit swelled. He lapped and aroused her until she whimpered, "Sinner."

He cracked a brief smile. He wanted her to lose herself in him, like he could in her if he allowed himself.

With his rough palms, he stroked the back of her firm, lean thighs and worked his tongue over her again and again. When she stopped murmuring and her breath came in short wispy pants, he edged his fingers around, wriggling them into the crotch of her panties. As he slid two fingers into her slippery folds, she groaned softly. When he teased her clit with his thumb, she swayed into him.

"Let's take this into another room." Resting his chin on her pubic bone, he looked up. Her eyes were half-closed slits of blue. Sultry. Sexy as hell.

"The bedroom," she whispered in a husky slur.

"Which way?" He stood, lifting her into his arms.

Without a word, Mercy pointed, and he carried her down the hallway, his strides long and fast.

Mercy wasn't sure if she was too breathless to speak or conserving energy for what was about to come. It didn't matter. Deep inside to her very core, which Sinner had inflamed so knowingly, she felt tonight was *the* night. The night she'd come.

He'd promised her a night of hot sex, and she was counting on him to deliver. By the time he flicked the floor lamp on and placed her on the white satin sheets of the king-sized bed in the guest suite, her body ached and throbbed with anticipation.

She stretched her arms out to him, but he remained standing, just out of her reach. She wriggled her greedy fingers toward him. "Time to make me scream."

He shook his head. "Not just yet."

"I didn't take you for a tease." She lowered her arms and dropped her eyes to his fly. "Unless it's a striptease."

With a flick of his fingers he unbuckled his jeans. She rolled to the edge of the bed and sat up. "Watching you strip has been a turn on I've dreamed of in this very bed." She stroked her hands across the satiny sheet to emphasize the point.

"Let's see about making your dreams come true." He moved closer and with slow, teasing moves edged his zipper open. Her breath caught with each click of the metal teeth. With every rasp, her body broke out in a feverish sheen—her forehead, her upper lip and between her breasts. She was already dripping between her thighs.

When his jeans were finally undone, she wanted to applaud. Hell, she wanted to tip him, throw dollar bills at him, wrap him up in the government-issued, green paper and unwrap him again.

With his tall, lean, hard body, he was better than any stripper she'd seen, which was only one, at her friend's bachelorette party in Philadelphia, and he'd been shared with every hungry, drooling woman in the Pleasure Dome. She'd barely gotten a pinch in.

Here was Sinner, all hers. No other hands or heads butting in her way.

As soon as his cock sprang loose from his jeans, she reached out and caressed him.

Hard, hot, smooth. She moved forward to lick him. He tasted salty and tantalizing. She couldn't stop herself from swirling her tongue around the head of his penis, again and again, until she heard him groan. She stopped just to tease him further before opening wide and taking in his entire length.

She liked this feeling of being in control. Sinner was confident enough to let her have her way with him. His eyes told her so with unblinking, smoldering contact when she looked up.

There was something commanding about meeting his smoky eyes while his cock filled her mouth. His pleasure lay in her power to give or withhold. She stopped sucking.

Should she continue?

His eyes shouted *yes*. His mouth said, "Yes," in a barely audible hissing sound. But his stance said he'd take whatever she gave him—or not.

If denied, he might shrivel but never complain.

She pulled with light sucking motions, and he arched his hips and groaned louder. Releasing him, she teased the tip of her tongue up and down his shaft. When she felt him quiver, she took him into her mouth again with even stronger suction this time.

She moved fast on him, then slow, then fast again, experimenting. He tensed, flinched, moaned. Her command over his reactions spurred her on. She caressed his sac and made love to his thick shaft. After all, his dick was going to take her where she'd never gone before. She wanted to show her appreciation beforehand, in case she wasn't able afterward.

Never having experienced an orgasm, she wasn't sure how bone-melting, mind-blowing, nerve-rending it would be.

When he tangled her hair in his fingers and guided her rhythm to one he favored, a slow but steady drawing up and easing off, she obliged him.

Until he pulled away. "Babe, we'd better back off and take it easy, or I might blow your head off." He grinned. "I've never held back this long before."

He stepped away and kicked off his jeans, but not before taking three condoms from his pocket and tossing them onto the nightstand. She smiled. Obviously, he was a man hell-bent on keeping his word. He began pulling his shirt over his head, and she stood and helped him out of it for the sake of speed. She didn't want the provocative heat radiating throughout her body to cool before she reached her goal.

Although the fire inside her felt as if it would take a lot of pumping to put out.

When he tossed the shirt, he stood before her naked and rock hard, looking sexy as hell and ready for action.

Her breath halted, and she shimmied out of her lacy bra and panties. When he cupped her breasts, one in each hand, lifting them, grazing her nipples against his, she moaned, relishing the friction but needing more. She wanted him to manipulate her peaked buds between his fingers and take the aching tips into his mouth.

"Touch my nipples," he murmured, saying the very words she desired to say.

She leaned away so that she could pleasure him, but he pulled her close again and repeated, "Touch me, Mercy. Make me hot."

She placed her thumb and index finger alongside his nipple, which was sealed with hers. While she rolled his hardened tip between her fingers, she squeezed her own sensitive nipple at the same time.

Closing her eyes, she let her head fall back as she plucked and excited them both. The softness of her skin against the roughness of his felt gratifying. She tweaked harder and faster. Heated sensations coursed through her body, pooling in her womb. The thrill felt erotic, different from anything she'd ever imagined. Like masturbating with a partner.

Her head spun, and yet she couldn't stop herself from rolling and pinching their joined nipples, driving herself closer and closer to the unknown.

Suddenly, she couldn't wait any longer.

"Come to bed," she murmured. She skimmed her

palms over his muscled biceps and down his strong arms to grasp his hands. Tugging him toward her, she reclined onto the mattress.

The slide of his naked body against hers felt more exhilarating than public sex on the park bench had been. The aphrodisiac of discovery wasn't what had driven her on the night along the river. It was pure Sinner.

He kissed her neck and nibbled her earlobe. She gyrated her hips, her pussy wet and lusting for penetration. She was about to find out if he had performance anxiety.

She crossed her fingers and tried to cross her toes. The feel of his hot, hard penis against her cleft must've sent fevered, crazy notions to her brain because she almost crossed her legs.

Chapter Eight

Giving an old Doriaism a new twist, Mercy figured, first come, first serve.

As Sinner possessed her mouth in a breath-stealing kiss, she boldly ran her hands over his strong back and tight butt. His muscles clenched and unclenched beneath her touch, her fingers grazing his buns, going lower with each stroke until she teased his genitals.

With a sharp intake of breath, he bucked his hips. His erection felt hard and eager between her thighs. The man's body was made for love. Lust, she amended, confident she was going to finally enjoy unbridled sex—with an orgasmic climax.

When he plunged his tongue into her mouth, she returned its primitive love dance. As if the passionate kisses weren't enough to drive her ever closer to the edge, he nibbled her ear, her neck, traced his tongue along her collarbone and suckled the pulse throbbing at the base of her neck.

Sensations assaulted her at an alarming pace. Her body blazed and then shivered. Heat and chills alternately raced to her erogenous zones.

She'd lost any control she had over the situation long ago. All she could do now was hold on for what looked like the ride of her life.

Grasping his neck, clutching at the longish hair at his nape, she kissed him anywhere she could. She nipped his earlobe, bussed his forehead, and nicked his nose, her kisses landing at random on whatever body part she could reach. His lips were illusive, remaining out of range.

His kisses landed where he willed. His mouth caressed the puckered tips of her breasts. Quick, hot licks of his wet tongue excited her as he moved from one to the other, leaving the abandoned, swollen nipple to shiver and ache for his attention.

"I—I think I'm ready," she murmured when she'd had enough of Sinner's teasing.

But he didn't seem to hear her. He trapped her wrists in his hands and had his way with her body. He suckled her breasts, pulling harder, giving her even more exquisite pleasure. As her body arched against his greedy mouth, she moaned, demanding some kind of relief.

He let go of her hands and moved lower, swirling his tongue around her belly button, dipping in and out, simulating fuck motions that had her gripping the satin sheets.

The man had a talented tongue. She wondered if his penis had equal talent.

"I'm ready now," she repeated in a raspy but louder tone.

He smiled up at her.

"You're going to be so easy," he growled, snatching a condom from the nightstand to encase his swollen dick.

"Oh, but it's never been—"

The word *easy* got caught in her throat as he slid between her open thighs and entered her, slowly edging in and then withdrawing. The heat of his smooth tip delved and inched into her again, followed by coolness, emptiness as he withdrew.

He played with her that way for several long tortuous strokes before he plunged his cock deeply and thoroughly inside of her.

She lifted her hips to meet him and felt totally filled.

Closing her eyes, she let the sensation of his possession carry her away. To the edge, where she clung for the longest time, meeting the push of his solid body, his hard length stretching her wide as he drove them both forward to...where?

Mercy wasn't certain, but she doubted she'd need her legs for the journey. Sinner seemed more than capable of taking her there all on his own. She wrapped her ankles tightly around his waist, pumping her hips in time with his and matching him thrust for thrust.

Restlessly, she traced her hands over his muscled shoulders, trailing down the slope of his back before grasping his firm butt and kneading. His breathing grew labored, and he gasped.

She flinched, wanting to scream *no*. That familiar male sound warned her he was going to jump off the precipice with or without her.

But unlike other men, Sinner didn't. Instead, he clenched his jaw, squeezed his eyes shut, and wrapped her in his arms, pulling her closer to him. His breath rushed hot on her face before he devoured her mouth with a kiss so fierce he sucked the doubt right out of her. Her muscles went lax as she yielded to his body and let him take charge, trusting he'd take her over the top with him.

And he did.

"Sinner," she shouted as her pussy clutched his cock and hot, spiraling spasms washed over her.

He plunged deeper and faster. Locking her ankles, she rode the delicious friction. His pubic bone met her clit with driving force. His harsh breathing matched her own. Her fingers clawed at his back as her body began to tremble. His skin was damp and hot. He murmured, "Come on, baby."

She tensed and closed her eyes. Her whole body pulsed, and with a low, whining sound, she moaned his name and shattered. Her vaginal contractions continued to milk him even as her arms and legs went limp, unable to hold onto him any longer.

He relaxed his tight hold, and his cock twitched in a powerful contraction as he came. He'd obviously used a lot of willpower to hold back while he waited for her.

"That was remarkable," she whispered against his ear. "You were remarkable."

His forehead rested against hers. "Yeah, it was good."

She stretched her arms over her head, a dreamy glow flooding her. "No, it was more than good." She smiled to show her admiration.

He grinned back. A twinkle lit his dark eyes. "No more compliments or it will go to my head." He chuckled. "Both of them. And I'll be ready again before you are."

"That soon?" Her eyes rounded. "But it will never be as incredible," she purred, satiated.

"Tell me what part was so incredible, and I'll be sure to duplicate it." His knuckles stroked lazily across her jaw.

"What was incredible was that I came."

She sighed. Her first orgasm. She was in love. Oh, not with Sinner. With the thrill, the euphoria, the total release of tension throughout her body.

"Don't you usually come?" Sinner caressed her neck, not sure he'd heard correctly.

"You're my first." Mercy smiled at him as if he were her hero.

"I didn't do anything out of the ordinary."

"Oh, but you did—"

He kissed her hard with a lot of tongue, hoping to erase some of the truth of her words from her lips.

She had been an extraordinary first for him, too. He'd encountered more than lust. From the minute she wrapped her velvety body around him, he'd lost himself in her skin, her scent, her softness. Her spontaneous inexperience.

He felt alive for the first time in almost two

years, and to tell the truth, it was a high he didn't want to do without again. But he couldn't indulge himself with anything more than brief encounters. He couldn't waste time. Suppose Parker skipped out, or worse, the old coot died before Spence cleared his name.

He looked down into her satiated eyes. Mercy wasn't interested in him as anything other than a vacation fuck. She'd go back East, and he'd be nothing but the stud who had made her come.

Chapter Nine

After disposing of the condom, Sinner returned. Settling himself next to Mercy's shapely form on the bed, he basked in her playful smile and the willing glint in her eyes.

Her body was all she was offering, and his body was all he had to give. He refused to think any deeper thoughts. "Ready for the second coming?" he whispered near her ear.

"To put a Doriaism to bad use..." She trickled her hand through the hair on his chest and down over his stomach to tease the tip of his dick with the soft pad of her finger. "Anything worth doing is worth overdoing."

Shivers rippled up his spine and testosterone shot through his veins. He stilled her hand with his. "Is Doria like Confucius?"

"Mmm," she sighed as he slid her hand between her thighs and slipped her finger along with his own into her wet, slick pussy.

"You are *so* ready," he said. "Want to try the top this time?" Her blue eyes blinked away his suggestion so he tempted her further. "You seemed to know your way around my lap the other night at the Riverwalk."

"Will I come that way?" She arched her back as he stroked her slippery clit with their fingers. "I'd hate to mess with such a winning system."

"Then mess with me." He released her finger and rolled onto his back next to her. "It'll be my pleasure."

"I hate to sound greedy, but will it be mine?"

Leaning over him, she rested her forearm on his breastbone.

"Why don't you find out?" he tempted, letting warm wisps of his breath fall against her lips before he grasped her hair in both fists and pulled her into a rough kiss.

He wanted her on top. The position was more sexual, less intimate. No arms wrapped around him in a loving embrace, no lingering kisses. Only vital body parts doing what came natural, working out their primal needs. No breath-exchanging climaxes while her mouth gasped beneath his.

On top, she'd be no different than any other woman who'd ridden him to orgasm. He'd remain distant from the longing she stirred in him.

He Frenched her, forcing himself to feel nothing but his baser sexual urges. She squirmed, her eagerness at the prospect of her second orgasm apparent. How unbelievable that she'd only come for the first time moments ago. What in the hell kind of men had she been going out with?

Assholes.

He shook off the anger and humiliation he felt for her at the idiot hands of the jerks. She wasn't his woman or his business.

Her urgent hands flattened his shoulders against the sleek satin sheets. "Riding you to climax has been another recent fantasy of mine. One I never imagined might come true. Until now."

She slipped her creamy thighs over his lap. Her pussy felt deliciously wet and hot against his dick. For all of a second.

Instead of getting right to the core of things, as most women did, she stretched her supple, trim body over his. Her smooth legs rested on his prickly haired ones, and she snuggled her curvaceous torso tight against his chest and stomach. Sliding her hands seductively along the length of his arms, she settled her gentle palms against his callused ones.

With her face next to his, her soft cheek caressed his. Strands of her hair tickled his shoulders. Her citrusy perfume mixed with the musky scent of sex.

Engulfed by her fragrance, her skin, her gentleness, he indulged himself. But if he let this go on too long, his heart would ache.

He breathed in deeply one last time, nudged his hips, and grunted, "This might work better if you sat up and straddled me."

When she lifted her head, her bed-tousled hair brushed his face like a caress. She smiled down on him, her lips pink and swollen from his kisses. Her eyes were heavy-lidded and glazed. Her golden lashes fluttered.

"You're my fantasy man come to life. I was savoring every inch of you. I'm sure lots of women have shown their appreciation for your body."

Appreciation. Yeah, right. Who did she think he'd been doing, Mary Poppins?

For a brief flash, he wanted to be more to her than just a hard body. He shook off the crazy idea by crushing her mouth with his, rougher than he'd kissed some of the unnamed women he'd satisfied himself with. When they insisted on kissing.

Mercy sat up after that. Shook her blonde hair to get it out of her eyes.

And into his mind.

The sight of her mussed hair, naughty body, and welcoming blue eyes branded itself onto his brain. He had to squeeze his eyes shut to blot out the image.

He concentrated with his libido. Her pussy lips felt hot and wet against his shaft, her ass, velvety and round on his thighs. And then he didn't feel anything—

What now? He flipped his eyes open just as her

cool, slender fingers began fitting the rubber onto him. His cock jerked with pleasure at the unexpected touch of her fingers.

Why in the hell did her attempts at sexual savvy turn him into a quivering dick?

To fight back any fuzzy feelings, he propped his hands behind his head. "No lip service this time?"

"Putting the condom on with my mouth would lose its suggestive impact if done too often." Her tone sounded matter-of-fact, like she'd read it somewhere.

He nodded at her reasoning, but watched, mesmerized by her sex-manual methods in action. When her upturned lips at last decreed she was pleased with her technique, she slid over his lap and gyrated her hips above his cock. Her lush breasts jiggled, enticing him to forget about coming for now, and instead taste her fragrant flesh.

He fought off the urge to lave her nipples until they hardened and she moaned his name. But she didn't know his real name. He'd like to hear her murmur *Spence* as she came apart at his touch, but he denied himself that intimacy.

The impulse vanished when she grasped his cock in her satiny grip and inserted him into her hot, tight pussy. Even he forgot his real name.

Spence's breath went ragged when her inner muscles gloved him like a fist and she moved her hips up and down and around.

"You move like a professional," he mumbled thoughtlessly, then gritted his teeth, bracing for the slap that was sure to follow.

Instead, she smiled proudly while she rotated her hips, grinding in a counterclockwise direction now. "Thank you." Flipping her hair off her damp neck, she explained, "Belly dancing classes."

He should grab her and kiss her for her forethought, but he didn't want to break her rhythm. Giving into the movements of her sultry body and the sway of her breasts, he cupped and teased the tender flesh and taut nipples.

A moan escaped her lips, and her vaginal muscles contracted with the sweetest, tightest hold he'd ever felt. As he kneaded her breasts, she clenched him tighter, her contractions milking his shaft. With each contraction, she moved more exotically and enticingly.

Soon his cock was dancing a wild hula. He'd never felt anything sexier in his life—nor would he in his next life, he was sure.

"Mercy," he groaned, unsure if he was calling her name or invoking relief from her torturous pleasure.

She crooked a questioning smile. "I gather foreplay's over."

If that was foreplay, he couldn't wait to see what came next.

She didn't make him wait to find out. She gripped his shoulders and began riding him like the bucking bronco Mark had broken to win his last championship belt buckle.

But Spence didn't want to think about Mark now. He was here to wipe the sad memory of his friend from his mind, for however short a time.

Gratefully, it didn't take long to forget. Mercy consumed him, body, mind, spirit. Her flesh, her willingness, her essence enveloped him.

His body responded. He grabbed her hips and arched, pumping into her wild gyrations.

Frantic, hot, and fast, she rode him.

Soon, he was wet with perspiration, and a sheen broke out across her face and breasts. Yet neither one of them let up.

Until she became convulsive, and he felt her begin to break apart. He let himself come then, joining her as they drove toward a spastic climax.

"Babe," he groaned after she'd collapsed on top

of him.

She reached up to peck him on chin. "You were right. I can come this way." She dropped her head back onto his chest.

More appreciation. He ruffled his fingers through her damp, tangled hair, massaging her scalp to assure her she'd done the job well.

Overdone it, actually.

"You deserve a break before we start up again." And so did he.

"*Mmm.*" She fingered the hair on his chest next to where her cheek rested. Then she stopped, and he could tell by her even breaths that she'd nodded off, hopefully forgetting about the promise of orgasm number three.

He closed his eyes. Grateful to doze.

Chapter Ten

Jay bolted for the front door to his apartment as soon as he hung up the phone. Damn computer geek had to call now, demanding he drop everything and come at once.

"I've got to run to the store for milk for my morning coffee." He blew a perfunctory kiss to where Cindy sat at his computer diligently posting pictures of his etchings for a catalogue he had no intention of producing.

"You could try drinking your coffee black." She flashed him what he supposed was a seductive smile before adding, "Hurry back."

Gawd. He hoped he wouldn't have to screw her.

Once outside he hopped into his Jag and tooled down the road. As he flicked on the DVD player to Enrique Iglesias and one of his lust-driven romantic tunes, it only enforced his determination to go through with the deal. His dream of a villa in Spain filled with all the Latin ladies his libido could stand was only a down payment away.

Thanks in no small part to Cindy and her gullibility. She'd been so easy to dupe. Using Rita to make her jealous had been his ticket to success. The talkative twit had been riding high ever since he'd chosen her over the office slut.

Before Enrique's second song finished, Jay swung into the lot of the darkened restaurant and spied a lumpy shadow of a man lurking near a tree. Killing the engine and headlights, he climbed out of the Jag.

"Did you bring the money?" the man asked in a

hushed voice as soon as he approached him.

"Sheesh." Jay waved his hand in front of his face. "What in the hell have you been doing, dumpster diving?"

"Some couple was doing it in their car when I arrived. I had to hide behind the trash bins until five minutes ago." He shoved his hands into his baggy pockets. "Where's my money?"

"Information first." He wasn't about to pay upfront. The geek knew Jay was computer illiterate. He could sell him anything.

"It doesn't work like that. Money first, research next."

"How do I know I won't get caught?"

"I don't give guarantees. You take your chances like everybody else."

"Hell." Jay swiped his hand across the back of his neck. Life was easier when he sold office memos instead of trying to go high-tech.

"Going to stop crying about it or do you need a hanky?" The guy stared at him through wire-framed glasses that magnified his red-rimmed eyeballs to look enormous.

Jay stepped to the left, downwind of the guy. The stench clung to his torn, grunge-styled T-shirt and was making negotiating difficult. "I lined up an unsuspecting employee who has computer access, like you advised. She's waiting back at my apartment, so could we wrap this up before she gets suspicious?"

"You're the one holding up payment."

"Damn, I forgot my wallet back at my place." Pretending his pocket was empty, he patted his pants where his tri-fold wallet warmed his ass cheek.

"Yeah, right."

"So what's next?"

"You mean aside from paying me?" The guy

checked his cell phone, maybe for a message, maybe for the time. He snapped it shut. "Can you get her password? It would make the process easier."

"I'll work on her." Jay forced himself to take the man's smelly hand and shake it.

****

Sometime later Spence awoke to fluttery kisses on his neck and underneath his stubbled jaw. Mercy was awake, and her eager lips were demanding orgasm number three. She hadn't forgotten.

"What time is it?" he asked, his voice groggy from sleep.

"It's late," she whispered, looking up at him with her bewitching eyes.

"How late?" He stretched before kissing her.

The titillating taste of her decadent mouth managed a jerk reaction from his satiated dick. When her sizzling lips skimmed down his neck, chest, and stomach, stopping to tease his belly button, his dick became less satisfied and more demanding.

"Anyone tell you how good you are at this foreplay stuff?" He shifted his leg, allowing her easier access to his lower parts.

"No." She swirled her tongue along his hipbone. "Neither of my ex-boyfriends was into foreplay or afterglow."

"They were jerks." He squirmed, his groin thrumming with anticipation. "Which would explain why you never had a climax before."

"I was beginning to think it was me. But thanks to you..." She dropped grateful kisses onto his cock.

Her warm, wet tongue grazed its throbbing head. Spence was wide awake now and raring to please the lady if it took all night.

Swiftly, he recalled he didn't have all night. He'd agreed to meet Google at one a.m., and that was a meeting he didn't plan on being late for. Even for the talented tongue of Mercy.

"What time did you say it was?" She hadn't said.

Crawling up his body, her pliant curves fitting him in all the right places, she glanced over his shoulder toward a night table. "A little before midnight."

"Shit." He bolted upright, clutching her to keep her from falling off the bed. She looked speechless and wide-eyed. "I have a meeting in an hour."

"You ranchers certainly conduct business at odd hours."

He chuckled. "It's due to long hours spent out on the range during the daylight hours."

Only he couldn't remember the last time he'd seen a range. Or lifted a bale of hay around the homestead he and Mark had owned—which belonged to him alone now. He couldn't ranch the place until he squared things with Parker.

"Makes sense," she murmured, believing him.

Naive. No wonder men took advantage of her.

He drew her closer and kissed her. She smelled like satin sheets and great sex. She tasted like late mornings spent in bed on rainy days. She tasted like forever.

He let himself get lost in the seduction of her mouth for several long moments before he pulled away and dropped a promissory kiss on her forehead. "Number three will have to be in the shower."

Snatching up the last rubber, he hopped off the bed and tugged her by the hand toward the bathroom.

She detoured at the door and led him into the hallway instead. Two doors down, she stopped in her barefoot tracks and swung a lacquered brown door open. "The Mesopotamia."

There sat the biggest, *girliest* bathtub he'd ever laid eyes on. Heck, the thing was pink marble for crying out loud.

He backed up. Shook his head. "Sorry, but I've got to take a rain check on the tub."

"Aww." She moaned with disappointment.

He'd only promised her three orgasms. No bathtub stipulations included.

Next to the tub stood a glass shower enclosure, large enough to fit a small herd of cattle, and the marble on the walls wasn't pink but brown. He pointed. "I don't have time to impress you with my showerhead techniques, but there's plenty of space for moving around."

Her lips curved upward slightly. "You can show me your ingenuity another night."

Another night. As much as his balls warmed to her offer, he'd have to shoot her down. But not right now.

He kissed her quick, snapping open the glass door and tossing the packet onto the shower stall shelf. Once he adjusted the taps, steamy water spat in every direction. The sprays held so much potential—and with him in too much of a rush to utilize them.

He gestured for her to step in. "Lady's first."

And she was a lady, despite the sexy look in her eyes. A part of him wished she were his lady. But things were what they were. Not that he blamed her, but women like her, and like his ex, didn't have staying power when it came to down-and-dirty circumstances like his.

He joined her underneath the streaming jets, and she handed him a sudsy bar of soap that smelled like some sissy bar drink.

"Pina Colada," she explained when he sniffed.

After sudsing up his dick, he rinsed and held out the bar of soap to her. Before she reached for it, he pulled back, remembering her limited sex life. She'd probably never showered with a man before.

"Let me." He could spare a few minutes to work her over with the bar of soap.

Soon steam and lather, and the scent of tropical islands, consumed the roomy space. He smoothed a thick layer of lather over her breasts until a cascade of suds dripped from the tips of her taut nipples. Gliding lower, he laved shimmering bubbles over her slick stomach and her patch of springy curls. With a sigh, she closed her eyes and opened her stance to maintain her balance.

Spence sucked in his breath at the sight of her luscious body, white and creamy, as if shot with his cum. She made an erotic image. His dick grew rock hard.

"Turn around, and I'll do your back," he urged to hurry things along when he'd rather linger over each sexually charged stroke.

Washing her shoulders first, he lathered his way down the length of her spine until he reached her very last vertebrae. He watched as the sudsy foam slithered between the perky cheeks of her ass.

His arousal grew even harder, if that was possible. Soon he sported the founding-father of all boners. Watching became too painful, and he hugged Mercy to him. The cleft of her glistening ass cradled his erection while his hands slid over her warm, slippery flesh.

Her breasts felt soft, her nipples nubby to the touch. He skimmed his thumbs over them, and she moaned. Slipping his hands lower, he glided his palms down her sleek stomach.

One at a time, he slid his fingers over her clit. The bud responded by pulsing and beading. She whimpered with pleasure.

When two of his wet fingers sank inside of her, stretching her wide, embedding knuckle-deep, she ground her ass into him.

He groaned into her ear. "Move forward."

She stepped forward into the shower sprays. Not to break contact, he followed.

The smell of coconut enveloped him. The hot water splayed from all three sides, hard and stinging against his skin, while her body felt soft and sleek in his arms. The contrast excited him, and he hurried to explain in more detail this time.

"Bend forward." When she reached for the wall, splashes of water slapped against them, leaving their flesh red and hot and ready.

She tossed him an eager smile over her shoulder, and he grabbed the foil packet from the shower nook where he'd tossed it earlier. In no time, he approached her quivering pussy from behind.

As soon as he slid between her legs and into her tightness, he grasped her hips from behind and pumped. At first he watched as his shaft entered and exited her pussy, but then he closed his eyes and gave himself over to the sheer pleasure of Mercy.

As she began to come, she reached around, grabbed one of his ass cheeks in her suddenly powerful grip and urged him on faster and harder. He'd probably be black-and-blue tomorrow, but her gratification—who was he kidding, his gratification—was worth it.

With two more plunges, she came and slackened her hold on his backside. As soon as he shot his wad, he withdrew and Mercy sank to the floor of the steamy shower enclosure. He slid down next to her. Dragging air in and out of his lungs, he reached up and spun the taps to off.

After he finally caught his breath, he said, "I have to go." He had to stay focused. Make it to his meeting with Google on time.

She nodded.

Water dribbled off his body as he exited the shower. Grabbing a towel, he flicked the thick terry over his hair and his body while heading for the door.

"Sinner."

When he looked back, she was standing, rosy and warm with a just-got-laid gleam in her eyes. Her hair was wet and dripping, plastered against her head in places, sticking up in others. Yet somehow, she managed to turn him on all over again.

"Yeah?" He stood as rigid as his dick had been earlier and waited for her to continue.

"You said you'd stay the night. Are you coming back?"

Hell, but he wanted to.

Hell, but he shouldn't.

He had street business to take care of. Dirty dealings. He didn't want to bring the stench back with him to the clean, sweet thing.

What he primed himself to say next would ruin any chance of his ever being inside her again, but he had to say it. He looked away before he walked away.

"You came three times. Our bargain's done."

Chapter Eleven

Mercy plopped her one-step-from-being-pruned body onto the cool, satiny sheets, which were still saturated with the smell of sex and Sinner. Nestling her head onto his pillow indent, she inhaled deeply of his masculine scent and squeezed her arms around her middle. She'd finally had an orgasm.

Three, to be exact. Every one better than the last. No, make that every one different than the last. With each torrid climax, Sinner had shattered her universe.

She sighed. He was so wrong. Tonight's bargain might be finished, but there were more bargains to strike between them.

He'd acted cool and detached, but she suspected he liked her well enough.

Otherwise, he'd have laughed her off the first time she approached him with her unpracticed, magazine-read attempts at being sexy. And what about his apology? He was sorry he let her slip from the bench to leave her unsatisfied, and he kept apologizing and coming on to her even when she'd ignored him.

Mercy didn't plan to ignore him again. He was going to be hers until she left for home. Somehow.

She ran her fingers between her thighs over her sensitive flesh, trying to re-ignite the sensation only Sinner seemed capable of evoking there. What she needed was a plan of attack.

Oh, she'd attack his lusty body all right, once she got him back into her bed again. But first she had to come up with a way to get him there.

She stopped her pointless stroking. Bone tired and sated from their vigorous tryst, she rolled over and reached for her cell phone. She'd promised to call Cindy.

She paused. Maybe she shouldn't bother Cindy. Maybe Jay was finally showing her more than his etchings. Maybe he didn't even have etchings.

Sliding off the bed, Mercy strode over to the dresser and pulled a pair of striped cotton pajamas from a drawer. Thinking better of her promise, she grabbed the phone again. Suppose Jay was as slow with his advances as ever and Cindy had given up for the night and was waiting to come home.

When Mercy flipped the cell phone open, three text messages beeped for her attention. All from Cindy.

Are you all right? Call me.
Are you there? Call me.
Are you alive? Call me.

When she punched in Cindy's number, and her friend answered on the first ring, Mercy shook her head. This didn't sound promising for Cindy. Or Jay.

"It's me," Mercy said. "I got your messages. All of them. I'm alive."

"So far," Cindy gushed. "You did tell the doorman to take a good look at Sinner in case you turned up missing or dead so he could identify the devil in a lineup?"

"Yes, and the doorman thanked me before he asked if I needed drug testing." Mercy groaned. "Cindy, I couldn't treat Sinner like a serial killer even for your peace of mind." Then she lowered her voice to a purr. "Now, lady killer, that's another story. He certainly knew his way around this lady."

"I can hear you smiling from here," Cindy screeched. "You can give me all the details tomorrow, but for now, I have to know. Did you?"

"Yes." Mercy nodded. "I came. And Sinner's gone

home." Or somewhere. But why bother Cindy with specifics that would only drive her wild. Or wilder. "How's your night so far?"

"Jay does have etchings if you were curious."

"I was." Mercy laughed while alternating between holding the phone with her shoulder and sticking her arms into the short-sleeves of her pj's.

"The problem is I've seen them over and over. We've been taking digital pictures of every one of his etchings from every conceivable lighting angle." Cindy yawned, sounding bored. "He's asked me to help him put together a catalog of his artwork."

"So you two will be spending more quality time together." Mercy perked her ears, fishing for info from Cindy for a change while she wriggled into her pajama shorts.

"So far, the quality hasn't been so hot." Cindy yawned again, louder. "Maybe it'll improve once we're past the picture-taking stage. But I doubt that will happen tonight. I'll be home soon, but don't bother to wait up."

Mercy flipped the cell shut. Poor Cindy. Her date with Jay didn't sound very exciting. Now Sinner...Mercy's pulse raced just thinking his name. Maybe he had a friend to fix Cindy up with.

Not a good idea.

Shaking her head, she buttoned her pajama shirt. In the immortal words of Sister Doria, that good deed wouldn't go unpunished.

****

"Psst."

The hiss came from the shadows near the rear of the deserted parking lot of the restaurant adjoining the *Starry Night*. Spence strode toward the sound, and Google emerged from behind the pecan tree, which concealed the garbage bins from the dimly lit street. A breeze kicked up, and the odor from the Dumpster followed the informant as he stepped forward.

"Hey, Killer," Google grunted.

In a flash, he grabbed a handful of Google's grungy T-shirt. He wanted to wring his pudgy neck and rattle a few of his too-pearly white teeth but thought better of the idea before it was too late.

"Wha—what was that for?" the informant spat out once he'd let go of him. "Why so touchy?" The snitch smoothed his crumpled shirt. "I've heard other people call you Killer."

"Not to my face." Spence scowled a warning at the man. He might be a sinner, but he wasn't a killer.

"Hey, I don't blame you." Google sneaked a look around the deserted macadam lot. "I wouldn't want to be branded as the man who killed his best bud."

"Mark. My buddy had a name." Spence shook the tension from his fingers. "That's why I'm paying you, to help clear up the misconception. Along with my name. So do you have anything?"

The heavyset guy shoved his hands into the pockets of his oversized jeans. His striped underwear bulged up around his waist. "I need the cash up front."

"Yeah." Spence reached into his shirt pocket for a handful of twenties and stuck them under Google's nose.

"I have high-tech expenses. Programs, mother boards." Google filched the money into his deep pocket so fast Spence was left holding out his empty hand.

Pulling it away, he leaned his palm against the sturdy tree. The bark bit into his flesh, reminding him he could feel. Most days a numbness, which had come in handy during his jail time, still lingered over him.

Google moved closer, lowered his voice. His breath smelled of onions and mint and clung to the humid air. "If I'm acting spooked, it's because this guy, Jay, stiffed me earlier."

Jay? Spence cocked his head. "Is he the corporate boy-scout who hangs out at the *Starry Night?*"

"That's him. The prick." Google removed his wire-rimmed glasses to rub at his eyes.

So Jay was dirty. And where in the hell had Cindy been during the transaction? Was she a party to Jay's corporate crime? Spence frowned—none of these things bothered him as much as Google's lack of caution. He had a loose mouth for a man who dealt in secrets.

"White-collared boys are all crybabies, but they do pay up eventually." Google wiped the lenses of his glasses on the tattered hem of his T-shirt. "Those designer types are used to paying through the nose for everything."

"I'm not." Crossing his arms, Spence rolled his back against the tree to scratch an itch. Google was talkative tonight. Maybe he'd have something worthwhile to say.

The snitch shifted topics quick. "Besides his studio apartment above the nightclub, Parker has a house somewhere in the city. I haven't located it yet, but it doesn't matter right now. He's out of the city. Out of the state," he amended. "He's visiting a sick friend. Real sick. Like dying sick. Nobody knows when he'll be back." He put his glasses back on and scratched his nose. "Probably when the guy dies would be my guess."

"Don't guess." He pinned the man with a stern look. The eyes gawking back at him were red-rimmed, probably from long hours at a computer monitor. "I need facts. Does he know about me?"

"He knows you're out of..." He hesitated to say jail, as if Spence were too delicate to hear the word. "Out and about."

"Let me know the second Parker's back in San Antonio. Hell, make that back in Texas."

"Sure thing. While I'm working on finding Parker's house in the city, do you want me to work on the dying man's name and where he lives?"

"If you can."

"I can." Google puffed out his chest, nearly bursting the safety pins holding the neck of his T-shirt together. "But it might take some time."

"One other thing." Spence aimed his fingers at Google like a six-shooter. "Put a password on my file and a zip on your mouth."

"I'd never talk about you, Kil—I mean, Spence. I—I only mentioned Jay in passing. I know you can be trusted. You'd never repeat anything."

He nodded, leaving Google to handle his end of the snooping. Spence had one more source to check out. Afterward, he'd sell his horse for payoff cash, and then he had nothing but time to kill until Parker showed up. He hated killing time. He'd done enough of that in jail.

As difficult as it was to move ahead before avenging Mark, he could busy himself putting the ranch and fences to right. During the day.

He hopped into his dusty pickup and started the engine. But what about at night?

Mercy popped into his mind.

As he drove across the city in the opposite direction of the small spread he and Mark had owned together, he couldn't shake Mercy's image.

Naked, willing, soft, and silky. Her skin. Her hair.

Her heart.

His breath caught. She'd forgiven him for ditching her on the bench. She really was sweet—and tart.

Feeling he had no right to her sweetness, he chose to dwell on her saucier side. Her musky taste, her lush scent. Just the memory of caressing her fragrant, shivering flesh with his mouth and his hands was making him hard again.

He adjusted the front seat to give himself more legroom and ease the tight confinement of his jeans. The recollection of Mercy's raw gasps as she came and her contented sigh afterward made his efforts worthless. The naughty twinkle in her blue eyes whenever he suggested something, anything sexy, was branded in his mind.

He fumbled on the dash for a suitable CD, slapping it into the player. Fast, ruckus music shouted out at him, the lyrics having nothing to do with a sexy woman or a man's heart.

Mercy was a lost cause to him, and rightly so.

After what he'd said before walking away tonight, without so much as a good-night let alone a parting kiss, there was no chance she'd ever show him her mercy again.

****

The next day, Mercy shopped the air-conditioned mall with Cindy, looking for a memento of her Texas trip for her mother. She pointed to a store called *Sew Good*.

"Mom's planning to turn my bedroom into a sewing room when I ship off for school. What do you think, Cin?"

"No sin," she replied, dreamily, taking Mercy's comment out of context. "Just a chaste good-night kiss."

"I'd take that as a sign of progress for the slow-moving Jay." Mercy grasped her friend by the shoulder and steered her into the fabric store.

"He barely kissed my cheek," Cindy droned.

"His aim will get better with practice." Mercy stopped to finger a bolt of polished cotton.

Cindy touched the fabric. "Jay seemed more interested in my skill with the computer catalog program from work than with any talent my lips might have had." She shrugged her hands to her hips and pouted out her lips. "What's wrong with my mouth? Or my body, aside from my 34B's in a 38C world."

"Only Rita's world is 38C, and I have my doubts about her." Mercy tugged a bolt of material free from the stack. "I wouldn't be surprised if she leaked saline."

"I suspected a boob job." Cindy pulled at the hem of her yellow sleeveless sweater, which matched her yellow platform shoes. "Let's forget about her. What about me?" Sucking in her stomach, she pushed out her chest.

"You're perfectly proportioned for your size and you have adorable pouty...lips." With a chuckle, Mercy went back to fingering material.

"So why hasn't Jay noticed?"

"There's nothing wrong with a man admiring your brain. He was probably so caught up with cataloging his etchings that his attention was on perfecting the snapshots. I'm sure next time you get together, you'll *really* get together."

"I hope so. A girl could get a complex working with Jay. And Rita. She's always got her lips to his ear, whispering." Cindy flipped through the material on the table begrudgingly.

"Well, he didn't ask Rita to his apartment to see his etchings, did he?"

"No." Cindy sounded placated as she yanked out a few red-white-and-blue Lone Star patterns.

"Do you think I should get my mother something more personal than quilting material?" Mercy rummaged through a container of commemorative thimbles decorated with oil wells, longhorns, cowboy boots, or cowboy hats.

"A thimble's good. Once you move, you can send her one from every place you visit or live." Cindy crossed one platform-sandaled foot over the other.

"I'll get this nifty pair of quilting shears, too." She held up a pair of titanium scissors with pink finger linings. "Mom can quilt my uncle a thank you for her coveted sewing room." Mercy shrugged, suddenly feeling hopeless and restless. "That's if Uncle Parker returns or calls and lends me the money to make my move."

Cindy patted Mercy's hand. "I know how stifling Lily Pond can be. It's like living in jail. But I have every confidence that you'll break out."

After Mercy made her purchases, they lunched in a western chain restaurant inside the mall. Cindy leaned her elbows onto the wooden table and heaved a loud sigh. "I'm so relieved you survived last night. I was worried about you taking Sinner back to the condo." She sipped her margarita, eying Mercy over the rim of the salted glass. "Was he worth the risk?"

Mercy burst with pent-up rapture. "I didn't know sex could be so enthralling, so exciting. So..." She paused, searching for the right word.

"Orgasmic," Cindy offered. "Well, I'm glad that's out of the way, and you won't be seeing the sinner anymore."

"But I want to see him again. Lots of him. I'm like an addict now that I know what ecstasy I've been missing all these years." Mercy picked up her margarita glass to ease the memory of her frustrations.

Cindy reached across the table and stopped Mercy's hand mid-lip. "Mercy, hun, he's the type to hit-and-run. You won't see him again. He got what he was after. I warned you. Remember?"

"I know what you said, but—"

"Forget the but." Cindy shook her short brown locks. "This isn't Lily Pond. In my travels, I've encountered a few like him. Oh, maybe not dangerous looking, but I guarantee he won't show up at the bar again. If he does, he'll ignore you. Nothing personal, Mercy. That's just how those dark, elusive types operate. That's why I'm going after Jay with his boy-next-door persona. Wholesome, and right now, sexually frustrating." She laughed.

"I intend to have another go at the elusive hunk." Mercy loosened from Cindy's grip and sipped the salty, alcoholic drink.

"How do you propose to do that?"

"I'm not sure. But he must have a weakness. Something that's such a turn on, he can't resist. Something sexy, yet sensual."

"That sounds tricky. Now, me," Cindy said, poking at her chest. "I'm going for cleavage. Something that lifts and separates."

Chapter Twelve

By their fourth store, things began looking up for Cindy.

Beneath the pink clouds and silvery feathers floating in the Angelwear Lingerie Shoppe, Cindy scavenged the Cleavage Galore bin, while Mercy scrutinized her own bustline for flaws.

Her T-top seemed snug in all the right places, and Sinner certainly hadn't complained. She flushed at the sensual indulgences she'd experienced at his urgings. How she'd plucked and teased both their nipples.

With a slight sigh, she moved on to browse the undergarments tucked in neat piles. Besides breasts, a person could enhance their hips, butts, and thighs.

Mercy checked her torso and legs in a nearby full-length mirror. Sinner had licked every inch of her. Apparently, what she needed to lure him back into her bed wasn't bigger body parts.

"I don't know." Cindy drew Mercy's attention back to bras. "There are just too many. Water filled, fiber filled, foam filled, gel filled, even saline filled."

"Try one of each." All in favor of comparison shopping, Mercy sniffed a sample bottle of perfume from a low-floating cloud. Too heavenly. Mercy's intentions were bent on sin and Sinner, and all the cravings he was capable of satisfying.

Her shiver of anticipation was interrupted by Cindy. "I'm going with the saline." She squooshed the bra cup. "This one feels almost like me. Only more."

After ducking into the fitting room, Cindy

emerged a few moments later sporting her new bust.

"Are you sure you're not going to topple over?" Mercy wrinkled her nose, sure that her friend was.

"No. I can balance." With a wobble, Cindy swiveled in front of a gilded mirror. "I've always wanted cleavage."

"You've got it now." If only she could find what she was after as easily. The perfect turn on for Sinner.

After Cindy paid and they were on their way out of the mall, a flashing neon sign caught Mercy's eye. *Fishnet Fetish*. She stopped dead in her barefooted sandals.

"Forget it," Cindy declared. "My legs don't need a thing. Besides those loud-colored designs will clash with most of my shoes."

"I was thinking about my legs. And Sinner." Mercy cocked an eyebrow at her friend.

"Oh. In that case, it wouldn't hurt to look."

There were all kinds of fishnets. Wide blocks, tiny squares, squiggly patterns, diamond designs. And colors. Purple, red, green, white, to name a few.

"I'd better start small." Mercy picked up a pair of stockings with small mesh holes in a basic black. "To go with my little black skirt."

"Oh, what the heck." Cindy grabbed a pair of the widest holed fishnets in green. "To wear with my floral wedgies." She shrugged. "As a backup, if the bra should spring a leak."

"Speaking of backups..." Mercy spotted something as colorful. "What do you think? Once I lure him to my bed, I'll need to keep him there." She snatched up a container of edible body paint.

At the checkout counter, Cindy added a bottle of rainbow body glitter to her purchases. "For my cleavage. To point Jay in the right direction."

"Did you find everything you needed?" the sales clerk lisped. "New piercing," she explained, sticking out her tongue to show off her barbell stud.

Cindy looked at Mercy questioningly. Mercy shook her head. No way.

On their way out of the store, Cindy argued, "Sister Doria said never to look a gift horse in the mouth."

Mercy rolled her eyes. "That one's a stretch, even for you, Cindy."

****

They were dressed to kill. Mercy wore her fishnets while Cindy packed her 38's. They decided to try their new look out on strangers before venturing into the *Starry Night*.

"I heard about this lounge, *Taboo*. Some of the people drinking coffee around the Bunn at the office were ooh-ing and aah-ing about the place."

"Sounds like a start."

After a cab ride across town, they got out in a high-end shopping district a few blocks from the nightclub. "We'll browse the shops and get our land legs," Mercy suggested. Climbing from the air-conditioned taxi into the late day heat, she was glad for the airy holes in her stockings.

"Your fish-netted legs are doing fine," Cindy observed after a few steps, "but I'm still a little wobbly due to the weight distribution of my upper half." With a jiggle, she realigned her modified bust. "Maybe I should've used a lighter hand with the glitter."

"I warned you about getting too top heavy, but I don't think the glitter's what put you over." Mercy grabbed hold of Cindy's arm and helped her stroll down the street.

After a few stares and a wolf whistle, they entered *Taboo*, and crossed into another world. Mercy squinted into the drab lighting, clouded with smoky sandalwood incense.

"I guess the darkness is supposed to add an aura

of the forbidden," Cindy whispered.

"As in taboo," Mercy choked. "I get it." She held onto Cindy as they groped their way toward the loud, synthesized music.

"Let's sit here." Cindy grabbed the first available seats they came across.

Following Cindy's lead, Mercy plunked down onto one of the short leather hassocks surrounding a small, circular glass table trimmed with chain mail. She maneuvered her legs at an angle to keep her fishnets from snagging on the metal.

"What will you have?" a monotone voice asked, emerging from the bleakness.

She peered up at a chalky-complexioned waitperson dressed in black, who looked like a cross between Vampire Lestat and a medieval damsel in distress.

Cindy pursed her lips. "What's the house specialty?"

"You mean the *aphrodisiac* of the evening." The dark-draped person stared at them through yellow-and-black contacts that resembled the eyes of a wolf. "Tonight's aphrodisiac is a Screaming Orgasm."

"I'll try one of those." Mercy's pulse picked up remembering Sinner's promise of a screaming orgasm and how satisfyingly he'd delivered.

"What's in the drink?" Cindy asked more cautiously.

"Three liquors." Their server's black-cloaked shoulders shrugged. "The bartender can also make you a Screaming *Multiple* Orgasm." Briefly, Mercy wondered what the bartender who made orgasms looked like, until she reminded herself they were only talking about drinks. "The multiple has cherries. For those who have lost theirs," the dark one sneered.

"I'll have the single." Cindy sneered back, tapping her fingers to the music before changing the subject. "What's this song called?"

"This gothic rock piece doesn't have a title. The house band, which comes on next, plays industrial rock *with* titles." The server drifted off into the murky haze of strong incense, leaving Mercy to wonder if titles were an improvement.

"What kind of place *is* this?" She blinked, trying to peer into the eye-tearing smog.

Cindy blinked rapidly. "I'm not sure I'm seeing what I'm seeing."

Two men appeared in front of them from out of the cloying darkness. Mercy could tell they were male by their bare chests.

Cindy spoke up first. "Nice pants."

Black leather. Tight fitting. One guy was wearing chains at his waist instead of a belt while the other sported a belt buckle fashioned like a gigantic spider.

Mercy cleared her parched throat. "That leather must be hot."

Which might explain why they weren't wearing shirts.

The taller man raised his pierced eyebrow and looked her and Cindy up and down. "Baby bats," he said.

The other man shook his head. "Corporate Goths."

"Neither," Mercy said, although she didn't have the foggiest what they were talking about.

She eyed the metal studding the men. Along with his eyebrow, the taller one had pierced his lip, nipple, belly button, and goodness knows what else. The shorter guy wore pierced earrings, kohl-black on his eyes, and a midnight-blue gelled Mohawk.

"Do you dance, drink, and do the dirty?" the one with the blackened eyes asked Mercy.

"Not in that order or on the first date." Mercy coughed, waving away the incense, wishing she'd tried the fishnet stockings out directly on Sinner.

The metallic man winked at Cindy, honing in on her cleavage. "You're a girl, huh? My name's Grunt." He thumbed his chest, missing his pierced nipple by a hair.

"Nice to meet you, Grunt." Cindy stuck out her hand.

He shook it awkwardly, apparently not sure if that's what was expected of him.

"Mine's Damien," the guy with the blue Mohawk said.

Mercy wondered if she should take that as an omen.

****

Spence had wasted most of last night searching in vain for a guy named Raven, who used to be called Clint in his former non-Goth life. He'd been a friend of Mark's during his rodeo days and before Clint's penchant for whips and chains had replaced lariats.

Before parking his pickup in *Taboo's* lot, he checked for Raven's black Jeep with the gold-winged insignias. It was there.

Hating to rely strictly on Google for information, he sauntered toward the entrance. Down here in the underbelly of San Antonio, lots of hearsay was bandied about, although most talk was kept amongst its patrons by some unspoken code of honor. But if Raven still felt any friendship or loyalty for Mark, he may give something up.

Spence entered the lounge and scanned the room. Once his eyes adjusted to the blackness—the black clad bodies, the black lighting, the black walls—he spied Raven at the bar. The man's arm was wrapped around the neck of a lady wearing a spiked dog collar that matched Raven's metal-studded belt.

He made his way toward the couple. Hell, it wasn't his thing, but they looked happy enough. If happy could be defined by a lack of frowns. Or smiles. He glanced around. Nobody in the place cracked a smile. Except maybe those two seated in the darkest corner near the band.

A loud laugh rang out from one of the women, and a chill ran up his spine. Cindy.

"Damn it." As he got nearer to Raven, he could make out the smiling face of the other woman across the room. Sure enough, those familiar lips were the ones he craved. Mercy's.

What in the hell was she doing here?

"Hey, Raven," Spence said as he kept one eye on Mercy.

What in the heck did she have on beneath that short skirt? Fishnet stockings. He closed both of his eyes briefly. Nothing good could come of this.

Chapter Thirteen

"Hi," the female said.

Playing it extra cautious, Spence merely nodded to the pale lady in the leather collar, figuring it wasn't in his best interest to speak to her unless Raven introduced her.

He leaned his elbow against the bar next to Raven. Amidst the gloomy atmosphere, the guy looked agreeable enough. Glad to see him, actually.

"Heard about Mark. Sad." Raven shrugged his shaved head, and a scar near his temple creased.

"Yeah." Spence squinted through the hazy incense burning his eyes and throat in Mercy's direction. Who was she with besides her friend, Cindy?

A man. She was talking to some young, bare-chested guy, and she had a cheery smile plastered to her lips.

Heat crawled up Spence's neck. He jammed his hands into his pockets. Getting hot under the collar wasn't smart or healthy, especially in a dive like this. But his blood boiled with jealousy, and he hated that the emotion ate at his gut.

"Sorry about your deal. Raw." Raven offered his tattooed hand. The Lone Star and an Egyptian cross intertwined, apparently in honor of his Western past and Goth present.

Spence obliged him with a firm handshake, keeping his fisted hand in his pocket while concentrating on not watching Mercy and the half-naked man on the other side of the room. "Thanks," he mumbled absently before he delved for information. "My bum rap's what I'm here to see you about." He looked Raven square on, trying to gauge if he knew anything he'd willingly share.

"Drink?" Raven asked, signaling for the bartender.

"Whiskey." Spence nodded.

"Three shots," Raven ordered, obviously including his nameless girlfriend in the round. "I figured you'd show sooner or later." He flexed his forearm and hand.

His hairy knuckles made a bone-cracking sound, causing Spence to wonder how much the man believed in his innocence. Raven's girlfriend reached over, her black lacquered nails drab in the dim light, and massaged her man's tensed, tattooed hand until he shrugged her off.

Spence crossed one booted foot while he bided his time. He didn't push Raven. His type would either tell what he knew or not. Bargaining wouldn't change the outcome.

Raven mouthed the name "Parker." Sneering, he narrowed his eyes that still looked enormous in his bald head.

"Yeah." Spence sucked in a breath of the stifling air. Looked like Raven had reached the same conclusion about the lying bar owner as he had. Perjury.

"His dying friend..." Raven waited. Spence nodded. "He's the slug who blind-sided you and Mark. From what I hear, Parker didn't see a thing. Wasn't even in the car that night."

Spence whistled a long breath, rustled his fingers through his hair. The situation was worse than he'd thought. He had no prior gripe with Parker. Why had the man set him up?

"Why?" Spence said aloud but mostly to himself.

"Damned if I know," Raven said through a snarl. "I wish I had the other scumbucket's name for you."

Silence fell amid the gloomy lighting as the bartender slid three shot glasses onto the scarred bar in front of them. Spence dug several crinkled bills from his pocket and flipped them onto the bar for the drinks. "Parker's supposed to own a house somewhere in the city. You happen to know where?"

The man shook his head. "Far as I know he lives above the nightclub."

"If you hear anything," Spence picked up his shot glass, "I'd appreciate knowing."

"Sure thing. You still at the ranch?"

"Yeah." Spence clapped him on the back.

Raven turned to his girlfriend. With a snap from his fingers, she picked up the shot glass and held the whiskey to his lips while he drank it down.

Spence downed his shot under his own power, figuring Raven had problems with his arm. Bad tattoo, rodeo injury, bar fight. Could be anything. Or he could be deep into the Dom/sub thing.

Not to wear out his welcome, Spence drifted toward an unlit spot near the dance floor where he could watch the band and Mercy. Her naïve curiosity and this dark den were a scary mix.

He spotted her fabulous legs, easily, even disguised by the inviting, kinky fishnets and blocked partially by the guy with the hairy, bare back.

Those sexy, silky legs had driven him and ridden him. As he pictured them wet and glistening in the roomy shower, he wished he could take back his hasty departing words from last night.

****

"So, what's your name?" Damien scratched at his naked chest as if he had fleas.

"Mercy." She wondered why she was wasting his and her time with introductions when the only man she was interested in was across town in the *Starry Night*.

As soon as her drink came and she paid, she was

un-jamming her legs from beneath the table—snags or no snags—and giving Cindy a kick to leave. It was time to test the fishnets where they counted. Sinner's reaction was the only one she craved.

Cindy was occupied, flashing her glittery cleavage and posing for Grunt, who expressed his admiration with a drooling grin.

"Come on." Damien shook his head, his blue Mohawk never budging. "What's your real name?"

"That *is* my real name," Mercy insisted.

He leaned in, blotting her vision with his bare chest and its matting of hair. Looked as if Damien was blond beneath all the blue gel.

Sinner's hair was coarser, his chest broader, his muscles harder. She sighed, determined to be the object of one particularly hard muscle of his before this night ended.

Damien leaned his taut arms onto the small glass table. His veins bulged blue, a shade lighter than his hair.

But the arms she was interested in weren't veined. Sinner's arms were firmer, stronger, more honed. So capable of holding her, molding her, possessing her.

A clunk brought her attention back to reality, as unreal as that seemed to be in this place. Damien's spidery belt buckle hit the glass tabletop as he crouched in closer. He wasn't wearing any weird colored contacts with cat stripes. His eyes were brown.

She blinked. But not as dark, or mysterious, or captivating as Sinner's.

"Want to dance?" He lowered his eyelids, trying for a seductive look that was pretty hard to pull off in his getup.

"To this?" The three-man band managed to give music a bad name. Or no name, according to their server.

Damien tilted his head to listen, and the skull-and-crossbones studding his ear scowled at her. She'd never danced with a man wearing earrings before, and she didn't plan to.

"Anything goes in here." Damien turned back toward her, a glint in his inky-ringed eyes.

"I've noticed." And on that note, she was exiting and taking Cindy with her. Drink or no drink. She'd leave money on the table. "Oh, look at the time." She stuck her wristwatch beneath Damien's nose before glaring at Cindy across the table. "What do you say, Cindy? Time to go."

But Cindy couldn't hear her. She was occupied by Grunt yanking her onto her stumbling feet.

"No thanks on the dancing," Cindy protested as he swayed in place with her.

"She said no," Mercy repeated for Grunt, in case the metal piercings in his ears were interfering with his sound waves.

Grunt grinned at Mercy, and continued dancing with Cindy, who stomped on his foot. But her platform-soled shoe was no match for his black, leather commando boot.

Mercy got up to assist her friend, and Damien somehow mistook her standing up to mean she'd changed her mind about dancing. When he grabbed her hand to lead her onto the dark dance floor, Mercy tugged away and tripped over the short hassock she'd been sitting on.

She waved her arms in fruitless circles as she plummeted backwards. Losing leverage, she closed her eyes and braced for the fall. But before she landed on her behind, a pair of strong arms caught and lifted her against a hard, masculine chest.

"I owed you one since your tumble from the park bench," a voice near her ear said.

Sinner.

Mercy twisted in his muscled, familiar arms,

looked up into his handsome face, glad to see him, sort of. She'd have preferred if Damien and Grunt weren't present.

Sinner smelled so good, so manly, like woodsy aftershave and whiskey. His body against hers felt hard and inviting. She didn't know if she should sigh or smile or kiss him. She did nothing, just let him continue to hold her.

"What's going on here?" he asked in a slow, low tone, eyeballing the other men.

Just then their server arrived with a tray and their drinks. "Two Screaming Orgasms."

Sinner's eyes widened. Mercy shrugged. Grunt put both hands up to indicate they weren't his drinks, which released Cindy, who paid the server before grabbing a glass and swigging down a large gulp. Damien hitched his spider-shaped buckle, and everyone started explaining at once.

Sinner listened for about thirty seconds before he kissed Mercy right on the mouth in front of everybody.

At first, his lips were tender and seducing. Once he slipped her his tasty tongue and began performing a carnal act with hers, the kiss became volatile. Heated arousal swept through her, and an insistent throb pulsed between her legs. She pressed her tingling nipples into his chest, wanting to get close to any body part of his that promised any kind of friction, in spite of the small audience watching them.

Was exhibitionism becoming a big turn on for her? Or was her passion for Sinner simply that overpowering?

Luckily, he had more restraint.

After kissing her, very thoroughly, with a lot of tongue, he pulled his tantalizing mouth away.

When Mercy opened her eyes, Damien was stepping into the dusky background. "Sorry, man, didn't know she was spoken for." Grunt followed his friend in a quick, vanishing departure.

"New friends?" Sinner met her eyes. His were soft with concern before he glanced at her legs and they turned dark and sultry. "Great stockings."

He poked a finger into the mesh of her fishnets, dragging his nail over the tender flesh of her thigh. She sucked in her breath to stop herself from moaning in front of Cindy and the people at nearby tables who'd taken an interest in the ruckus. But his bold touch was hot and welcome. She clung to his neck with both arms while a single, brazen thought raked through her.

His naked, hard body taking hers to orgasm.

With a knowing smile, he let her slip from his strong arms, placing her firmly on her high-heeled feet. Her knees felt weak, her legs rubbery. Grasping his toned biceps did nothing to ease her erratic pulse or her sizzling aroused state. The muscles beneath his smooth skin felt so solid and able.

She'd never cool down if she stayed in his sexually stimulating proximity. Mercy let go of his arm as soon as her balance steadied.

"If you two are ready to leave, I'll see you out. Or home." His voice was an alluring rumble.

"Home," Mercy coughed out. Looked like sinful things were coming her way. "I need a dose of cough medicine after this overdose of incense."

"You can drop me off at the *Starry Night*," Cindy said after taking another long sip from her drink. "Thanks for helping us make new friends, keep the old, and all that."

"Confucius or Doria?" Sinner furrowed his brows.

"Doria." Mercy snatched up her purse from the tabletop.

After she righted her skirt and Cindy readjusted her low-cut knit top, Sinner tucked Mercy's arm in his. But once they edged around the table toward the glow of the exit sign, he pulled back.

"A screaming orgasm, huh?" He tasted the tall, frothy drink. "I've had better." He winked at Mercy. "And recently."

She smiled at him through heavy-lidded eyes as her insides melted like warm, oozing marmalade.

Oh, yeah. Sinner had weaknesses.

Chapter Fourteen

Spence walked Mercy to the front door of her friend's swanky apartment. It wasn't in him to just drop her off on the street since the incident at the *Taboo* club with the Goth warrior-wannabes.

He had a need to protect her and a conflicting need to run hard and fast from the responsibility. Taking care of his own messed up situation was all he could manage right now.

"I never thanked you properly for coming to my aid."

Mercy leaned her supple body into his, reached up, and captured his head in her slender fingers, skimming a sensitive area behind his ears with her fingernails. Tingles ran the length of his spine to congregate at the tip of his dick.

When she touched her mouth to his, her lips felt warm and soft. No, more than soft. He'd kissed women with soft lips before. Gentle, that was it. And comforting.

And he was reading too much into the simple kiss.

He pulled away, but instead of leaving his warring emotions on her doorstep, he found himself asking, "Does thanking me include inviting me in?" He teased his fingers across the swell of her breast, touching her naked skin where her neckline dipped.

"Mmm," she lowered her eyes, turned slightly, and unlocked the door. She left it open wide as she entered the marble foyer.

Her hips swayed with her every high-heeled click across the polished floor. He groaned, knowing full well the feel of her hips naked and grinding beneath his.

Had saving her enticing butt from the Goths vindicated him? Had she forgiven him his hasty words from last night? Was the curve of her tight ass in her short skirt his invitation to enter?

Or was she seeking revenge by cockteasing?

While he debated her intent, his eyes trailed the black seams of her fishnets downward to skim over her well-shaped calves and her trim ankles. And swiftly back up when she reached to hang her purse on a brass coat hook. Her hemline took a slow ride, inching up until more than the lacy tops of her stockings were exposed.

Her black skirt barely concealed the tantalizing vee between her legs. Did she have panties on?

His ragged breath built to a low growl, and he stepped inside the foyer, kicking the door shut with his booted heel. Hearing the slam, she shifted on her high heels and tossed him a come-hither look over her shoulder. His dick hardened, and his blood thundered in his ears.

Oh, yeah. His foot, or rather his boot, was back in her door again.

His body throbbed, aching to take her here, up against the cool marble wall. But his mind was set on stripping off her stockings while she writhed on her satiny sheets.

"I'd like to peel those stockings off with my teeth." He rested his eyes on her milky thighs, which looked all the more tempting winking at him through the fishnet of her stockings.

"I'd like you to." She was so damn sensual and enthusiastic. Always ready for a new sexual adventure. A man could fall for a woman like her if he didn't watch his step.

He strode forward, secure that his heart was steeled and cold. Not just by the people he'd met in jail and on the streets. Or even those who'd set him up. But deadened by his losses. The woman who swore she'd wait but ran out before the trial started. His parents, gone in an automobile accident while he'd served his unwarranted time. Mark, his best friend, slain for no apparent reason other than walking a woman to her car.

His heart was frozen but safe.

He came up behind Mercy, wrapping his arms around her waist and hugging her to him, settling her pliable ass against his rigid, ready dick.

Her curves were made for love. No, he meant fucking. She fit him perfectly, and he ground his hips into the cleft of her round ass to prove the point.

"Why don't we go into the bedroom and you can show me how talented your teeth are?" Her breath a wisp of mint, her tone smoldering.

Lightly, he bit her neck. She laughed and bent her head, giving him better access to the tender flesh. Her skin felt smooth and tasted like honey as his teeth drew her in.

He nibbled higher and tugged at her earlobe, imitating what he planned to do to her stockings with his teeth. She shivered an encouraging response, her throat vibrating in a husky moan.

Damn, but she got to him. He was rock-solid by the time she took his hand and led him into her bedroom.

Mercy positioned her sensual body on the scented, satin sheets and held her slender arms out to him, coaxing, eager. He looked down at her, so seductively beautiful.

He didn't have the right. But also he didn't have the will to leave. He knelt on the mattress in front of her, sliding his palms up her calves, over her thighs and down again. He teased her responsive flesh several times, enjoying her shivers beneath the meshy fishnets and his hands.

He traced kisses along the same path, up her long legs and back down, heating her cool, sleek skin with his mouth. When he started upward again, he worked his tongue into the cobwebby fabric of her stockings and tickled the tender flesh behind her knees and on the inside of her creamy thighs. She moved restlessly, and her skirt hitched higher on her hips, revealing a seductive flash of her black panties.

But he restrained himself from going right for the tasty target. Darting his tongue through the holes of her hose, he licked a slow trail up her leg and ran his open mouth over the exposed flesh at the top of her thigh-high stocking. Mercy's skin quivered beneath his touch while her breathing quickened into soft, steady pants.

Still, he took his time, taking hold of the spidery top of one stocking with his teeth and tugging downward. She moved her legs wider apart to assist him, and he lost his cool midway to her knee, quickly backtracking to her inner thigh. With her skirt up around her waist, he had easy access to her irresistible pussy.

He wriggled the slinky material of her panties aside with his index finger and slipped the tip of his tongue inside. He teased at her clit, lapping his tongue over her slickness several times before grating the tasty morsel with his teeth and tugging rhythmically.

Her moans told him how much she delighted in his vigorous efforts. He stopped to tease her further. "Do you prefer tongue or teeth, babe?"

"Both. Don't stop." She tangled her fingers in his hair and directed him back to where she wanted him.

He chuckled and went with little resistance.

She was moist, sweet, and ready. Her sensitive nub had swelled and hardened. She arched, grinding against his mouth.

He stopped again. "I haven't finished with your stockings."

"Oh, yes, you have." She rolled toward the nightstand where a shopping bag was stashed beneath. Digging in she pulled out a pair of sewing shears. Handing the scissors to Sinner, she demanded, "Either peel them off or cut them off."

"In a hurry, huh?" He loved her spontaneous reactions. Unlike other women he knew, she was unrehearsed and genuine in her desires.

He eased one blade underneath a netted hole near her toe, clipping slowly, allowing the sleek metal to tantalize her sensitive flesh, especially the closer he inched up her leg toward her inner thigh. She shivered. Her breath halted. The danger, the excitement, the innate trust involved in the act wasn't lost on her. Or him. His nerve endings tingled. His cock twitched. With the sharp, pointed tips of the shears aimed threateningly toward her silken-clad pussy, he snipped through the lacy top of the stocking and the fishnet fell away.

"Hurry. The other one." She sounded breathy, arousal evident in her sultry voice. While lifting her still-stockinged leg, she wriggled her other free of the shredded remnant.

Her wiggling made it difficult to slip the sharp tip of the scissors into the fishnet on her upraised foot. "Don't move," he commanded, clasping her calf in his other hand. She stilled, her immediate compliance a turn-on that tightened his sac. He snipped upward, the black flimsy stocking giving way to reveal a growing slash of her creamy skin that whet his lust.

By the time he finished, an idea glinted with the hovering scissors.

"What about your panties?" He waited for her reply.

"Yes." Her blue eyes blazed with sexual

excitement. She lifted her hips and stilled her breathing.

Carefully, he worked the blade beneath the narrow strip of fabric at her crotch and cut.

With a gasp, she exhaled. "I've always wanted crotchless panties."

He smiled. She was full of unfulfilled fantasies it seemed.

With a grin, she snatched the scissors and dropped them onto the nearby night table. With her free arm, she cradled his neck and pulled him down on top of her.

"I take it you're ready," he muttered.

She answered him with her mouth, sealing her lips to his, lashing at his tongue with hers, then stopping to nip at his chin and jaw.

Spence didn't bother to strip her naked or to undress himself. Hurriedly, he worked at his fly, unbuttoning and unzipping to free himself. Her nimble fingers rushed to assist him, and with both their hands in action, they were protected in no time.

When he entered her, she wrapped her taut legs around his waist and suddenly he wasn't so frantic. She felt tight, wet, and hot, but she also felt different. Different from any woman he'd ever been inside. Like he was in too deep. Yet wanted to stay all night.

Staying the night was not a practice he indulged.

Attachments could only slow him down. He had to keep his mind on the prize. On justice for himself and Mark.

He refocused, and with slow, easy strokes, he rebuilt the urgency to a smoldering height. She clung to him, arched up to meet him, urging him into a wilder tempo with her fingernails and her heels. In a pulsing sensation, his cock flexed and his cum flowed. He continued to pump until her body shuddered and he brought her to orgasm.

When his arms collapsed, he lifted himself up onto his elbows to brush a damp strand of blonde hair from her glistening forehead. Smiling, he uttered, "That was nice," before he could stop himself.

He didn't want nice in his life. Especially not *nice* sex. He had to stick to down-and-dirty and concentrate on getting Parker or his friend, and frequenting whatever smutty places that involved.

None of which were anywhere near Mercy's clean sheets and sweet body.

"That was more than nice," she gasped, catching her breath. "I can't believe I came again. I thought the other night was just a fluke."

"A nice fluke." Which he needed space from before he said *nice* one more time. Rolling away, he slipped from the bed. "I'm thirsty, what about you?"

She propped her head on one hand, watching him from beneath a questioning brow. "There's bottled water in the fridge."

After detouring to the bathroom to flush the condom, he thought about grabbing his jeans. But with Cindy out chasing Jay there was no need. Spence headed for the kitchen bare-ass naked.

When he opened the door to the fridge, a surprise jerked his head back. There, spotlighted in the glow from the bulb and looking as fresh picked as a Spring day, was the corona he'd bought Mercy.

He lifted the circle of flowers and sniffed at their faint fragrance. Why had Mercy kept them? He thought women only kept flowers from men they cared about.

The patter of her bare feet made him glance her way. He sucked in his breath. Mussed yet sexy, in a light blue, silky robe that brought out the brightness of her eyes yet opened to expose her dewy skin,

Mercy somehow managed to look pure and nasty all at the same time.

Sliding her arm around his waist, she joined him in front of the open refrigerator. "Find anything good?" She touched the hand holding the corona of flowers.

Her filmy robe against his naked skin felt sleek and smooth and her body underneath accessible. His urge to have her again was overwhelmed by a silly impulse to kiss the top of her head.

"I was surprised to see you'd kept them," he said to stop himself from following through with the affectionate gesture.

Mercy looked up at him. She didn't answer. She bit her bottom lip, not quite sure how to reply. Flowers from a man who measured his words and actions were not something she'd throw away.

"Flowers are nature's way of smiling." She quoted the Doriaism, then decided to come clean. He deserved her honesty. He was always forthright with her—bluntly so at times. "Although my pride was hurt because you left without an explanation, I knew missing the bench seat and landing on the ground was an accident." She pecked his cheek. "Even Cindy's nagging couldn't change my mind."

He placed the chilled flowers on her head, arranging the halo so the ribbons streamed down her back. The cool edges tickled her spine through the thin robe when he tilted her face up to his for a warming kiss. "Flowers are for wearing, not for saving."

Before she could reply, he grabbed a green, long-necked bottle of water and slammed the refrigerator door shut on his unexpected sentiment, the glimmer in his eyes, and the gentle tone of his voice, leaving them both in the dark.

The soft fragrant blooms and the blackness raced Mercy's imagination. She removed the flowers from her hair. Leaning back, she held them between her and Sinner's naked torsos, letting the dangling ribbons tickle his groin.

He slid her silky robe from her shoulders and tugged the material, pulling her down to lie with him on the cool tile floor. "I can think of a few body parts I wouldn't mind paying floral tribute to."

She sought his eager mouth in the darkness. "That's why you're my dream guy."

Chapter Fifteen

Hours later at the front door, Sinner leaned a work-scarred hand against the jamb. He felt lost for parting words. Probably because he didn't want to leave her.

Mercy didn't seem to have the same problem.

"Good night," she gushed. Smiling sweetly, she pecked a kiss to the corner of his mouth and reached for the door latch. She looked tired from their rigorous lovemaking and cocksure where to find him tonight—in his usual spot at the *Starry Night Club*.

Before thinking it through, he heard himself say, "I can stop by later with takeout for dinner."

Shock widened her eyes and froze her fingers to the latch.

Damn, his offer had come out sounding like a date.

"Or I can see you at the Riverwalk, at the *Starry Night*," she amended.

Yeah, he'd scared her all right. She obviously wanted things between them to stay on a casual track.

And so did he. Despite his sentimental lapse in judgment earlier. Why should he care if she'd kept his flowers?

As she groped at the hardware, she studied his face, probably wondering why he was suddenly acting like a man misled by a satiny bed. He knew the score. There wasn't anything between them but sex.

Grabbing onto the doorknob, she twisted it.

He shoved his hands into his jean pockets, his

tall frame blocking her from opening the door. "Do you like Chinese, Italian, or Mexican food?" he pursued when he probably should've dropped it.

But food wasn't a date. Her serious eyes were reading too much into his simple offer to feed her.

"Food can be downright erotic," he said, and her blue eyes took on a sultry edge. He had her interest peaked. And his own. "Take dessert, for instance." He whispered near her ear. "Hot fudge. Warm and slippery and sweet. Dribbling onto sensitive body parts before being licked away."

She dropped her hand from the brass knob and licked her lips. "Surprise me."

"Should I bring enough for three?"

Her eyes went blank. It took him a moment to catch on. He chuckled. "I wasn't hinting at a threesome."

She shook her head. "Good because that isn't a fantasy of mine."

"Do you think your roommate will be here and hungry?"

"Oh, Cindy." She smiled. "You meant in case Cindy decided to stay in." Mercy pointed to the triangle-shaped clock on the wall that read two a.m. "She might *still* be out."

"Give me your number, and I'll check before I come over."

Her smile dropped.

He should have known. Wanting her phone number sounded too date-like. But he couldn't back down now. It would make it seem significant.

With a tight fist, she scrunched the throat of her robe and recited her cell number.

He didn't bother to repeat it, and she didn't seem to care that he didn't. She'd probably prefer if he forgot it and she caught up to him at the club, like before.

Where nothing resembled a date.

"Good night." He lowered his head and kissed her on the mouth. Too light and too sweet.

But he'd worry about that later. He had all day to get his feelings back under control. Hell, he had until Parker showed up. After that, he'd bet his lone horse other emotions would take charge. Bitter, angry ones.

He turned and let himself out, hearing her click the lock as soon as he closed the door.

****

Mercy flicked her tongue along her bottom lip, tasting the aftermath of his kiss. With a slow slide, she let her feet give out from under her until she ended up sitting on the hard, marble floor.

"Whew." That good night kiss had been scary. Too soft, too tender. If this affectionate, non-sexual side of Sinner persisted, she'd have to set him straight. She wasn't about to fall for the dark, perplexing man.

Forcing herself to stay grounded, she labeled their sensuous acts with the most vulgar term she could think of...they'd fucked. That was all.

Sure, he was tall, dark, and desirable. Humorous at times. Gentle on occasion. But all those attributes had to do with sex, she assured herself as she pushed to her feet and headed for the shower.

An hour later, Cindy arrived home from the *Starry Night* to a scattering of petals across the kitchen floor and more questions than Mercy cared to answer.

"I'm supposing the flowers fell out of the fridge, knocking over the water, and the barefooted smudges along with several unrecognizable body imprints were caused by..." She closed one eye as if gauging the scene. "Stop me at any time if you feel I'm off base here." Cindy giggled from her spot on the kitchen counter where she dangled her legs, her clunky shoes tapping.

Mercy worked the mop across the floor, erasing the remnants of her rousing romp with Sinner before Cindy got any more graphic with her speculations. "Just good clean fun is all."

"Calling a sinner good is a stretch of my imagination." She frowned. "He still worries me. He's so secretive."

"I'm seeing him again," Mercy stated, not about to be deterred.

After a long pause her friend ceded. "My evening with Jay, on the other hand, was wholesomely clean with very little fun."

"Aw, Cindy, I'm sorry." She rinsed out the mop. "Didn't he notice your enhanced endowments?"

Cindy shrugged. "When he left me off, he looked as if he was going to grope me, but instead pecked a quick good-night kiss that landed near my top lip."

Poor Cindy. "He's getting closer to your mouth."

She waved it off. "Let's talk about you and the marks on the floor you're so frantic to polish away."

"Unlike your relationship with Jay, mine and Sinner's is purely physical. My future doesn't include any serious dating with the cowboy, regardless of how hot he is. I have life-changing plans to cement as soon as my uncle comes back or calls."

Cindy crinkled her brows.

Mercy shook her head, adamant to affirm her point. "Our relationship is strictly sexual." She nudged the mop handle toward Cindy's chest. "What happened after Jay *almost* grabbed your saline sweeties and *almost* kissed you?"

"He suggested we get together tonight to finish cropping the pictures for his portfolio."

"At his place again?" Mercy raised her brow. "That has potential."

"Not enough. I've decided to pull out the big guns."

Mercy's eyes widened. Not a bigger cup size!

Cindy nodded her head, determined. "The Mesopotamia. He's never seen it other than in publicity shots. So if you insist on seeing Sinner and have any designs on the tub, you better go for it tonight." She eyed Mercy, curiously. "Looks like he's staying the course until the end of your vacation. I was wrong about him bolting after one or two trysts." Cindy scratched her head. "Makes you wonder, doesn't it?

"Made me wonder," Mercy said in all honesty, unsure of the unexpected changes in Sinner but positive her future didn't include him.

****

Fresh from the shower, Mercy slipped on jeans and a tank top before joining Cindy in the living room. "I left my cell in here. Did it ring?"

"Nope." Her friend's bra-enhanced knockouts were showcased in a red, vee-necked sundress. She was meeting Jay for drinks at the club before heading over to his apartment to finish their digital photography, and she was apparently dressed to give his pixels some stiff competition.

"No calls. That's good." Mercy nodded. Sinner had said he'd call before arriving for their date-that-wasn't-a-date so she was able to breathe easy. She was more than happy to let things cool between them until he snapped back to his usual, less affectionate self.

Her cell phone rang, and her spine stiffened. When she flipped it open, she was grateful to see her mother's number displayed.

Skipping over the hellos, her mother zinged right to the core of her concern. "I haven't heard from your Uncle Parker. He said he'd call this week."

"I haven't talked to him either, but as far as I know, he's still out of town."

"He's never broken his word to me. Why is he

acting like this?"

She pictured her mother wringing the phone cord and picked her words, careful to ward off what sounded like a panic attack on her mother's end. "He's visiting a sick friend. I'm sure he'll turn up soon."

"He promised to show you and Cindy around San Antonio. He never breaks a promise."

"And I'm sure he won't break this one either."

"Call me as soon as you see or hear from him."

"You can count on it."

When she hung up, Mercy turned to her friend. "She's upset about my uncle not showing us around. It's out of character for him not to keep his word when it comes to family and friends."

"I'm sure she's worried about more than that. There's the matter of your uncle and the loan. It's important for her to see you happy."

"I was so busy calming her down I didn't question her reasoning. If I have to, I can phone him when I get back home, even though I'd much rather borrow money from him in person."

"Maybe you should call her back."

"I'll wait until tomorrow. If she hasn't heard from him by then, I'll persuade her that I don't mind asking for a loan over the phone." But she crinkled her nose at the thought.

"Are you going out like that?" Cindy raised both brows. "You'll have to hurry if we're sharing a cab."

"I'm staying in tonight."

"Better watch out. Absence makes the heart grow fonder," she teased.

"I hope not." Mercy hooked elbows with her friend and walked her to the foyer. "I'd just as soon avoid Sinner since his lapse in character."

Cindy jerked her arm free. "What has he done now?"

"Made plans with me ahead of time. I don't need

a boyfriend. I need a sex machine."

"So he's considerate *and* sexy." Cindy shrugged, grabbing for the door handle. "Maybe you brought out some long dormant manners in the guy. Don't freak over it. Enjoy it. By the time he lapses back into his demon self, you'll be home in Pennsylvania." She flung the door open. "Oh, hi."

There stood Sinner about to ring the bell. Tonight, he didn't have a stitch of black on. He wore washed out blue jeans and a gray T-shirt. Mercy's heart flipped. He wore them so well.

He stepped aside and let Cindy dart by. "Goodbye."

Slamming the door, he greeted Mercy with a passionate liplock that took her by surprise. His lips were firm yet sensual, and the taste of him drove her wild. Stretching up on her bare toes, she maneuvered her neediest body part up against his solid, inviting fly.

How could she want him this much and this soon after last night's more than satisfying encounters? Who was she kidding? The kitchen floor had barely dried when she had wanted him again.

Now that he was here, why deny herself?

With a moan, she snuggled into his groin, grinding her hips in suggestive motions. Both his mouth and his zipper reacted, hot and eager.

Once she left Texas and Sinner, who knew when she'd meet a man who measured up again. If ever. She imagined a woman was only entitled to such volatile sex once in her lifetime.

He pulled away. "Let's save this for dessert."

She looked behind him on the floor for the takeout containers. "Where's the hot fudge?"

He laughed. "I was mending the corral fence and lost track of time. I figured we'd walk down to the local deli for something."

"I'll fetch my sandals." She hurried, greedy to

get the eating part of the evening out of the way and begin the sweaty, naked part.

In no time, they were outdoors, walking down the sidewalk like any ordinary couple, strolling hand-in-hand in the early evening. At first, she chafed at the boyfriend/girlfriend image reflecting back at her in the storefront windows. But she and Sinner were not an average twosome—once indoors, he'd take her to heights of ecstasy that were anything but typical.

She looked up and met his dark eyes. His barroom pallor was sun-kissed from his workout today while repairing the corral. A warm breeze brushed through his black hair, giving him a sexy, mussed appeal. She itched to get her hands in it, all over him really.

He crooked a smile as if reading her mind and chucked her under the chin. "Hungry?"

"Very."

His hold on her hand tightened. He entwined his fingers with hers. Noise from the nearby traffic hummed in her ears but couldn't drown out the thrum of her heart, beating with a sexual hunger they both meant to satisfy after they ate. She sped up their pace. The canopied entrance to the deli couldn't come into sight fast enough.

When they finally arrived, he held the door open for an elderly man and woman who both used canes. Next, a party of six, led by a red-headed woman, barged through ahead of them. The last person in the group, a tall, thin man, greeted Sinner when he brushed by. "Hey, Killer."

Sinner's jaw muscle tightened.

With a slight chuckle, Mercy ducked under Sinner's muscled arm, teasing, "It's no secret you're a lady killer."

He shook his head, his eyes dark and brooding.

Why was he insisting he wasn't a ladies' man?

119

Was he becoming infatuated with her? She didn't like that idea and decided to do something about it.

Grabbing hold of his tense arm, she turned so that her breast brushed against his ribs, enticingly. Her tone became suggestive and drew his focus back to where she wanted it. Strictly on sex. "Let's hurry and eat."

He glanced to where the group was being seated. "Let's not stay."

Good. Eating at a cozy table-for-two was too romantic to her way of thinking.

"We can eat alfresco in the park across the street." She lowered her voice. "Under the lamplight. Where licking each others' fingers is more acceptable."

His dark eyes devoured her. "I seem to recall fresh air and park benches have a horny effect on you."

Her body heated to an instant glow. She had her sexy Sinner back.

Chapter Sixteen

In the dimly lit park, Mercy bit into a piece of crunchy celery, then gripped the short stalk between her teeth while she peeled the waxed paper from her sandwich.

Spence sat across from her on the wooden bench, the white deli bag between them. His appetite forgotten.

The jerk from the restaurant had pissed him off. Calling him Killer, and in front of Mercy. The guy was damn lucky she'd been there or Spence would've taught him some manners.

The scent of roast beef wafted as Mercy waved his sandwich under his nose to urge him along. Instead, he grabbed hold of her wrist, leaned in, and bit at the piece of celery in her mouth. When his lips grazed hers, she tasted wet and welcome.

She had a way of taking his mind off anything but her, and right now that's exactly what he needed. Pulling back, he crunched the crispy veggie between his teeth, chewing slow and deliberate to entice her. He flicked at his lip with his tongue, much the same way he'd licked at her clit last night before he penetrated and made her come. With her eyes riveted on his mouth, she sighed, and the stub of the celery fell from her lips.

A shopper bustled along the nearby walkway so he let go of her wrist and took the sandwich. When he didn't unwrap it, Mercy offered him a bite of her ham on rye. He shook his head. "Rancher's prefer beef."

"Being from the northeast, I've never seen a

ranch, other than on TV." She grinned. "Or a rancher, until you."

He chuckled. "You've seen plenty of me."

"Not enough, apparently. I have an uncontrollable desire to eat faster, talk less, and grope more."

"I'll toast to that." Digging in the bag, he grabbed a carbonated beverage and popped the cap. The cold liquid sprayed and dripped down the sides of the bottle, wet and glistening beneath the streetlight.

They both licked at the foamy drops, the tip of his tongue meeting her velvety one on the smooth glass. He allowed the sensation for a moment and then pulled back to tease her and leave her wanting more.

Disappointment flickered in her eyes before she lowered her lashes, but when she gazed back up, challenge replaced dissatisfaction. Her flashing blue eyes warned him two could play his game.

She toasted with a demure smile. "Be good or be good at it."

Was that another Doriasm?

She clasped the bottle with the same reverence she paid to his cock when she stroked and mouthed him. Mesmerized, he watched her tongue caress the circumference of the bottle lip. He let out a low groan before he could stop himself. At the sound, her eyes took on a wicked glint. Forming her moist mouth into a perfect O, she rested the bottle opening against her lips before inserting the longneck an inch and then another, and finally drinking. Her throat thrummed as she swallowed, and by the time she stopped, his mouth had gone dry and his dick rock hard.

"Lose your appetite?" She gestured to his sandwich.

"No." He shredded away the paper, took a big

bite and chewed, while keeping his stare trained on her, wondering what she was up to next rustling through the food bag.

Soon her hand reappeared, clasping a kosher pickle so large its size rivaled his own. The smell of vinegar and dill tinged the air. "I get first dibs on the pickle," she announced.

He chuckled, but knew she was capable of wiping the smirk off his lips. When she took the long, cold pickle into her mouth, toying with it and sucking it, his smile drooped and the crotch of his Levi's bulged.

She grated her teeth along the shaft of the dill-delight with light, teasing strokes while he shifted on the bench and stretched his legs out, seeking some comfort from his confining fly. Her tongue, pink and slick, was about to swirl around the rounded head of the kosher-king when he'd had enough. Sitting up, he growled, "Do you know what I'd like to do with that?"

No. She shook her head, the pickle wobbled, and a car horn honked from out on the street.

"I'd like to eat it from your lips...bite by bite...from between your legs."

By her familiar glazed-over look, he knew moisture pooled hot in the very area he'd mentioned.

Abruptly, the picnic ended. She tossed their leftovers, pickle and all, back into the white paper sack.

"Second dibs, coming up."

****

Back at the penthouse apartment, Sinner lived up to his words. The hard, large pickle was a poor substitute for the real thing, but his tantalizing lips and teeth and tongue made up for it. When he inserted the cold, briny vegetable into her pussy, she shivered and her muscles clenched to hold it tight.

With each nibble, the pickle shifted and teased

her insides. Lust prickled in her belly, exciting her, making her moan. His soft hair tickled her inner thighs, and his rough-shaven chin grated her flesh as he moved on her. The combination of sensations was overwhelming, as was the final crunch before he tickled her cold, sensitized clit with his warm, dexterous tongue.

Afterward, replacing the dill stub with his penis, he ardently pumped and brought them both to a potent orgasm.

The man fulfilled Mercy's every sexual fantasy, and she'd had years to store them up with no outlet. A part of her never wanted to let him go. Another part understood not to open anything more to him than her thighs.

She still knew little about him. He wasn't the verbal type. Dark, mysterious, and sexy. Perfect for her vacation-gone-wild, before she settled down to the seriousness of retooling for a new career and a life with bigger horizons than Lily Pond or sinners.

"Mercy." He lay next to her, sexy and sated and drowsy amidst her tangled sheets.

Poor man. Too much sun fixing fences, not enough bedtime.

"Hmm." She teased her fingers along his hard-muscled chest and sleek ribs, raking her nails through the wiry hairs surrounding his nipples. Touching his body delighted her.

"Do you want to see a ranch? My ranch?" His usual confidence sounded slurred. His voice kind of rusty. "Tomorrow afternoon."

He was normally so cocksure, and her heart went out to him for risking her rejection. Despite the fact that she shouldn't go, that his home might reveal more than she needed to know about him, she heard herself say, "I'd love to."

They both fell silent. Minutes ticked by. The quiet became awkward.

"Want to take a warm, relaxing bath?" she asked.

"Why not?" Spence asked when it was the last thing he wanted to do. But it beat lying here listening to the quiet following his clumsy invitation.

What was wrong with him? Asking her out to his place? And in broad daylight, too. First, he'd asked to see her tonight, then he'd asked for her phone number, and now this. He was acting like a boyfriend.

He shook loose from her arms and hopped out of bed, anxious to put space between them, even if it included the damn bubbles from the bath.

"I have a surprise," she said, after she'd lit a slew of candles and they were both seated in the large, empty tub.

"The utility company shut off Cindy's water or something," he said glibly, facing Mercy in the pink, marble tub, his toes touching hers. Their naked bodies dry as a bone.

She reached onto the shelf behind a stack of pink and brown towels and lifted out a cellophane-wrapped package. Her eyes sparkled with mischief and expectation.

He snatched the box, holding it up, squinting in the dim candle lit bathroom. "Body paint."

"Edible," she said, proudly.

He shrugged, giving the idea a chance to sink in. The woman was insatiable with her desires. But then, she'd been love-starved for years. What would it hurt to oblige the lovely lady while she was in town and he had nothing better to do?

Once Parker showed up, reality would turn ugly fast enough.

"Dessert's on me," she teased.

The sexy glow in her eyes made him hard against his better judgment that anything sexually enjoyable could take place in a pink tub.

Surrendering to her carnal charms, he ripped open the cellophane with his teeth. Accommodating her might be fun. He couldn't remember the last time he'd had any fun. Probably his last night on the town with Mark. They'd laughed and teased right up until the deadly incident.

He blanked out the intruding memories by concentrating on Mercy and her dancing blue eyes. She was fun. They'd laughed at the bulls-eyes they scored last night in the kitchen with the corona of flowers and certain sexy body parts. And earlier in the park, he'd enjoyed teasing her before his hard-on took over.

Her rosy lips urged him to flip open the box. "What's your pleasure?" he asked, unfastening the lids from the jars and handing them to her one at a time.

She read the labels. "Seductive strawberry, penile pineapple, blueberry bliss, and cherry crème. I hope you like fruit."

"What's the recommended daily allowance?" He winked and she grinned. She was so easy to please. In and out of bed. His heart lurched. There was no denying his attraction to her, which could prove fatal. He'd fall; she'd leave for home. Safe for her but unfortunate for him.

But he was a big boy. He could risk it.

With a final sniff, she selected a jar, and he licked the rim. "Tastes good enough to eat."

Sticking his index finger into the container, he came away with a thick glob of strawberry paint that he tapped to her nose and traced onto her lips. She lapped at the goo before sucking his finger into her warm mouth, simulating a rhythm they both knew well by now.

Once she let up, she draped her arms around his neck and smudged her painted mouth against his. The invigorating flavor of strawberry mingled with her intoxicating taste. He savored the satiny texture as he suckled her lips until they were clean.

"My turn now." She dipped four fingers into the yellow paint jar and smeared a slippery, citrusy path down his chest. Her slick yellow palm wrapped itself around his dick, sliding up and down until his erection throbbed.

"I hope you're planning to clean that mess up." His voice sounded thick and syrupy.

With a nod, she dipped her head and her tongue touched his chest like a flame, licking at his nipples, flicking in and around his belly button before her hungry mouth descended onto his shaft. His hands tangled into her hair, and he thrust his hips, urging her to engulf his full length. Pleasure built fast, and he groaned when her hot, wet tongue allowed him entrance into her throat. His cock pulsed with lust.

He untwined her silky hair from his fingers and broke their contact.

She looked up, her eyes heavy-lidded, her frustration apparent.

But he couldn't let her taste his cum. Didn't she realize the binding trust and commitment involved in such abandonment? He took the bond seriously. He couldn't allow her to become that important to him.

"What else do you have?" He grabbed up a jar and the box to read the directions.

Tattoo stencils and feathery paintbrushes fell from the carton. Picking up one of each, he traced a blueberry tear onto her cheek. She giggled with each tickling stroke and the teardrop ended up looking more like a blue pear.

His artwork took on a more original bent when he drew a freehand star over her breast. She didn't giggle with those brushstrokes. Her nipple tightened into a tempting bud. Resisting, he moved on to paint a rosebud on her belly.

Leaning back, he closed one eye to admire his creativity. "Stand up so I can finish."

"No thorns," she warned, getting up.

He curled his finger. "Come closer."

She edged nearer.

Again he gestured. "Closer." Another step and another command. "Closer."

She straddled his waist. Her legs spread, her thighs open wide, exposing her glistening swollen lips and clit to his view and his paintbrush. Her willingness shot heat to his groin. He drew a thick blue line between the folds of her labia. She shivered with the contact but didn't move. The slickness of the paint matched the slickness of her desire, and the scent of musk and berries meshed. Each touch of the soft bristles caused her to shudder. Her breathing came in pants.

She grabbed at his hair, directing him to put his mouth on her, bring her to climax.

He ducked away. "I'm not done painting."

She raked her fingers across his scalp before letting go to stand there, open to him, steady and waiting. Re-dipping the brush, he printed the letters of his name down her thigh, like an artist putting his signature to a masterpiece. Something primal stirred inside him at the thought of her being his.

Wishful thinking.

Looking down, she slanted her head to make out the letters. "S-P-E-N-C-E," she spelled out. "Spence." She blinked and stared at him. "Is that your name?"

He nodded with his eyelids.

She dropped down onto his lap and hugged him around the neck, locking her gaze to his. "That's a sexy name."

He licked at the blue-painted tear on her cheek, her eyelashes fluttering shut. "Nothing's as tempting as Mercy."

Chapter Seventeen

Mercy painted a few abstract smudges onto his chest, which resembled a bad Picasso in the flickering candlelight.

"Ready to rinse?" She flicked a finishing touch before dropping a quick, sliding kiss onto his paint-smeared lips.

"Yeah." He reclined, smirching a rainbow of colors against the sleek, pink porcelain.

After turning on the taps, she added a capful of clean-scented bath beads to flush away the clashing smells of berries, pineapple, and cherry.

Cherry had been her favorite. Spence had been creative with more than his paintbrush when he drew a smiley on her buttocks with his cherry-dipped penis before spreading her sex lips and taking her from behind with the deepest penetration she'd experienced yet.

He filled her totally, then withdrew fully. The feeling of heat followed by cool air urged her hips into action once he gratefully plunged again, opening her wide to his erection, making her moan while he played her clitoris like a fine-tuned harp with his cherry-tinged fingers.

Sated now, she looked at Spence and wondered why he'd revealed his name after all this time. She hoped it wasn't more of his recent intimacy, which had been closing in around her like a dark cloud.

He'd not only asked for her phone number, but now he wanted to take her out to his ranch. What was wrong with him? She preferred him aloof. He wasn't the kind of man a woman got involved with on a serious basis. With some luck, he'd forget about the invitation, lose himself in fixing fences again.

Snapping the lid shut on the bath beads, she grabbed a washcloth and a glimpse at a brighter picture. Daubed in multicolored streaks and swirls, the sight of him made her laugh.

"Don't think you *don't* look like an escapee from a Jell-O factory," he said from beneath lidded eyes. With a chuckle, he splashed foamy, warm water at her.

As bright-colored dribbles streamed down her chest and arms, she scooped up water. But before she could splash him back, he snatched her into his strong but colorful arms and pulled her onto his lap where water pooled in a murky, purplish shade.

Taking the washcloth from her hand, he sloshed it under the running spigot. After dabbing at her face, he ran the thick terry over her arms and body. His touch was light, the cloth soft and warm, the experience mesmerizing. Mercy closed her eyes. Her muscles slackened beneath his ministrations. Her mind mellowed, her resolve weakened, her heart softened.

Lucky she only had to stay on guard until the end of the week when she left Texas and Spence. Otherwise, she could fall for him, big time.

"I have some chores in the morning," he mumbled.

"Uh-huh," she said, without opening her eyes, glad she had nothing to do tomorrow but recuperate from their vigorous lovemaking.

"Is noon okay?"

"Noon?" She opened her eyes, crinkled her eyebrows.

"To pick you up to see the ranch."

While she nodded, she grappled to put a sexy spin on it. A roll in a haystack was a pretty fantastic fantasy. "Do you have hay?"

"Is that a deal breaker?"

She smiled.

"I have lots of hay," he teased. "Do you have something particular in mind?"

A classic Doriaism popped to mind. "You can bet your boots on it."

****

Dressed for the office in a blue, tailored suit, but wearing pink-striped platform shoes, Cindy bounced into the kitchen the next morning. "How was your night? Mine sucked. We cropped photos, and Jay missed my mouth by a mile when he kissed me good night." She poured a cup of coffee from the automatic pot she set each evening before bedtime. Suddenly, her forehead puckered. "Why are you up so early?"

"I called my mother. You were right, Cindy. She's worried about my loan and ticked at her brother. He's never been out of touch except during the Vietnam War, and that was beyond his control."

She gulped her coffee down. "Maybe we could ask around the club and find out the name of his sick friend for her. But I can't tonight. Jay's coming over so I can show him the Mesopotamia tub."

"I'll stop by the *Starry Night* later." Mercy leaned her back against the granite kitchen counter, bracing herself with her arms. "Spence is taking me out to see his ranch this afternoon."

Cindy's cup hit the saucer with a clank. "Who's Spence? Where did you meet him? Where's his ranch? And I'm glad you finally ditched Sinner, even if he helped us out of that bat cave, Taboo, they call a lounge," she spouted in two long breaths.

"Spence *is* Sinner, and he owns a small ranch outside of town."

"Ooh." Her enthusiasm drained in one elongated vowel. "Given his sudden first name status with you, I take it the Mesopotamia was a success with *Spence*."

"Let's just say the tub's no longer virgin," Mercy replied evasively.

Cindy raised her brow and then her eyes to the wall clock. "Sheesh, look at the time." She rushed for the doorway. "Jay better plan on getting more than his feet wet tonight."

****

Spence was still railing at himself. He wanted and liked Mercy way too much for his own good. And showing it to boot. What with giving out his real name and making dates in the afternoon.

Not to mention phone calls, he berated as he dialed her number. As soon as her sexy voice answered, "Hello," his stomach did a flip. Oh, yeah. He had it bad.

"I'm running late again. Flat tire." He leaned his palm against the door jamb, taking in the view of the mesquite trees outside the dusty window shade. While he rubbed at a smear of grease on the white-painted molding with his thumb, he wondered if he should've cleaned the place up a bit.

Right, and next he'd be changing the sheets before any sex had taken place on his bed.

"Can I bring something? Food? Wine? I can pack a few things while I wait until you get here," she sing-songed. So sweet, so agreeable, so not what he needed at this point in his life. Her tenderness could only distract him from his goal to find Parker.

"I have food," he grumbled. She'd have to take him as he was. He stopped rubbing at the dirty mark. She'd settle for what he had to give. Or stay away.

And why did that idea sound like he was running scared, hoping she'd back off?

Because he sure as hell was.

"Then I'll just come as I am." Her voice suddenly sounding smoky and turned on. Or maybe it was the way she said *come* that made him think so.

132

"Damn." He was still muttering to himself as he drove over to the condo after fixing the tire. At least her going back East at the end of the week would take care of what he didn't have the willpower to do. "Stay away from her."

He jammed on the brakes, parking next to a shiny BMW. He was outclassed in this neighborhood and with Mercy. She deserved someone successful, established, someone who hadn't served time and didn't mingle with the likes of the people he'd met in jail or on the streets these past weeks.

"Scum." He swiped at the filthy fender of his truck for emphasis before heading up the stairs.

Instead of ringing the bell, he banged on the door to let out his frustrations. Before his knuckles rapped a third time, the door swung open and the slim-figured beauty stood before him, shiny-faced, her head haloed by her blonde hair.

"I'm ready." She smiled and the world tilted, and he felt young, and eager, and hopeful.

All things he could never regain.

Along with the woman he could never attain.

But for now she was his.

He claimed her with his lips, branding his mouth to hers. She tasted sweet, like the spoon full of sugar he stirred into his coffee each morning. He let his tongue roam her open, welcoming mouth, savoring every flick at the warm, wet flesh, glad to be inside her body.

When he pulled away, he twisted a curl of her hair onto his finger and studied her sky-blue eyes. She smelled like fresh air and sunshine. Things he'd missed in jail. Everything about her was sparkling and filled with promise. While his tomorrows were too distant to even ache for.

"Ever been rolled in the hay?" he asked with a slight grin, seeking from her only what he knew he could lay claim to.

"No, but I'd roll with you just about anywhere." Her laugh sounded hesitant, as if unsure of her sexual prowess.

He un-spun her hair from his finger. Ran his knuckles along her delicate jawline. "The hayloft will do for starters."

"How about a tractor? I've never ridden a tractor."

He chuckled and grabbed her elbow. She flipped the lock on the door, and they were on their way.

As they left the building, Spence got sucker-punched by the first streak of blinding daylight. Mercy in the sunlight with the beams glancing off her shiny hair and her bright eyes was even more amazing than Mercy at night.

He sucked in air to ease the ache of wanting more of her than he deserved. The smooth softness of her skin as he took her palm in his and helped her up onto the worn passenger seat of the truck did nothing to help the pain.

Still, Mercy rated an admission of how heart-breakingly special she was, especially after the idiots she'd dated, and Spence decided to be the man to tell her.

"You take a man's breath away, even in stark daylight."

She tilted her head. Touching her palm to his rough-shaven cheek, with a sweep of her lashes, she murmured, "I'll remember who said those words all my life."

Too much sentiment. He broke away and slammed the door shut. His throat felt tight and he swallowed hard.

By the time he came around and climbed behind the steering wheel, gratefully, the mood had changed. She sat with her hands on her lap and a sexy gleam in her eye.

That's when he took in her well-washed jeans

and her vee-neck T-shirt. "Shirt matches your eyes," he said, cranking over the engine. Then before she could get all moony-eyed on him, he added, "How about your underwear?"

"I'll show you mine when you show me yours," she replied coyly.

"I'm not wearing any."

Pulling away from the condo, he steered the truck toward the highway leading out to the ranch, and to the haystack, and the tractor.

Hell, he planned on showing her everything he had.

Chapter Eighteen

Wooden frame house, dirt yard, no flowers. It wasn't Southfork.

"Your ranch is...interesting," Mercy said for lack of a more enthusiastic word as Spence pulled to a dusty stop in front of the porch.

Hopping down from the truck, she coughed and waved away the small cloud of grit his tires had kicked up.

"Needs paint." He shrugged his hands into his pockets when he came to stand beside her, studying the ranch house as if he'd just noticed its faded, chipped, once-white paint.

"The place has a lot of potential." A coat of paint, dark shutters, green grass, and some colorful wildflowers clumped near the front door would do wonders. Maybe a wicker porch swing. It needed a woman's touch.

She backed up a step. But not this woman's.

Shading her eyes, she looked beyond the house, across the flat green horizon. A few straggly trees, a crisscross of fences, no livestock. "No horses?"

"I had to sell the last horse for expense money."

Start up cash, she imagined. But he did have a tractor parked next to a weathered barn. Sort of a rusty, green-colored machine.

He followed the line her eyes had taken. "I didn't sell the tractor."

She flashed an admiring smile. "Big tires."

"Big customized seat. I'll take you for a ride later." He draped his arm across her shoulder and led her up the three wooden steps and across the porch to the screened front door.

Inside, the house felt dark and cool, the shades pulled partially against the heat of the day and the sunlight. Aged floral wallpaper decorated the entryway, and the dining room and living room, which were both visible from the hall.

"Original," she said, agreeably. Even the dust. Except for the hallway, a fine layer had settled on the floors and furniture. A musty smell permeated the closed-up rooms. "Seems like no one's lived here in awhile."

"I just moved back in a few weeks ago. Except to sleep, I haven't spent much time here."

She left the comfort of his arm to gaze at some wooden-framed pictures hanging randomly on the wall. Through the hazy glass and the dimness in the hallway, she squinted at a smiling, elderly couple. By the large number of blazing candles, they might've been celebrating a sixtieth birthday party. In another frame, in a photo blown up to nine by twelve, stood a handsome, grinning cowboy, sporting a shiny, large belt buckle.

"Family photos?" She glanced at Spence over her shoulder.

He looked down for a moment before he met her eyes. "Those are my parents," he said, proudly, pointing to the happy couple. "They passed away. My best friend, Mark." He tapped the glass of the other one. "He's the rodeo hero. He's dead now, too."

"Oh." Sympathy for the hurt lurking behind his brooding eyes swelled in her chest. "I'm sorry." Focusing on a picture of two boys holding fishing poles, she asked, "Are these your brothers?"

He chuckled. "No, that's me and Mark when we were kids. Neither of us could catch a trout, but we had heaps of fun trying."

She grinned. "I can tell by the fondness in your voice you miss him."

"Yeah." He sauntered away, down the hallway toward the kitchen.

After studying the picture, she determined the taller boy was Spence. His dark eyes were the giveaway. She followed him into a linoleum-floored kitchen with seventies, avocado green appliances.

"Is this your family homestead?" she asked.

The muscles in his back rippled as he filled a glass with water from the spigot. He turned, leaned against the sink, and crossed one booted foot over the other. Through narrowed eyes, which made judging his emotions impossible, he simply said, "No." Putting the glass to his mouth, he drank while watching her over the rim.

She stared at his mouth, his moistened lips, his throat as he swallowed. Walking over to him, she tugged on his belt loops until he stopped drinking, and then she took the glass from his lips. Straddling his legs, she sipped a mouthful of water, leaning back slightly so that her hips met his lean ones.

He was right. Enough nosy questions. Before she discovered more than she cared to know about the mysterious man. That he was good in bed was all that should interest her.

She pressed herself against the thick zipper of his blue jeans, straining into him further as she reached around to clatter the glass onto the drainboard. The movement effectively increased the pressure of her pubic bone against the hard heat of his cock beneath the denim, and she moaned.

He held her tighter, his masculine scent of soap and outdoors soaking through her pores as his strong hands spanned her waist. He notched his fly to fit against her crotch. The roughness of the denim and the metal of his zipper grated against her delicate sex lips, but the ache felt delicious. Her clit swelled and her fluids pooled between her thighs. Her breath quickened.

"I wouldn't mind a peek at the bedrooms." She closed her eyes, enjoying the thrill running through her veins, firing her nerve endings.

His fingers dug into her spine, pulling her even closer, until she gasped with want. "Spence," she hissed and forced her hand down between their bodies, rubbing the heel of her palm against his hard-on while the back of her hand excited her own crotch.

"That feels good," he said, urging her on.

She tried to slip her hand down the waistband of his jeans but failed. "I want to feel you." She fumbled at his zipper while working her leg along his hip, centering her pussy against his fly. Unable to get close enough, fast enough.

Blood pulsed in her eardrums, her heartbeat throbbed loud. She heard nothing and everything. Music—strange erratic notes of a classical nature.

"Your cell phone, babe." He loosened his hold.

She groaned and pulled her cell free from her jeans. "I'm shutting it off." When she flipped the phone open, checking to see that it wasn't her mother or uncle before she hit the power button, she heard the screech of Cindy's voice.

"Mercy. Mercy, are you there?" she spurted, a frantic edge to her voice. "Answer me if you are. It's urgent."

"I better take this," she mouthed to Spence, holding up a finger to indicate it wouldn't take long. "Hello," Mercy croaked, her throat dry.

With a sigh, she eyed Spence's hands, missing his wild embrace while they'd primed for the ride of her life. His life.

"Are you with *him*?" Cindy whispered.

She wished she was with him, *naked*, but Cindy had interrupted that. "I'm at the ranch."

"Get out of there. Now."

Not sure she'd heard right, Mercy smiled at

Spence and turned away so he wouldn't overhear her whacky friend running off at the mouth.

"Why?" she asked, tolerantly.

"Killer." Cindy paused. "They call him Killer because he was in jail for killing a person."

"Are you crazy?" But her throat tightened. Either answer her friend gave, yes or no, was a losing proposition.

"No, I haven't lost my mind. They don't call him Killer because he's a lady killer. Well, maybe he is, but not in the sense we thought. He's a real murderer."

Real murderer. Mercy's heart pounded out each word.

Her hand shook. "Who's filling your head with this nonsense?"

Catching Spence from the corner of her eye, she saw him wander to the window, apparently to give her more privacy. He lifted the sash with a flip of his strong wrists, letting a warm breeze of sweet-smelling air filter through the stuffy room.

"Someone at the *Starry Night* told Rita he served time in jail for killing a person, and she waited until lunch break to tell me. Grr...I should kill *her*." She sucked in a quick breath. "You'd better get out of there right now. Are you stranded? Should I call the cops? Should I hitch a cab ride out and get you myself?"

"Calm down." Mercy needed time to think. She pinched the bridge of her nose to staunch the burning sensation building behind her eyes. The sound of Spence breathing from a few feet away only messed with her concentration.

Cindy groaned. "Why couldn't you date someone safe like Jay? But not Jay, because he's mine." Then she changed her train of thought. "Go outside so you have room to run...until I get there...or send the cops."

"No," Mercy rasped. "Whatever you do, don't send the police. There must be a logical explanation. If he was going to harm me, he'd have done it long before this."

"I don't know." Cindy exhaled. "Although, Sister Doria always believed a person is innocent unless proven guilty."

"I'll talk to him. Ask him."

"No," Cindy protested. "Suppose questioning him riles up his killing instinct."

"I'm not going to accuse him of anything." Especially not murder. Mercy sighed. "I'll handle this. Don't worry."

"Don't ask him anything until you're outside so you have a better chance at escaping. Are you sure I shouldn't call the police? And a taxi, in case I have to claim your body."

"Get control of yourself," Mercy said in a hushed tone to calm her friend. "I'll be fine. Don't overreact or call the cops. Wait for me to call you back." She snapped the cell phone shut.

Spence turned at the sound. "I heard your friend screeching from across the room. What's got her panties in a twist now?"

"Long story." Mercy eyed the tall, rugged cowboy. He was gruff at times, but she doubted he'd fatally harm anyone. He bought sentimental flowers, opened doors for old people, painted teardrops. He'd saved her and Cindy from the Goth night-clubbers. Still, she'd assured Cindy she would talk to him—outside. "Let's take a walk."

He agreed by yanking on the porcelain doorknob of a warped, wooden door leading out onto the backyard. With a loud squeak, he held open the battered, screen door. She filed past him, blinking against the sudden sunlight after the dimness inside the house.

At the bottom of the narrow steps, he joined her.

He matched his strides to hers as they strolled down the dirt path toward the barn.

The ground felt hard and gravelly beneath her sneakered feet. Cowboy boots definitely served their purpose, she thought, absently. After several yards, she cleared her throat, not sure where to start the unsavory subject.

"Remember the other evening when the man at the deli called you Killer?" Spence's booted feet crunched down hard on a stony section of the path. He didn't reply so she forged on. "And I thought he was referring to your prowess with women."

Silence. She glanced up at him. His eyes were fixed on the horizon where the cloudless blue sky met the distant green meadow.

She tried again. "Cindy called to warn me that the nickname meant something far more dangerous."

He nodded. "As in, I killed my best friend."

Chapter Nineteen

Mercy stumbled, and Spence grabbed her arm. *Did you kill your friend?* she wanted to ask.

But fear choked her windpipe and the question died in her throat. Forget Cindy's suggestion to run for her life. Panic froze her feet in place.

She and the supposed killer stood in the middle of the dirt pathway, yards from the barn and the fenced field. The only life other than them was a drab-colored rabbit, scurrying for cover. The air gripped heavy, hot, and still, as did his hand on her forearm.

Mercy studied his black, hollow eyes, seeking answers to questions she dared not voice. His expression remained unreadable. Quiet stretched between them for long moments, splintered only by the twitter of a swallow.

To break the intolerable suspense, she touched the tips of her fingers to his broad hand. When he loosened his hold on her arm, she didn't move away. Standing her ground, however weak-kneed, she offered him vindication. "But you didn't kill anyone." Her voice sounded faint.

"The DA's office claims I killed Mark. I was sent to jail for manslaughter." He stated the facts in a monotone. His eyes flat.

For a moment, she couldn't wrap her mind around the meaning of what he said. Although he could be grim or distant, she'd spent enough time with him to see his lighter and kinder sides. He laughed, he hurt. He helped some people, he avoided others. He cared.

"Mark was your childhood friend. You loved him," she murmured.

"That didn't matter to the twelve people who voted me guilty."

Her heart caught mid-beat. How horrible to have his best friend killed, to lose him forever, and then be accused and convicted of the crime. Shaking her head with incredulity, she thought of herself and Cindy. "I can't believe you did it."

"I didn't, and I intend to find out who did." He smiled, slowly, the corners of his mouth turning up slightly. His eyes crinkled. "I wish the jury was as trusting as you."

"The jury didn't know you like I do," she said.

"Let's hope not." He chuckled.

"Do you want to talk?"

He shook his head. "It's obvious there's enough talk about me and Mark to go around."

"Cindy made an honest mistake. She was misinformed by Rita, her coworker from the office. You must've seen Rita around the *Starry Night*. She's the one with big—" she faltered, undecided between saying boobs or breasts.

"Don't go shy on me now." He cracked a grin. "I've seen her. She has healthy lungs and hangs around Cindy's boyfriend."

"Cindy, Jay, and Rita work for the same company," Mercy explained.

He kicked a stone from the path. "Cindy's a good friend to you. Let's let it go at that."

She rested her hand on his, sad for him at the loss of his best friend. She didn't know what she'd do without Cindy. "I'm sorry about Mark. How did it happen?"

He clasped her hand. They began walking down the path toward the barn and the field. A mild breeze wafted hot.

Grief for Mark weighed heavily on his mind, but

Spence wasn't used to voicing his sorrow. Could he trust Mercy when he hadn't trusted anyone since the trial?

She squeezed his hand to encourage him.

He wanted to share his sadness, his anger. And Mercy was compassionate. If he didn't talk to someone about the emotional events of that evening, he feared he'd explode or, worse, break down and become useless in finding the true killer. Mercy was probably his safest outlet. Within the week she'd fly back to Pennsylvania, and both he and his story would get forgotten in the bustle of her everyday life.

"We were out on the town," he began, "celebrating Mark's championship bull ride. He was reminding me how always keeping an eye on the prize pays off." Spence blew out a breath at the irony. "That was the motto Mark lived by. He was laughing, happy to be alive and in one piece after riding a bull called Steam Roller. The buckle bunnies were all over him. Us."

"Buckle bunnies?" She puckered her pretty forehead.

"Rodeo groupies. Mark had finished dancing with a blonde beauty." Spence smiled. "But not as beautiful as you."

The image of the woman came to mind in vivid detail, along with Mark clinking his beer bottle to Spence's before saying, "The gorgeous chick I was two-stepping around the sawdust wants me bad. But she's got a friend."

Spence had stepped back and groaned. "I know where this is leading. I'm not leaving with Dracula's daughter, buddy or not."

"I'll admit she's a little long in the tooth, but you don't have to kiss her. Not open-mouthed anyway." Mark chuckled while Spence eyed the woman. Her eyeteeth could've opened bottle caps.

"Maybe after I have another brew." He downed

the last of his long neck and held up his empty to signal the bartender for another. "But you've got to explain to my girlfriend how I'm only helping you out. Things are going good between us, and I'm not about to screw it up."

"I'll drink to that." So Mark had another beer, too.

Maybe one too many, looking back.

"We both had too much to drink that night." He looked at Mercy. "Next thing I knew, we were rambling down a dark street outside the bar, showing the ladies to their car when all hell broke loose.

"The beauty screamed, a speeding car attempted to mow us down, and all four of us hit the macadam like a pile of discarded rag dolls. I got clipped by the bumper on the way down."

He heard Mercy's intake of breath, but kept on, wanting to get it all out now that he'd started. "Before any of us could recover and get to our feet, a big guy built like the bull, Steam Roller, hopped out of the car. But he wasn't coming to help. Mark was the first one up and the first one knocked down. A blow to his chest. It turned out Mark had an undetected heart problem.

"When I got up, my head still reeling from the bumper, I managed to ram the guy. There was more screaming. This time from both the blonde and her friend. Then I went down. The lights went out. No more screams. No sound at all."

"What happened after that?" Mercy asked, her voice little more than a whisper.

"When I came to, an EMT from the ambulance crew was working over me, giving me oxygen, strapping me to a gurney. A police officer rode with me in the back of the ambulance to the hospital. After I was diagnosed as fit and released from Emergency, the cop handcuffed me and read me my rights. An eyewitness had stated I'd walloped my friend in the chest and killed him. The buckle bunnies had disappeared. So had the driver." He looked Mercy in the eyes. "I'll recognize him to the day I die."

Mercy's eyes widened. "Why would the only witness lie?"

Spence snorted. "That's what I'd like to know, along with why we were jumped. Why would a stranger testify that I hit Mark and killed him? Why would he swear under oath that he happened upon the fight and no car or other persons were at the scene?"

Spence had spent eighteen months in prison on a manslaughter charge thinking about it. And nothing added up.

She shook her head. "I have no idea."

"Mistaken identity. An irate boyfriend." He shrugged. "Hell, I don't know, but I'm damn sure going to find out." He clenched her hand. "I'm not taking my eye off the prize until I clear my name and find Mark's killer."

His chest heaved. Perspiration dotted his brow. Just when he was about to pull away from her entwined fingers, she raised his hand to her mouth and kissed his tensed knuckles.

Damn woman. He couldn't let her get to him. If there was a remote chance at spotting Parker, he'd have to abandon her and go after the man. Parker getting away while Spence did Mercy on a Riverwalk bench couldn't happen again.

Gradually, he untangled his fingers from hers.

She nodded, as if understanding his need for space.

They'd reached the end of the path. He rested his elbows on the split-rail fence and stared out across the fallow field. He and Mark had been going to plant hay and alfalfa. Raise horses.

Her gentle hand rested on his shoulder. Tension seeped from his muscles. He glanced at her. "Want to take a ride?"

"Riding you would be my pleasure." With a teasing smile, she fluttered her lashes and nudged her hip against his.

"I meant a ride on my old John Deere."

"That might be just as gratifying. Something about huge, heavy machinery turns me on."

"I have just such a piece of machinery, waiting to be turned on."

He wrapped his arm around her waist and pulled her close. Kissing her, he swept his tongue inside her mouth, testing her desire, tasting her want. He kissed her with just the right amount of pressure to make her forget about anything but getting off on his body.

When he broke away, he lifted her over the wooden railing of the fence, dropping her to her feet alongside a cluster of wild daisies. He hopped over next, and in no time they stood beside the tractor, Mercy slightly dwarfed by its size.

"It's been field modified." He pointed to the mismatched fenders and a makeshift seat. "In other words, repaired with whatever parts were on hand."

She touched the dented fender, quickly jerking her hand away, the metal hot from the midday sun. Next, she trailed her fingers along the sidewall of one of the large, rubber tires. "Rough yet smooth," she purred. "Like sex with you."

His insides tightened.

He climbed up onto the wide seat, patting a spot on his knee for her to sit. She squinted against the sun as she looked up at him and smiled a helpless gesture. He reached out and hiked her up onto his thigh. Her butt snuggled tight against his body as they peered out across the rough terrain of bunch grass and rocks.

She reached over and stroked the fender again. "I like it up here."

"Want to touch something you'll like even more?" he whispered near her ear.

"Yes." She glanced down at his fly and he laughed.

"I meant the steering wheel."

Grinning, she gripped the wheel in her fists. "It feels smooth and hard and hot." She sidled a glance at Spence. Electricity arced between them.

With a flick of his wrist, he cranked the engine over. The smell of fuel and exhaust fumes mingled with the meadow-sweetened breeze. The motor jounced, the vibration shaking her bottom and evidently revving her engine, from the way she squirmed on his thigh.

"Kind of like foreplay, isn't it?" She winked at him.

"I like my foreplay naked," he dared.

She took his dare and began unbuttoning her jeans. "Stop me if you have neighbors you don't want to shock."

He didn't stop her.

His eyes trailed the steamy actions of her hands as she skimmed her sneakers and jeans off, tossing the pants onto the hood of the engine and jamming her feet back into her canvas shoes.

"Are you going to watch or drive?" she asked.

He engaged the gears, and the tractor edged forward with a thump. While sitting on one of his thighs, she dug her fingers into the other for balance. His muscles flexed taut beneath the denim fabric. She closed her eyes and lifted her face to the sun.

After bumping along for a few feet, her eyes flicked open and she stared at him over her shoulder. "You must be hot."

Without waiting for his reply, she busied herself

with his T-shirt. Working the soft-washed cotton up over his flat abs and broad chest, she kissed along his collarbone. His skin tasted salty and provocative beneath the hot sun. She snaked one of his arms out of the armhole but snagged the other on his elbow before working it loose to whip the shirt over his head, quick, so he didn't steer the tractor too far off course. Flinging the shirt next to her clothes, she tugged at the waist of his jeans.

"Can you help me out by throwing the gears into neutral or park or something until I get you stripped?" she asked.

He pushed on the gear shift. "I don't plan on getting caught with my pants around my knees." But while the tractor idled, he obliged her. With a lot of jostling on both their parts, he heeled off his boots and shimmied out of his jeans. Once he was naked, he tugged his boots back on and gunned the sputtering engine to a crawl while she picked his pocket for a condom then tossed his pants on the pile with the rest of their clothing.

As the large tires plodded along, crumbling the earth beneath them, he chuckled at her determination. Laughing, she swiveled around to climb onto his lap. Straddling him, while trying not to block his view as he steered, caused more than a few tickles to his ribs, adjustments of her legs, and nudges of both their chins and necks.

When she was settled with his chin nestled on her shoulder and their chests fitted snuggly, nipple to nipple, she lifted her hips to give her sole attention to his hot, hard, pulsing dick.

He groaned when her fingers grasped the head of his cock.

"You're a good driver," she said, maneuvering her hips over his erection and momentarily blotting his view of the rocky field.

"I hope this isn't an accident waiting to happen."

He veered the wheel to the left with a jolt.

"That's a Doriaism." Her voice bobbled, coming out in short blurts, as her torso bounced and she fought to keep upright and not injure his dick while she dug her knees into his waist.

His hard-on survived.

Once they were steady again, Mercy kissed his sun-warmed neck, which tasted of soap and smelled woodsy. "This is nice, but could you hit one of those smaller rocks for a bounce we can appreciate."

He swerved the tractor. "This one's for you, babe."

When the bounce hit, his erection tickled her G-spot with enough friction and force to send a thrumming sensation through her entire body.

"More," she demanded, eagerly.

Soon he was driving erratically around the field, no longer dodging rocks but aiming for them. Talk about rocking her world. And all the while, the hum of the motor and its vibrations increased the stimulating pleasure. The anticipation of not knowing when a rut would titillate her next only added to the exhilaration.

Finally, Spence pulled up next to the fence. The tractor idled. A faint whiff of acrid gas and the smell of wildflowers mixed. Gripping her hips in his capable hands, he arched into her. As he bucked and she plunged onto his stiff cock, faster and firmer with each frenzied stroke, they both surrendered to their orgasms.

Panting she collapsed against him, hugging his neck in her sticky arms. The sun beat hot on her back, perspiration trickled down her spine. Her breasts clung to his matted chest hairs.

He heaved air into his lungs. "I'll never use a tractor again without thinking of you."

She gasped. "Me either."

He chuckled. "As if you'd ever."

Sylvie Kaye

As their breathing evened, he took her face
between his hands and kissed her mouth, gently,
slowly. No urgency. The day stretched out like an
endless summer.

When he separated from her lips, he stared into
her eyes. In the sunshine, his weren't as dark brown
as usual. His lashes fluttered as he blinked against
its brightness. The breeze tousled a lock of hair on
his forehead, giving him a boyish, carefree
appearance. The smell of wildflowers carried on the
air. Along with the smell of man and sex and
machinery.

"If circumstances were different—"

"But they're not," she said lightly, not wanting
to think about feelings or affections. She touched her
hand to his shadowed jaw. "Don't feel as if you owe
me explanations or accolades."

He nodded, his eyes and brows speculative.

Relieved, she reached behind her and handed
him his shirt from the bedraggled pile of clothing.
When he took it from her, she lifted herself from his
lap to squeeze toward the fender and away from
him.

He slipped the T-shirt over his head, his muscles
glistening in the sun, rippling with his motions. His
hair was mussed and his shirt wrinkled but he
looked good. Good enough to do again. Would she
ever get enough of him? She heaved a sigh and
watched as he peeled off the rubber and heeled off
his boots to tug on his jeans.

After sticking his feet into the legs of his pants,
he hefted the waist of his jeans upward until all too
soon his muscled thighs and tight butt were covered
from her view.

"Aren't you going to get dressed?" He looked
over at her watching him jam his feet into his boots
once more.

"I was enjoying the show." She grinned. It

152

wasn't everyday she got to look on as such a hunky man undressed and dressed for her pleasure. In stark daylight, no less. Actually, it was never, until today.

Spence snatched up her clothing and hopped down from the tractor. Holding them just out of her reach, he teased, "I'm enjoying your nudie show even more."

With a laugh, she lunged, joining in the fun by grabbing for her clothes while he switched them from hand to hand.

When she was pressed against him, flailing for his arms, he asked, "What would Cindy say about your panty-less tractor ride with an alleged killer?"

"Cindy! I forgot to call her back. She'll be frantic with worry." She gestured to her jeans. "My cell phone's in the pocket."

He handed her jeans over and helped her wriggle her legs into them, when a screech filled the air.

"Stop right there, *Killer*. Let her go."

Spence glanced over his shoulder to see Cindy high-stepping down the path in her shaky shoes, waving her arms, and whirling her handbag like a bolo.

Mercy stopped squirming and went still.

"I see I got here in the nick of time. Don't think about using violence on her," Cindy warned. "I have pepper spray and the cab driver is on alert to call 911. One whistle from me and he'll radio for backup."

He stood in front of Mercy, blocking her friend's view while she finished shimmying into her jeans. He hoped she'd hurry dressing because he didn't want to tangle with Cindy. A sheen of perspiration broke out across his upper lip and forehead. As soon as Mercy shoved her feet into her sneakers, he sidled away so Cindy could see her friend was alive and unhurt.

As Cindy closed in, Spence moved to stand behind Mercy. Safer to let the ladies fight it out.

"Calm down, Cindy." Mercy held up her hands. "I'm all right. Everything is all right. A big misunderstanding is all."

"Has he forced you into saying that?" Cindy scowled in his direction, aiming the spray. "Do you have a gun to her back?"

"No." He held up both empty hands.

"I should've called," Mercy said. "Time slipped away."

Cindy squinted, taking in Mercy and Spence's rumpled appearances. "They call him Killer. It must mean something."

"His friend died, and he's searching for the killer. It's all a sad misunderstanding."

He hoped Mercy's words penetrated her friend's floppy-haired skull. But Cindy continued to glare at him, so Spence pointed toward Mercy, gesturing with his finger to believe what she said.

At last, Cindy eyed Mercy again. "If you say so." She lowered the hand holding the pepper mace.

"Thank you for coming to my rescue." Mercy hugged her. "Even though it wasn't necessary. Now, we'd better get back up to the house. The meter must be running on your cab." They linked arms. "I insist on paying the taxi fare."

"No," Cindy protested.

"No." Spence agreed. Digging some bills from his pocket, he said, "I'll pay."

One way or another he was sure he would anyway.

Chapter Twenty

What had he gotten himself into?

On the trot back to the ranch house, Cindy continued to vent while Mercy insisted, "He's harmless."

Spence bit back his bitterness. He didn't need anymore people in his life who didn't believe him. The twelve-person jury, along with the prosecutor and the so-called eyewitness, Parker, had been enough. Deep in his bones, he felt it was only a matter of time until Mercy's friend turned her against him.

He didn't want to let go of Mercy just yet. He didn't want to be alone with his thoughts and memories. During his jail term they'd haunted him constantly. Probably would again as soon as she was gone from his life.

She brought him smiles and brightness, and he meant to enjoy her until she flew back home. He stood aside when she stuffed Cindy into the cab.

With the taxi door open, Mercy turned to him. "About Cindy jumping to conclusions...her intentions were well aimed."

"So was her pepper spray." He was eager to put Cindy behind them and show Mercy his rumpled bed sheets.

"I'm going to ride back with her. It's the least I can do after she came all the way out here." She met his eyes. She was the only softness or kindness to happen to his life in a long time.

He gave a slight shrug. "I'm sorry about the misunderstanding."

And he was. Neither woman deserved the scare the rumors about him had caused. And that was a prime reason he shouldn't fool around with the none-too-streetwise Mercy.

But was he fooling?

Only himself. His heart hammered. He wanted her, like a man wanted a woman he'd never let go.

But he couldn't pursue a serious relationship until this nasty business with Parker was settled, which looked like it may never happen.

"I'll apologize to Cindy for you, once she's calmer."

"When will that be? She doesn't seem like the calming down kind." He peeped into the cab, where she sat still holding her container of pepper mace.

Not any time tonight would be his guess. He might as well track Google down. See what news the snitch had for him, if any.

"I didn't get to see your haystack," Mercy teased, lightening the heavy mood.

"Next time." He wanted to kiss her but held back. Not now, when he wasn't giving her the whole truth.

There wouldn't be a next time at the ranch. Mercy in the nighttime was one thing, but Mercy in the daytime was heartbreaking. He couldn't let her into his home and this close to his heart again.

"Will I see you tomorrow?" She turned and climbed into the cab.

"You'll see me," he promised, admiring her tight ass.

By the time the taxi disappeared into a cloud of dust, he'd mooned over her enough. He had to focus on his goal.

****

Jay punched in the numbers to Cindy's cell. The twit had left work early and hadn't returned. What rotten luck. Just when he'd worked up the gumption to screw her, she'd gotten ill.

He needed her, now. Pressure was mounting and big dollars were on the table. His company's biggest rival required the plans for the new line within the week while they had plenty of time to retool for next year's production. Cindy's password was key to getting into the file untraced. If the break-in was ever discovered, she'd end up taking the fall. Or so Google had guaranteed him.

"Hello," her shrill voice sang out, grating his nerves like chalk on a blackboard. If she was the type who talked during sex, he wasn't sure he could maintain a hard-on.

"Are you all right?" he asked with faked concern.

"Yes," she cooed, falling for his artificial anxiety. "Mercy needed my help."

"Are we still on for tonight?"

"My place at six."

"Everyone's gone for the day." He dug into his desk drawer for his antacids. "And I'll be leaving shortly."

"I'll be here, waiting," she sing-songed, off pitch and piercing. He held the receiver away from his ear, wondering if he could talk her into a ball gag.

He shivered, and not with anticipation. Dread ate away at his gut. He wasn't used to kissing up to any woman who didn't turn him on. Loosening his tie, he popped open the bottle of antacids, wishing it was Viagra. The lid flew and landed in a corner of the hardwood floor.

"Should I bring a pizza or something?" He doubted he could eat with his stomach burning this way, but he had to offer to make it look good.

"I ate at the club with Mercy. She stayed on while I rushed home to get certain things." Her tone turned sickeningly sweet. "Things like the tub and the candles set up for this evening."

"I'm really not hungry anyway. I ate a late

157

lunch," he lied, tossing back two pills and chewing.

"See you soon," she chirped.

No sooner did he say good-bye than Rita slinked into his office. Rita was his type. Beautiful, built, well dressed, and easy. Unlike Cindy, who was loud, flat-chested, tasteless, and easy. Rita plopped her rounded ass onto the side edge of his desk and leaned toward him, flashing her tits.

"Hiya," she whispered.

"Hey, yourself. I thought the building was empty." He reached out to brush an imaginary piece of lint from her open neckline, letting his fingers linger on the swell of well-displayed cleavage.

"Naughty, naughty." She inched away but added in a seductive tone, "We're the only two here."

He figured now was as good a time as any to find out why Rita was suddenly so hot-for-his-hose. She'd been sniffing after him ever since he'd started paying attention to Cindy.

"Ever do it on a desk?" he asked, playing aggressive defense.

"Not on yours I haven't," she drawled, wrapping her lips around the words.

Silly question on his part. She was a lousy junior-executive. Her naked butt must've polished half the desks in the company to get promoted this far.

With an unexpected sweep of her manicured hand, the papers cluttering his desk surface scattered. Pink and green and blue antacids bounced onto the floor as the plastic bottle toppled. She didn't even blink. Before the last pill stopped rolling, she yanked on his tie, pulling him to his feet.

He went along, curiosity coursing through his veins.

Once she had him situated in front of her short skirt, his groin nestled between her creamy thighs, she kissed him, hard and hot. Her tongue swept his mouth and tangled with his tongue. As hot as she was, as promising as she tasted, as horny as he became, an alarm went off in his brain.

"I've got to go." Business first, especially his lucrative side operation.

She effectively gagged his protests with her tongue. After a thorough tongue-lashing, he gave in. What the hell was a quickie? Cindy could wait. And what difference would ten more minutes make in the scheme of things.

As he unzipped, Rita slithered her panties off. Her musky femininity tantalized his nostrils, and he hurried to dig a rubber from his pocket and protect himself. Through narrowed eyes, she watched, slowly spreading her thighs wide, and then even wider.

"Uh-uh." He shook his head and turned her around, bending her over his desk so that her lush ass was positioned at just the right height for his penetration.

Splaying her hands the width of the desk, she gripped the edges. With a provoking wriggle, she egged him on.

Yielding to impulse, he slapped her sassy backside with his open hand.

"Ouch," she yelped. "That was deviant but *nice*."

Her pert cheek turned pink and felt warm beneath the palm of his hand. Gratified, he smacked his hand to her other cheek with the same amount of pressure, and it blushed the same shade of pink.

"Is that all you've got?" she challenged, waggling her butt with a seductive shake.

He smacked her bottom harder this time. First one side and then the other. Twice more until her buttocks was red and hot and she whimpered, "Fuck me. Fuck me," after each slap.

From behind, he slipped two fingers into the folds of her vagina. She was drenched. Her pussy milked his fingers, anxious to be penetrated. When he withdrew them, he spread her moistness between the cheeks of her rear end, his slick fingers zeroing in on her puckered hole.

"Do you like it this way?" he taunted, sure that she did.

She moaned. "Yes. Give me all you've got."

He slipped the tip of his finger in, and she stiffened for a second. Then she pushed against his hand and ground her ass into him. He was in knuckle-deep, when she demanded, "Quit playing around and stick your cock in me."

Withdrawing his finger, he sunk the pulsing head of his dick into her and halted. She felt tight and wet.

"Don't stop," she hissed.

With his hips, he lunged forward and her muscles parted, giving him easy entrance. He grabbed her hips and plunged, burying himself to his balls. Her bottom gyrated and set a frantic pace. Hard and fast, he drove himself into her. Over and over, flesh slapped flesh. Grunts and groans stole his air.

Giving as good as she got, she slammed her soft, hot cheeks against his hard pubic bone. Between thrusts, he worked his hand around to her clit and urged her to a climax by flicking his fingers over the engorged nub. Soon, she let out a scream. Her arms went limp and her breasts flattened against the desk. She rested her face to the side and gulped for air. His cock jerked, once, twice, and then he released.

"You were great," she gasped, in what sounded like a practiced phrase. Stretching one arm across the desk top, she flicked her fingers until she had a grasp on the tissue box.

He moved away and disposed of the condom while she cleaned herself up. By the time he was zipped and tucked, she was dressed.

He noticed she didn't park her butt on his desk this time. Her ass was probably still cherry-red and on fire. She stood alongside him as he stuffed some papers he'd scooped from the floor into his briefcase. He checked his wristwatch. He had to get going or Cindy would be miffed. She was hard enough to take when she was in a good mood.

"Are you going to the *Starry Night?*" Rita asked.

"Not tonight."

She raised an eyebrow. "You aren't taking that loudmouth in the clunky shoes out alone somewhere, are you?" Her tone was tinged with suspicion.

"I might be. What's it to you?" He clicked his case shut, met her eye to eye.

She stroked her hand down the length of his tie. "I'm not stupid. You can't possible be interested in her. There must be something in it for you. I know it can't be her social standing; she has none. Other than at a seedy bar on the river. So," she purred, "it must be work related."

His stomach began burning again, but he wouldn't give Rita leverage by scavenging the floor for his antacids.

"You have a wild imagination," he bluffed. "You should keep it on what you're good at." He glanced down at her crotch before brushing by her.

She trailed after him. "You're up to something, and I want in on it." He opened the door and strode down the hallway toward the elevator. "I won't rest until I figure out what it is." Her voice echoed through the empty offices.

"Bitch," he mumbled under his breath as he punched the *down* button.

****

"You're here." Cindy shrieked and jumped into Jay's arms right after he rang the bell and she flung the door open.

161

He forced himself to kiss her on the mouth but refused to go so far as to use his tongue. He had to act and soon. With Rita nosing around, he couldn't waste any more time and risk the deal going sour, like his gut. He'd get what he came after tonight. Fortified with enough antacids to stomach the job, he proceeded to seduce Cindy.

He groped her breast over her gaudy blouse. His fingers sank into the crisp, neon-green cotton material and something squishy. She continued kissing him as if she was numb to his advance.

He squeezed harder, until finally he pressed into pliant flesh, and she moaned in response. That must be one hell of a bra she was wearing. Unfortunately, he'd find out soon enough just how padded.

Back to the business at hand, he asked, "Where's the tub?"

"Through there," she croaked like a frog and pointed down the hallway, and he tugged her by the wrist in that direction.

When they entered the spacious bathroom, he slipped the knot open on his silk tie and flung it onto the sink. Next, he shrugged out of his jacket, dropping the expensive garment onto the cold marble floor. Hell, he'd probably have to burn all his clothes when he returned to his apartment after performing the dirty deed with Cindy. He didn't want any remembrances of this night, other than her password.

With performance anxiety and Cindy foremost on his mind, he noticed the Mesopotamia almost as an afterthought. "The tub looks better than it does in the sales pamphlet."

He was sure next year's model would look even more impressive and worth every buck the competition was paying him.

He turned the brass spigots and water poured forth, warm and steamy. Maybe the room would fog up enough to blur Cindy from his vision. Then he'd pretend she was Rita while he boned her. Rita had definitely lived up to her 'ravishing' nickname. His hand rubbed his cock in reverence.

"You're certainly in a hurry," Cindy said, massaging his shoulder. "Bad day."

"Yes, I can't wait to put it behind me," he said in all honesty. Grabbing the lighter from the shelf, he began putting a flame to the dozen candles circling the tub.

What did she do, buy out the damn store?

While humming some dumb love song, she dumped bath salts into the water. The stench of flowers choked his airway, and a headache throbbed in his skull.

The ache eased somewhat when she flicked the light switch and the room dimmed. Between the steam and the candlelight, he could barely make out her features. Pretending she was another woman would be easy.

Stepping in front of Cindy, he hastened to unbutton her blouse. She offered no resistance. Once he had it off, he flung it to the side, not looking where it landed nor caring. After that he reached behind her back and undid her bra. The darn thing weighed about five pounds and hit the floor with a *thud*.

"They're saline," she said, hugging him and nipping at his chin.

"Too chicken for implants, huh?"

"Are big breasts important to you?"

"No." He clasped one of her small mounds in the palm of his hand while he lied. "Everything over a mouthful is a waste." To prove the point, he suckled the nipple on one of her deflated tits.

"And to quote a woman I know, you've said a mouthful." She arched her back, making it easier for him to nibble.

"It figures a woman said that," he mumbled. A small breasted one, he'd bet.

With a *pop*, he broke suction. Enough with the foreplay.

"Let's get wet." He didn't wait for her to reply but started flinging the rest of his clothes off.

She followed his lead, and soon they were submerged in the smelly, floral water with the whirlpool jets whining. He managed to manipulate their positions so that he sat straddling her back and not facing her flat chest. She leaned against his chest, her eyes closed. She seemed content. Maybe he wouldn't have to screw her after all.

He ran the washcloth over her shoulders and neck, splashing warm water over her fair, freckled skin. She seemed complacent enough so he went for broke right away.

"Maybe we can work on my portfolio at the office, during our breaks and lunch instead of wasting our off-hours."

She peered over her shoulder. "I'd see a lot more of you then."

"Oh, yeah. Our evenings would be free to do more of this." He was lucky she couldn't see his eyes. They surely expressed his disinterest.

She nodded. "I'd like that."

"My office is too central, though. We should use yours. You don't mind sharing your computer and password with me, do you?" He feigned an affectionate tone.

"I'll tell you mine if you tell me yours," she purred, then blurted out, "My password's peanut butter."

"I'm changing mine to jelly," he crooned in her ear. "First thing in the morning."

She laughed, her delight apparent.

Leaning back, he gave his tight muscles and taut nerves over to the relaxing water jets. He couldn't believe finagling her password had been so simple. He didn't even have to gaze into her eyes lovingly. Or screw her.

****

"Over here." Huddled in the darkness of a sprawling live oak alongside the river, Google waved Spence toward him with a penlight.

In the still air of the humid evening, a musty smell of dust and electronics and close quarters clung to the bespectacled man.

"Glad you could see me." Spence cocked his ear toward the opposite bank of the river where a thick mist hung low on the water. He listened for noises, wanting to ensure they were alone. Voices carried on the water.

When the only sound came from an owl hooting somewhere down river, he turned his attention back to his informant.

Google stuffed one hand into the oversized pockets of his oversized pants and shrugged his slouched shoulders. "Not sure how much help this is, but I promised to pass along whatever I came across."

"I appreciate it." He clapped Google's shoulder, soft from too many hours at the computer and no apparent type of manual labor. "One man's trash is another's treasure," Spence muttered, wondering if that qualified as a Doriaism.

He smiled inwardly at the warming reminder of Mercy. She'd ingrained herself into his stark life in a short amount of time. He'd miss her when she flew back East. His craving for her was never far from the surface, no matter how deep he tried to bury the emotion.

Google opened his mouth, his pearly veneers catching a glint from the penlight when he fumbled deeper into his pants. "I was hacking vehicle and license bureaus last night when I came across a registration for a boat in Parker's name." He fished a scrap of paper from his voluminous pocket. "Here's the make, model, size. She's called *Mermaid*. Thought it might be something."

Spence took the crumpled, raggedy scrap of paper and tucked it into his shirt pocket. "Can you find out where the boat's docked? Parker could be as close as the nearest marina."

"I'll keep working on it. I've made your case my pet project. I was called a geek back in high school so I know about persecution firsthand." He shrugged. "I can relate to yours."

Spence dug a few bills out of his jeans, but Google shook his head. Pushing his glasses back onto his nose, his wire-rims gleamed against the jogging penlight. "I'm okay right now. I made a kill—ing," his voice stammered on the last word. "The corporate rookie I mentioned the other day finally came across with a password and the dough. He needs my special brand of computer savvy, and I demanded megabucks for making me wait." He poked his chest out with pride. "Consider the tip on the boat a freebie until I find out more."

A nerve in Spence's cheek jumped. What kind of scam was Cindy's schmuck-of-a-boyfriend pulling that relied on computer hacking? Was she in on it, too? A rustle on the other side of the misty river wiped his curiosity away, fast. He had his own nemesis to worry about.

"Thanks," he said, grateful for Google's generosity.

Looked like he'd sold his horse for expense money too soon.

The snitch's cell phone let out a muffled ring from inside the pocket of his roomy pants. "Gotta take this?" he apologized. "Check back with me tomorrow. Same time, same place."

Chapter Twenty-one

"My mother called while you were in the shower," Mercy said, savoring the fresh-perked aroma of her morning coffee while waiting for her bagel to toast.

From across the room, seated at the circular glass-topped table, Cindy flashed an eager grin over the rim of her cup. "Did she mention me?"

"Yes, she sends her love and misses you. She said to give you this." Crossing the kitchen, she hugged her parent-starved friend. "She's vexed because she still hasn't heard from my uncle, and I had nothing new to offer. I talked to Lenny and a few of the other employees and regulars last night. Nobody knew the name or whereabouts of my uncle's sick friend."

"Not to trivialize her distress over his exact location, but Parker's probably wrapped up in concern for his ailing friend. She's just uptight over you having to return home without a check to finance your future." Cindy frowned. "If he stays away too long, you'll miss this year's college semesters."

"Let's talk about something more pleasant." She'd already talked the subject into the ground with her mother. "How did things go with Jay? I noticed melted candles in the bathroom."

Cindy flitted her blue-mascaraed lashes, which matched her blue platform shoes. "We cuddled. We kissed. All by candlelight in gardenia-scented water. It was *so* romantic."

Mercy smiled. "I'm happy for you."

"Not to preach, but when you date a good guy you get romance and permanence." She gestured to the toaster where smoke poured out.

Mercy popped the burnt bagel and scraped butter onto its blackened surface while Cindy chatted on about Jay. "To give us more time to spend with each other in the evenings, Jay suggested we access my computer at work to produce his art portfolio."

"Is that wise?" Mercy asked.

"I remote in from home when I work on projects for the company over the weekends."

"*For the company* being the keywords." She hoped Jay wasn't taking advantage of her friend's good nature.

"I wish you'd pursue someone as solid and secure as Jay." Cindy waved away the seared smoke circling their heads.

"Spence suits me fine for now." Heat thundered through her body at how well he suited her. Mercy bit into the charred, buttered bagel for the sake of something to do other than stand and shiver with delight at the mere thought of his sexual abilities.

"Better to be safe than sorry," Cindy tossed out the Doriaism. "You can't blame me for wanting to see you in a safer relationship. Someone without Spence's life experiences. Jail. Death. What do you talk about? I mean, you have nothing in common."

"He's just like everybody else. A person with problems, and he opens up to me." She stood at the granite counter instead of sitting where Cindy could see the concern that certainly tainted her eyes.

With a clunk, Cindy dropped her cup onto the saucer and shook an accusing finger at her. "You're falling for him, and after I warned you."

Denying that he'd gotten to her, that her heart not only empathized with his emotions but twisted in love knots whenever he let his façade down,

Mercy shook her head. "He seems needy in the friend department. I thought we might remain friendly. Phone, write, or maybe email if he has a computer. After I get back to Pennsylvania. Or when I'm away at college. Or from wherever I may end up once I launch a new career."

"You want more than a pen pal. You want to stay in touch with him because you're falling in love with him."

Mercy brushed imaginary crumbs from the front of her nightshirt and checked her toenail polish for chips, looking anywhere but at her friend. "I care about his well-being," she said. "What kind of person would I be if I engaged in intimate acts of passion with him but didn't feel any compassion for his misfortune?"

"However heroic his cause may seem, it'll lead to trouble. When you leave, don't look back. Promise to forget him."

"I can't promise."

"I was afraid you'd say that."

****

When Spence arrived that evening, Mercy hustled him right back out the door. "We can't stay. Cindy's expecting company."

"I thought I smelled the scent of female attack dog in the air."

"Ha. Ha." Mercy swatted his arm but hooked hers through it on their way to the elevator and down to the parking lot. Once they were settled in his truck, she asked, "Are we going out to your place?"

She did like the comfy feel of his house, and the relaxed persona Spence took on when they were out at his ranch. So what if she liked him more than she wanted to admit? She suspected he liked her more than he'd admit. Why else would he confide in her?

Besides, all that 'liking' between them certainly

hadn't hindered either of them in the sex department.

"Nope," he said, an odd edge of determination in his voice. "How about a movie instead?"

He never failed to surprise her, in bed or out. "A movie?"

"The rectangle screen with moving pictures in living color with surround sound." He gestured with his hands, forming an oblong before starting the engine to the truck. "Bigger than a TV, smaller than the barn."

"Smart ass," she mumbled. But the prospect held some promise. A dark theater, plush seats, groping hands, heavy breathing. She licked her lips. "Great for foreplay."

He chuckled and leaned over to kiss her before pulling out of the lot.

And that was as close as she got to any foreplay. The cinema was dark all right, except when bombs and fireworks exploded on the screen, which was throughout most of the film. The plush seats were hard and narrow. The only groping fingers were slicked from buttery popcorn. Lots of heavy breathing went on though, with the audience sucking in their breath and exhaling during the multiple on-screen pyrotechnics and battles.

Toward the end of the feature, Mercy managed to push her disappointment aside. The evening was the most low-key she'd spent with Spence, yet felt kind of nice. He smelled great, like a woodsy aftershave. And familiar. His soft, husky-voiced comments sounded companionable while his arm resting on her shoulder felt comfy.

She was beginning to feel warm and fuzzy over him. And far too loving. She wiggled away. Absently, he reached over and pulled her back.

After the show, she figured him for some action, but...

"It's too far and too late to drive out to the ranch," he said. "And I have to meet someone within the hour."

She noted he was dressed in black again, which meant he had late night business in the city. With a snap of an idea, she smiled, digging through her handbag until she came away with a crumpled piece of leather, initialed with a P, attached to a shiny gold key. "My uncle has a place in the city. We can go there."

"I didn't know you knew anybody in San Antonio besides Cindy."

"I do. And he's not home." She jangled the key.

"I'll have to be minuteman." Spence flashed her a provocative smile. "What's the address?"

She told him and relaxed against the seat while he maneuvered the truck into the busy traffic. His nearness in the movie house had been a tease, only stirring her appetite. She craved to feel his powerful arms hold her tight against his chest while she matched her breathing and her heartbeat to his. She wanted to feel his hot flesh and bone against hers.

Which all sounded more romantic than lusty. But a little romantic fantasy along with the sex could only spice things up, couldn't it?

****

Once Spence passed a few cars and steered the truck into the right lane, he asked Mercy, "How did you like the show?"

"The licorice Nibs were good."

He laughed. "I suspected you weren't into action-adventure when you spent more time at the concession stand than in your seat." But she'd been a good sport and hadn't whined, like some women he'd known before his jail term. The movie had been a great distraction for him. For the first time in ages, he'd felt like a normal person enjoying an ordinary amusement.

"Let's just say I didn't mind going for the popcorn and drinks." She leaned toward him when she spoke, and he caught a hint of her perfume, or maybe it was the shampoo she used. But she smelled seductive.

"Here I thought you lived to serve me." A few services she could perform for him ran through his mind. He loved the way she serviced his cock. Her mouth fitted tight over the head, pumping with her hand at the base while she ran her tongue along the throbbing vein of his shaft. His dick itched with desire at the mere memory.

"I do live to serve you, for several more days anyway." She flitted her eyelashes demurely.

"We'll see." He let his voice dip into a thick, sexual tone, shying away from how much he'd miss her when the week ran out.

And not just sexually. He'd miss her smile. The way she made him feel when he held her hand or kissed her. The way she made him feel by merely walking or sitting beside him.

Somehow, being with her blurred his hard edges, made him feel softer on the inside. Not callous and cold like he'd become over the past two years.

Mercy responded to his suggestive tone by reaching over and stroking his thigh. Her hand felt hot through the dark denim of his jeans, and she succeeded in giving him an instant boner.

"Later, babe," he murmured, shifting on the seat to ease his discomfort.

"Later." But she didn't let up.

"Nice part of the city." He nodded toward the houses shadowed by post oaks and pecans to divert her attention until they reached their destination and he could act on his carnal appetite.

As she peeped out her side window, she stopped massaging, but didn't remove her hand from his inner thigh. His hard-on stayed on alert.

Mercy squinted through the windshield to make out the houses in the dark. "That one has a nice stone front," she said, kneading his thigh muscle again, and his revived erection began getting harder to deal with in his seated position.

He missed the street and had to circle back. "What house is your uncle's?"

Her pretty blonde hair shimmered in the streetlight as she shook her head. "I'm not sure. I've never been here before. My uncle's been away since I arrived. But he left an open invitation and the key."

"8082, 8084, 8086," he recited the house numbers as he downshifted the truck to a crawl.

"There it is." She pointed to a tree-lined, brick driveway with a house set well back from the street. 8088. He pulled the truck into the empty drive and shut the motor off.

The neighborhood was quiet. The shrill of katydids and the rustle of a stray cat prowling in the shrubs were the only sounds other than their own breathing. The sweet aroma of oleander drifted in through the open window, but once he helped Mercy from the truck, her scent filled him, seeping into his pores, pulsing the blood in his veins.

At the front stoop, she plopped the key into his hand without touching his palm. But her very presence and the heat from her body were enough to keep him turned on.

Jiggling the lock, he opened the door and halted. "No alarm." He groped along the wall in the foyer until he hit a light switch. A dim-lit chandelier glimmered above them.

"I imagine the bedrooms are in the back of the house," she whispered, her voice low and luring. She moved ahead of him down the hallway.

He slapped the door shut and followed her. Catching up in a few strides, he grabbed onto her wrist and tugged her backward every few steps to kiss her neck and cop a feel.

Her breasts were a handful, the flesh soft and firm, her nipples hardening in immediate response to his flicking thumb. Each time he smacked a light kiss to her tender neck, she laughed. He liked the tinkling sound. It sounded wholesome and sincere.

The women he'd been with since he'd served his time had faked their laughter, along with their orgasms. He hadn't cared then. But since Mercy, he'd be hard set to go back to the way things were.

He'd been celibate in jail. He could do so again, until he settled up with Parker and then what? Nothing. His heart slammed at the answer.

Mercy peeked into one room and then another, opening and shutting doors. Finally, she kept one open. "This must be the guest bedroom. There's nothing personal in sight."

She was right. No pictures, jewelry, books. They entered, leaving the glow of the hall chandelier behind. As he shut the door to the bedroom, darkness closed in around them, except for the sliver of moonlight filtering in through the curtain. She stood still, apparently waiting for her eyes to adjust.

Leaning against the door, he encircled her waist with his hands and turned her to face him, tugging her lush figure up against him. He groaned at how her supple curves fit his body sexually. His half-hard cock sprang back to life with a raging stiffness. Evidently, her persistent hand during the truck ride had been more than enough foreplay for him.

He jerked at her blouse and pulled it over her head and off. Bunching the soft fabric in his hand, he held it near his face and inhaled her sensuous scent.

An aroused glint shone in her eyes. While still holding the blouse, he captured her slender wrists and tugged them behind her back.

She arched her spine and thrust her breasts

forward until they rubbed against his chest with a slight but provocative friction. Her nipples peaked pebble-hard against the silky material of her bra. When she tilted her chin upward, her breath fanned his jaw, moist, heavy, and sweet.

Tempting as she was, he didn't take her mouth yet. He twisted her blouse around her wrists and tied the fabric off into a knot behind her back.

Brazenly, she moistened her lips, running the enticing, pink tip of her tongue along the seam of her mouth with deliberate slowness. Then her tongue slipped from sight, and she sucked her bottom lip between her pearly teeth, baiting him to make her open up to him.

He twirled a blonde strand of her hair around his fingertip, letting the curl spring loose to brush her cheek and neck while he gauged his next move and her response.

With a shiver, she swallowed hard. He dipped his head and licked at the throbbing spot on her throat. Tension lay just beneath the surface of her creamy flesh. She arched her neck, urging his mouth to kiss her throat, but he resisted, denying himself the pleasure of sucking her silky skin between his teeth and nipping.

Instead, he flicked at the front closure of her bra with his index finger, teasing her. Her eyes glimmered with heat and want. Her lashes fluttered, shadowing her cheeks. She wavered, swaying forward, nudging the plastic snap onto his finger.

He retreated and trailed his finger down her torso, stopping at the waistband to her slacks. Gently, he let his fingertips crawl beneath the material until he stumbled on a narrow strip of elastic.

Thong panties. His interest sparked. His fingers yanked the elastic band upward to her belly button with just the right amount of pressure to stimulate her clit and make her spread her legs. She emitted an audible sigh from deep within her throat.

Nudging his knee between her thighs, he rubbed against her with a slow, grinding motion. She spread her legs wider, gyrating against his leg, pressing harder, moving faster, thrashing.

He cupped her bottom in his palms and lifted her against his rigid groin. His erection and balls tightened, heavy with his desire for her. The green numbers on the digital clock-radio flickered, catching his attention. He'd lost track of time. He had little more than a moment before he had to leave to meet Google.

She gasped, stilling her hips to ward off her apparent spasm.

"Go for it," he coaxed, slipping his hand down her pants to hurry her orgasm along. "We're out of here soon."

"But I want to come with you inside me."

"We don't have the time."

"What about you?"

"I can wait," he said.

She stilled his hand. "Then I'll wait, too."

Damn soft-hearted woman.

Chapter Twenty-two

Once they were back in Spence's truck, Mercy checked her cell messages. "There's a text from Cindy. Jay cancelled their date."

So Mercy got dropped off at the condo. No sooner did she unlock the door and flick the light switch than Cindy stumbled into the foyer, wearing her pajamas and a pair of pink, fuzzy, wedged bedroom slippers.

"Did I wake you?" Mercy asked. "I'm sorry."

"No. I must've fallen asleep on the couch. Looks like I had a four-hour nap." Rubbing the sleep from her eyes, Cindy cracked a grin. "But that means I can stay up four hours later and we can chat. What with me settling in at the San Antonio office and meeting my new coworkers, and both of us dating, we haven't spent much time together this visit."

Mercy heeled off her shoes and smoothed her hands together in glee. "I'll get the ice cream and spoons."

"And I'll find an old movie on the TV. A black-and-white one."

Once they were settled, they scooped ice cream from the carton, watched the flick, laughed, cried, and gossiped about old friends from back home during the commercials.

When the show ended on a schmaltzy note, Cindy wiped her tears away with the sleeve of her pajamas. "This was fun. Like old times."

"Uh-huh. I'm glad Jay cancelled."

"Me, too. We needed this time together." She grinned. "He's coming by tonight, though."

"Of course. I figured as much." Mercy stretched and yawned. "I guess my Uncle Parker didn't call, or you'd have mentioned it."

Cindy shook her head. "He didn't, but your mother did. She wanted to know if you'd heard anything. I told her you'd let her know as soon as you did. Despite her frequent calls, I think she's trying not to ruin your vacation."

"Thanks for handling the situation. I don't know what to say to her anymore about her absentee brother."

"I told her to think positive." Cindy stood and gathered up the spoons and empty carton, tossing Mercy an encouraging glance. "I'm sure your uncle will show up by flight time with a fat check to secure your future and get your mother off your back."

"I wish I could assure her sooner. Save her the long-distance phone bill." Using the remote, Mercy flicked the TV off.

On her way out of the room, Cindy pivoted at the doorway. "Where did you and Spence go?"

"Spence took me to a movie. Later we ended up at my uncle's place." An idea took root. "We should have dinner there this evening. Spence hasn't had a home-cooked meal in...in a long time."

"Since jail time." Cindy arched her eyebrow.

Ignoring her friend's cynicism, Mercy asked, "Can you cook?"

"Grilled cheese and scrambled eggs. I have one special chicken recipe for company."

If Cindy could prepare the specialty, how hard could it be?

"Could I borrow your recipe? You know my mother. She barely let me near the kitchen. Microwave dinners and toast are the extent of my cooking."

Cindy laughed. "And I know you like your toast smokin'." She crinkled her nose and quoted, "The way to a man's heart is through his stomach. You're falling for him, and don't say I didn't warn you."

"Repeatedly," Mercy muttered.

"Why him, Mercy?" Cindy whined. "He's a convict."

"He's not a criminal, just a man who was in the wrong place at the wrong time. He's a victim in all this."

Cindy shrugged. "All I'm saying is that you're kidding yourself if you think it's still only about the sex."

"I have a lot of years of sex to make up for."

Her friend shook her head before nudging her chin toward the kitchen. "If you must, there's a wooden box next to the blender. The recipe's easy to find. All the other index cards are blank."

****

What Mercy had with Spence was purely carnal. Cindy was wrong.

As if to stress her point, Mercy dabbed perfume to her pulse points and an extra dash to her inner thighs. Slipping into a low-cut sundress, she pushed aside Cindy's warning and concentrated on her grocery list instead. Recipe in hand, she took a cab to the market and then to her uncle's house.

In the daylight the place looked more spacious. The foyer was high and airy, the hallway wide, the kitchen compact with a well-planned work area with industrial appliances and heavy-lidded pots and pans. Her uncle must've liked to cook at one time, but the kitchen looked like it hadn't been used in a while.

While unpacking the perishables from her grocery sack and stashing them into the refrigerator, she noticed his under-stocked supplies. Soft drinks, bottled water, aged cheese. He obviously ate out or at the club.

Mercy moved on into the oh-so-familiar guest

bedroom to strip the bed and freshen up the musty sheets. Upon opening the door, she caught a hint of Spence's familiar male scent lingering in the closed-up room. Heat rushed to her belly. Everything about the man turned her on. His smell, his look, his touch, his voice.

She jerked the linens from the bed before she was too hot and bothered to concentrate on making dinner. After tossing them into the washing machine, she decided to acquaint herself with the rest of the house. With a soft slap, slap of her sandals, she wandered through her uncle's masculine living room with its bold-colored stripes and nailhead-trimmed leather chairs.

From there she entered his den and sat down behind his large mahogany office desk. While she rang Spence's number, she studied a picture of her uncle, standing next to a taller, broader man on a fishing boat called *Mermaid*. Both were smiling with their arms clasped around each other's shoulders. She wondered if the hearty-looking man was her uncle's now sick friend.

"Hello." Spence's deep voice reverberated through her body like a spasm, causing her sex lips to shiver and cream.

Shameless. And in front of her uncle, too. She flipped the framed photo face down.

"Can I tempt you?" She paused for a provocative effect. "With a home-cooked dinner?" Twirling the phone cord around her finger, she bobbed her foot up and down in a sensual rhythm.

"Will you be wearing an apron?" His voice dipped low, sounding salacious and intoxicating.

"Nothing but." Her nipples tightened, and she untwisted the cord while conjuring up all the possibilities of kitchen sex. Textures and temperatures of food, from smooth, hot sauces to cold, hard cubes of ice. Bodies positioned against the counter, on the tile floor, or straddling the armless, chrome chair.

"Aprons are an unfulfilled fantasy of mine." He sounded sexier and grittier than usual.

Her clit quivered. "What time?" Mentally, she was already searching the kitchen for an apron. If the cupboards turned up empty, she'd need to take another cab ride, to the mall this time.

"Hmm," he said, thinking.

The throaty sound of his voice sent more scorching excitement through her body, centering in the very core where she sat. She uncrossed her legs and hoped she could learn how to cook while in such an aroused state.

"Is six o'clock okay?" he asked. "A man who's helping investigate Mark's murder didn't make our meeting yesterday. He left a message on my machine to be there tonight at eight."

"Oh." Even though she knew any lead into who killed his friend was important, disappointment sank her voice.

Could they eat and perform both of their kitchen fantasies in so short a time?

"I could come back afterward." His tone sounded steamy and suggestive, like she was hot-fudge fondue and he had a sweet-tooth fetish.

"Yes." Her hand tightened on the receiver as her wayward heart trembled in her chest. Spence was coming back to spend the whole night with her.

Spence, sleep-mussed with his dark, liquid eyes half-lidded. Her waking, cradled in his strong arms. She'd never woken up with a man before. Her heart fluttered at the idea of Spence being her first.

Her grip loosened once he hung up. She was reading too much into their affair, into him. She squeezed her eyes shut on the image of lovers entwined in the blush of morning light.

She wasn't falling in love with him, as Cindy so

often persisted. She merely desired a little romance with her lust for a change of pace.

The meltdown around her heart had more to do with his fight against injustice than love. She was a sucker for a heartfelt cause and an underdog.

Although, Spence was anything but.

He may be a victim, as she'd pointed out to Cindy, but he was still tall, strong, proud, and tough. He'd come out a winner. With or without her heart's entanglement. Or any other involvement on her part.

Resolve in place, she bucked up her chin and marched toward the kitchen to find an apron and somehow prepare chicken cacciatore.

****

At six sharp, Spence rang the doorbell. Mercy let him in, wearing the denim, bibbed, barbecue apron she'd found in a kitchen drawer and nothing else.

"Wasn't exactly what I had in mind." But his smoky gaze slid over her, simmering and slow.

In a flash, even the skimpy covering of material felt too hot and heavy next to her skin. The coarse denim aroused and peaked her tender nipples while the tie at her waist begged for release.

Holding her arms away from her body, she gestured. "This is the best I could come up with on short notice." She smiled, sure visions of a French-maid apron had danced in his head. But he whistled all the same and spun her around, stopping to plant a succulent kiss between her shoulder blades. Chills rippled down her spine. She hadn't been aware that the spot was an erogenous zone of hers.

"Can you cook as well as you wear that apron?" He patted her bare butt.

"You'll have to take your chances and taste test for yourself." With a twist of her torso, she latched onto his thick, muscled arm and led him into the dining room.

"You set a mean table." His dark eyes took in the fresh pink carnations she'd bought earlier and the shimmering pastel candles she'd lit.

His tall, lean frame, standing near her in the candlelight, looked so devilish and handsome. She brushed her hip and breast against him to prove to herself he was real and she had the right.

"Sit here." Moving away, she pulled out the wooden, armed chair at the head of the linen-covered table.

He smiled at her, affection warming his dark eyes to a milk chocolate.

An unprecedented impulse *not* to jump his bones on contact coursed through her. To enjoy a leisurely dinner instead. How strange. Especially after the past two sexless evenings they'd spent together. Oh, not that she didn't have fantasies she wanted to explore, but she wanted to relax and dine with him, first. Indulge in his humor and his companionship.

She ducked into the kitchen, puzzling over what it all meant. She liked Spence. She cared about him. But love? She shook her head. Cindy couldn't be right?

Lust or love? She rolled the words around on her tongue, coming away with 'lusty love.' Was there such a beast?

The stove's timer went off and she jumped. Donning a pair of clumsy, silver oven mitts, she pulled the oval casserole dish from the oven and gingerly carried it into the dining room.

Spence leaped to his feet and jockeyed both the mitts and casserole from her, plopping the hot dish onto its serving cradle in the middle of the table with ease. He lifted the lid and sniffed, glancing at her curiously.

"It's chicken cacciatore. I may've added too much spice and herbs and not enough chicken." Suddenly, she wasn't sure cooking dinner for him had been the delicious idea she'd thought it would be.

He flicked the silvery mitts aside and sat back down. "I like chicken."

Good, because she was feeling chicken at the moment.

Exposed and vulnerable in too many ways, she slipped her naked butt onto the cold, hard, wooden chair.

Chapter Twenty-three

Spence looked down at the contents of his gold-rimmed china plate. The aroma of the chicken and spices wafted up warm and pleasant. Mercy had gone out of her way to prepare the meal for him. Hell, she'd taken a cab to the grocers and then out to her uncle's house. She'd fussed big time.

"I may have added too much wine to the sauce," she apologized with a smile, seeking his eyes.

With a clinkety-clink, her knife and fork hit the edge of her plate. She was nervous. She cared what he thought. His heart clenched at her concern. Picking up his fork, he dug in.

"It's delicious," he said after several mouthfuls.

Not bad. After prison food, even his boot would taste good with enough salt and pepper. But he bit back the remark. This wasn't the time to rag her.

"Thank you." She fingered the stem of her goblet, her wine untouched. "I've never cooked a meal from scratch before."

He lifted his wineglass and with a ting touched the delicate crystal to hers. "You do everything beautifully."

Especially make love. He studied her over the gold rim of his glass. The way her lashes fluttered and her lips pursed. The way her throat tilted as she drank. Through lowered lids, she looked at him with a gaze that shot pangs of want through his body.

He leaned across their plates and kissed the sheen of wine from her lips. She tasted from grapes and her own flavor of sweetness mixed with sexiness. The combination heated his blood, along

185

with his heart.

And muddled his brain more than any glass of wine could. He settled back and downed the remaining alcohol.

She sipped again before she seemed relaxed enough to taste her food. "Mmm." She looked up, surprised. "Not too bad for a beginner."

With a smile, Spence returned his attention to his plate. He intended to tamp down any urges she stirred in him until he'd eaten his last bite. He'd keep his mouth and hands off her until he showed his appreciation by finishing the meal she'd prepared especially for him.

He ate with the proper amount of gusto to keep her grinning. When he had his fill, he stretched out his legs and sat back, watching her pick at her plate. She was cute in her sauce-splashed apron. Heart-softening cute, and his heart wasn't immune. Warmth spread through his chest, thick and syrupy.

When she put her fork aside, he hastened to get the rest of dinner out of the way. "What's for dessert?" Afterward, he'd strip her of her adorable apron and get his sappy emotions under control by replacing them with lurid ones.

She raised her hands in a helpless gesture. "I don't know how to bake."

But she sure could cook. She was the hottest and at the same time the sweetest woman he'd ever met.

"You can be dessert." When he clasped her hand in his to help her from her chair, an agreeable glint lit her eyes. "Now where's that bedroom you showed me last night?" He winked, but the hammering of his heart was giving his baser emotions a race for their life.

And his libido was losing. All of a sudden, something had changed. He wanted more from Mercy than just sex.

He wanted to make love to her.

With each stride, he came closer to his amorous objective. But his booted steps didn't falter as her silken hand led him into the dimness of the guest room. He resigned himself to follow his heart and brood over the outcome of the foolish endeavor later.

In the cool darkness, he let his gaze flicker over her face and form. Her no-frills apron was all she wore, covering her in the front while exposing her from behind. He pulled her up against his body, cupping her naked bottom in his hand and kneading her pliable cheeks. She moaned in response. Pressing herself against his groin, she rode him with slow, tantalizing movements.

"I need you," he admitted. His mouth touched hers ever so lightly before nibbling her lush bottom lip, teasing the flesh between his teeth. When he broke away, he licked her lip to ease the sting he'd caused there.

She arched her back, fitting herself tighter against his fly and meeting his eyes. "How?" Her sexual appetite for adventure was apparent in her slurred word and the darkening of her blue eyes.

"Straight, plain, old-fashioned, missionary style." He watched her eyes widen with each of his proclamations. "No fantasies, no tricks, no gymnastics."

"Why?" With her palms resting on his chest, she licked at her lips, her pink tongue wet and glistening.

"Because I fancy you that way, Mercy." Not giving her a chance to question him further, he trapped her hands against him and sealed his lips to hers. He explored the warm, wet inside of her mouth with his tongue until she was breathless with desire.

Reaching around behind her, he untied the apron at her waist and her nape. When he edged away, the material slithered down between their bodies, landing on the dusty tips of his boots and her pink toenails. Her bare feet, her naked flesh, and the heat from her body engulfed his senses. She palpitated with female sensuality.

Even as his heart sighed at the sight and smell of her, his dick hardened with need and passion. His seed surged to the head of his cock, eager to lay wet claim to her in the most primitive, age-old way. He throbbed to be inside her, making love to her.

"We can't fool around," she demanded, flicking at the metal snap to his jeans. "You have to leave within the hour to meet...whoever." She didn't sound like she cared who he was seeing afterward. Her concentration was centered on her busy fingers.

With a quick zip, the metal teeth gave way, and she hurried to work his penis free. He stayed her hand with his. "Slow down, babe. We've got enough time to do this right."

"Once we're naked on the bed, we can slow to a crawl if you like." She kissed his lips and chin and jaw while shimmying his pants down over his hips.

He indulged her by heeling off his boots and stripping off his shirt. Her frenzied hands wriggled his jeans down and shucked them aside. With a thump, his back hit the door when she grabbed his shaft in her smooth, delicate palm and stroked him. Up and down, up and down. She added her second hand and more pressure to pump his sensitive flesh to its fullest arousal. He groaned, and the back of his head banged against the wooden door as he gave himself over to her administrations.

Salacious jolts licked at his nerves, all converging at the crown of his dick. He groaned. This wasn't going the way he'd expected. He wanted gentle and tender. He wanted to make love to her, worship her body, inside and out. She was going after flat-out sexual satisfaction, as always.

"Let's try that bed crawl, you mentioned," he

mumbled through strained vocal chords. It took a lot of willpower to stick to his guns, break her loose from his erection, and hold her away by her bare shoulders. Her skin felt satiny next to his callused hands and so irresistible. His fingers twitched beneath the effort.

When she nodded her assent, he slid his palms down her arms to encircle her wrists. With a nudge of his hips against hers, he backed her over to the bed. Her eyes glittered with passion as his hard-on throbbed against her inner thigh with each step. She was so easy to read. So sexy. So tempting. So achingly sweet.

In one easy push, he tumbled her onto the mattress. Holding her open arms out to him, she curved her mouth into an inviting smile. Her lips were moist and enticing. Sexual anticipation fired her eyes, their heat drawing him in. He wanted to lose himself in her eyes. Her mouth. Her body. Her heart.

He shifted onto the bed and straddled her legs with his thighs. He let the heaviness of his cock settle between her thighs, the tip resting at the downy entrance of her slit. With a faint whimper, she attempted to spread her legs but to no avail.

Propped on his forearms, he gazed at her face. Her blonde hair sprawled onto the dark coverlet, shimmering in the waning light slashing in through the window blinds. He pecked kisses onto her eyelids as they fluttered shut. He grazed the corners of her mouth, teasing her, before he sucked the sound of a sigh from her lips.

Cupping the back of her head in his hand, he made love to her mouth, kissing and sipping at her lips, dipping his tongue into the warm, wet flesh. By the time he broke away, his breath came in ragged gasps while her hips ground against his, restlessly. He slid a moist trail downward. With a gentle tug of

189

his teeth, he drew the smooth skin at her throat into his mouth. She purred and stretched, bowing into the love bite, receptive to his touch.

He licked at the base of her throat where her pulse pounded, rapid and aroused. With the tip of his tongue, he traced lower to her breasts and swirled slow circles around her tightening nipples. She tasted of salt and spice and sauce. He smiled, and her skin shivered where he broke contact. Digging her fingers into his hair, she urged him to continue the foreplay.

For now, he resisted. "I love the way you feel and taste." He rested his chin on her solar plexus and stared into her smoky gaze, branding her beauty onto his mind. For later, when she was gone.

"Taste more," she coaxed, her nails grazing his scalp as she directed him back down on her.

"I aim to." He went willingly.

With a slight pull, he sucked one rigid nipple into his mouth. Letting it loose, he allowed the cool air to tantalize the turgid bud before heating it with his moist, hot mouth again. And again. He restrained from his natural impulse to pluck and roll the nub between his teeth while she writhed in her eagerness. He wanted tonight to be memorable. Different in every way from the lusty encounters of their past evenings.

She arced into him, hissing and demanding, "Harder."

His need to make love to her, instead of fucking her this side of brainless, stopped him. His urgency for tenderness became more desirable than getting his rocks off. Probably because he'd had less of it.

He drew her other nipple into his mouth with care, bridling his inclination to grate the swollen bud with his teeth and gratify her groans. Instead, he titillated her senses with gentleness, indulging his hunger for love and caring, giving it instead of receiving it.

After lapping with feathery strokes and tantalizing her beaded rosette with TLC, with a last, delicate pull, he stretched her nipple out long, before releasing it.

She squealed, "Don't stop," and stroked him behind the ears, encouraging him to suckle more.

He shook his head. Her fingers grasped at his ears, attempting to halt the negative motion. He chuckled. "If I don't move on, I won't have enough time to kiss you all over. And I plan to kiss you all over."

Her eyes glazed over, intrigued. She released him and dropped her hands to her sides, limp and compliant.

After kissing the delectable flesh on the inside of her breasts, he moved on. He traced his tongue over her stomach and tickled her belly button and hipbones. She squirmed, attempting to spread her thighs, but still trapped by his.

"Can I do something for you?" he taunted, knowing he'd do just about anything she wanted.

"While you're down that way..." she cooed, gripping the sheets.

"I plan on getting around to it. I'm going to make love to every inch of your body," he promised.

With a satisfied sigh, she grasped for the nightstand before relaxing her limbs. She wilted into the mattress, trusting him to keep his word.

He liked that.

Liked it a lot.

He knelt between her legs, nudging them open and wide. "Nice curls," he murmured, trickling his fingers through the dark blonde hair on her mound, which was wet and shimmery with her cream.

"They're natural," she croaked, lifting her hips into his touch, her stomach muscles quivering.

He withdrew his hand and draped her thighs

over his shoulders. He blew on her clit, and her body jerked closer to his mouth. Her impatience excited him, but he kept his control. With light movements of his tongue, he lapped at the opening to her pussy. She bucked her hips in immediate response. Pressing on her stomach, he stimulated her clit with his thumb while his tongue flicked into her vaginal folds. With a soft touch he licked her until she cried out.

"Spence." Her voice sounded ragged.

Moving his thumb aside, he took her clit into his mouth and sucked gently, the taste of her musky, slick, and his for the taking. His.

Normally, he didn't endorse the exchange of body fluids, but Mercy was different. He wanted her juices in his mouth, and the trust that came along with that particular desire. He wanted to taste her as she came and have her taste him.

His breath caught. Hell, but he had it bad.

"Spence," she called his name again. This time more urgent and frustrated.

"Babe, I can make you come this way."

"I need to feel you inside of me."

He didn't want her needy, he wanted her loving. So he snaked his way back up her body. Bracing his arms alongside her head, he kissed her, tender and long before taking her in his arms.

On a breathless sigh, she said, "Here." She opened her palm to reveal a condom packet.

Glancing toward the nightstand, he noticed a handful of foil squares. Now he knew what she'd grappled for earlier, and it wasn't any proclamations of love.

He sheathed himself and started over. He kissed her for the pure pleasure of it. Over and over, until her breath came in gasps and his cock was too hard and heavy to ignore.

He entered her with a slow, rhythmic rocking of

his hips. Kissing her mouth, he inhaled her honeyed breath as she moaned.

She wrapped her ankles around his waist, squeezing him tight, and he sank in deep. She felt good. Right. Like she was his.

To the hilt she was, and he reveled in his possession of her.

He pumped in and out, slow and steady. He loved the feel of being inside her. Loved her silky skin gliding damp beneath his and the feel of her fingers and nails as she clung to him.

He relished the warmth of her breath as she panted and the fragrance of her body heat. She enveloped him. Her hot, wet core sucked him in and held him on the edge. Pulsing, throbbing need drove him on when he would've stayed as they were, sweaty, entwined, possessed.

But who possessed whom? His muscles jerked. His cock twitched. Did Mercy have him by the nuts—so to speak?

Yes. The instant the answer formed in his brain, he released. Tremors shook his body.

Fear or satisfaction?

A powerful spasm rocked him, twinged his muscles, drained his fluid.

I love you. He swallowed the words, the thought, the feeling welling up around his heart. Instead, he moaned her name, "Mercy."

Soon she shuddered in his arms, reaching her own peak of gratification. He let the wave of her orgasm subside before gathering her pliant body against his rough-planed one. She fit him too damn perfectly. His heart ached with the sweet irony of her leaving him at the end of the week.

But it was what they both wanted. Wasn't it?

He clenched his eyes shut and held his breath to break from her spell.

After a moment, he said the first unsentimental

thing that came to his mind. "If we hurry, I can help load the dishwasher."

"Don't worry about cleaning up." She pressed her soothing lips to his in a lingering kiss.

He pulled away from her just to make sure he was capable of doing so. With bravado, he asked, "Would you deny me the chance to play house?"

He forced a chuckle, but he wanted to do everything and anything with her from washing dishes to sexual acrobatics.

No, his brain shouted. He had other, more urgent demands. He had to keep his eye on his goal as Mark had so often reminded him. Playing house with Mercy here or anywhere else stood in the way of Spence's obligation to get Parker.

His breath halted. When had evening the score with Parker turned from a need into a duty?

Chapter Twenty-four

"Sorry I couldn't make it yesterday, but my car petered out on the Kelly Parkway." Google lifted his hands in a helpless gesture.

"Hey, shit happens." Spence glanced up at the moonless sky and across at the river bank. All appeared dark and quiet.

"I intercepted an email to Parker. He isn't on his boat yet, but he's planning a ceremony aboard. No date or destination. I'm hoping for more details when he replies."

"Good job." He surveyed the river again. The only life he detected was a bat swooping the water for insects. "Do you know who sent the email?"

"Not yet. But I'm working on it." Google thumbed his glasses to his nose.

"How soon 'til you find out?" He dug into his pocket to pay the informant off.

"I'll call as soon as I have it." Google waved away the money. "I'll run a tab for you. We'll divvy up when it's over."

"Thanks." Spence nodded to the man.

"Probably not important until Parker gets back in town, but I found out his house address. It's 8088 Windy Hill Lane."

Spence felt like he'd been punched in the gut. The street address was Mercy's uncle's house. What in the hell was going on? What was she—they up to?

Parker wasn't averse to using women for his dirty dealings. Was she really Parker's niece, or another bimbo who'd disappear after she did her damage, like the buckle bunnies Mark had picked up

195

before his death?

Spence's mind reeled, but he managed to mumble, "Can you check if Parker has a niece?"

"I'll get right on it." With a wave of his hand, Google scooted toward the path, leaving Spence to stew alone.

Looked like when he went back to Parker's house tonight he'd have to confront Mercy. Forget making love. What a fool he'd been.

Forget fucking her, too. He wasn't into payback sex. He had no intention of screwing her to bury his anger or seek revenge.

She had questions to answer. For one, where was Parker? And what was she to the snake, a relative or his paid hustler? Would she lie about her connection to him?

Spence watched a bat pounce the water, diving on its prey while others hovered above in silence. He raked his hands through his hair and stared down into the inky water.

Since Mark's death, lies seemed to circle him like bats in the night.

****

Mercy dabbed at her eyes with a tissue and hopped off her uncle's oversized sofa when she heard Spence's truck pull into the driveway. The hum of the engine had barely sputtered to a stop when she flung the front door open wide, letting in a blast of warm night air and the sweet scent of oleander.

"Spence." She threw herself into his arms, glad he'd come back so soon. She hated that she missed him this much, that his welcoming arms felt so warm and secure.

"Hey, babe." He leaned down to look into her teary eyes. Taking her bare shoulders in his strong hands, he kissed her mouth with a soft lingering kiss that, for no particular reason she could fathom, felt kind of sad and melancholy.

Like a final goodbye. But that was days away.

"How did your meeting go?" she hiccupped. His mouth tasted salty from her tears.

He didn't answer but asked, "Why are you crying?"

"Oh." Feeling embarrassed, she forced a smile and crumpled the damp, shredded tissue in her hand. "I'm watching a very sad, very romantic movie." She pointed toward the TV in the other room where a woman in a chiffon dress chattered about underarm deodorant. "There's a commercial break right now."

He thumbed a tear from her cheek, his touch gentle.

"I'm not sure how it will turn out," she whispered, gazing into his dark brooding eyes.

"Let's have a look and hope for the best." His voice sounded odd.

Taking his arm, she placed it around her waist and shut the door against the night and the heat. As they walked into the living room, her barefooted steps lightened.

He was hers for the evening. He'd come back to spend the whole night with her, into the morning. She intended to enjoy whatever time they had left for all its worth. She intended to take enough physical loving back with her to last a lifetime, in case she wasn't entitled to such an intense affair of the body again.

Body. Who was she kidding? Despite her best efforts and denials, her mind and heart seemed to go along with her body. She was having a difficult time separating them.

When Spence settled next to her on the cushy sofa, Mercy tucked her bare feet beneath the hem of her cotton sundress and cuddled into the shelter of his protective arm to enjoy the rest of the movie.

The power of his nearness, the strength of his

virile body, the movement of his hard chest as he breathed, everything about the potent man distracted and aroused her.

He seemed untouched by her presence and totally immersed in the show. He didn't utter a word until another commercial. Then, studying her face and holding her captive with his somber eyes, he said, "Tell me about you. All I know is that you're from Pennsylvania and you're here on vacation."

Spence wasn't one for conversation. His intense gaze gave nothing away. She wanted to keep up a correspondence with him after she left, and this looked like the ideal starting place to make that happen. He needed someone who was into more than his hunky, handsome, but solemn exterior. And heaven help her, his well-being concerned her.

"Let's see." She re-tucked her dress. "What might interest you about Lily Pond?" After a moment, she shook her head. "I don't suppose you golf."

"No."

She reached up and touched his cheek, but he pulled away.

"Don't stray from the subject."

Dropping her hand, she shrugged off his seriousness. Moistening her lips, she began, "I moved in with my mother for monetary reasons and because Lily Pond is so small the only apartments for rent are across the street from where we live, which sort of defeated the purpose anyway."

He chuckled. "Go on."

"I've dated two men over the course of the years. Neither relationship has been satisfying, as you know." She snuggled deeper into the crook of his arm, yearning for the sizzling sensations he was able to wrest from her willing body.

She feathered her nails over his chest and abs, dipping down toward his fly, but he stilled her hand with his large one. When he released her hand, she missed the warmth and rough feel of his palm on her skin.

"You're straying again," he cautioned. "Tell me about you and your uncle."

She rested her hand on his firm thigh, inches from her goal. After her bio, she'd have another go at his zipper.

"I've been thinking about a drastic career change. Something less isolated and more people oriented than a transcriptionist. Something in the financial field. I'm hoping my uncle will lend me the money for tuition and living expenses."

"Ah," he said, dragging out the sound.

She touched her fingers to his throat just for the thrill of feeling his delectable skin vibrate. He smelled of a hint of spicy aftershave and the fresh outdoors. "That sounded more like an *aha*," she said. "Although I can't imagine what would surprise you about anyone wanting to move away from Lily Pond to start anew."

"I knew you weren't the typical tourist." His tone was tinged with disapproval. "You didn't take in many of the local, historic sights."

"You're my main attraction," she teased, massaging the arm he had draped over her shoulder. His muscles flexed tense and rigid beneath her persistent touch.

"I'd bet your uncle has a lot more drawing power than I do."

"If you mean the loan—"

"I mean the money."

Confused, she fell silent. He didn't sound jealous. More accusing, as if she'd done something wrong.

She searched his eyes, trying to read his emotions. She supposed his traumatic experiences over the past two years with the death of his best friend and his jail sentence required some coddling on her part.

Before she could assure him of his importance to her, the commercials ended and Spence refocused on the screen. The movie started back up where it had left off, in the middle of a dramatic scene between the lovers.

The gangster husband hung up the phone after finding out that his beautiful bride had betrayed him. Not to the police, not to another mob boss, but by having an affair with another man. A nobody in the mob scheme of things.

When the handsome husband smiled and hugged his wife in a loving embrace, the tension broke and Mercy sighed. "He's forgiven her." What a man. What a lover.

Then, with a squeak, she covered her mouth.

As the husband caressed his wife, a knife glinted in his hand, and he stabbed her in the back. A splotch of dark red blood spread across the back of the woman's white dress, and she went limp in her killer's arms.

"I like happy endings." Mercy reached for the remote, but Spence stopped her.

"Let's see it out until the end."

She waited as the scene changed, flashing to a crowd gathered in a cemetery by the woman's gravesite. The husband was shaking hands with the mourners.

"The rat."

"She betrayed him." Spence's voice sounded bitter.

"That's no reason to murder her," Mercy protested.

"He's dead, too, on the inside."

"He'd have to be to kill her." Mercy squirmed on the cushion alongside Spence. The movie had lost all of its romantic appeal. She flicked the remote, stopping at a comedy show.

Comfortable once again in his secure arms, she nestled her head on his chest. By the time the first skit ended, she'd dozed off to peals of laughter.

When she awoke, the sound of static and a flickering screen greeted her. Rubbing the sleep from her eyes, she stretched. How long had she slept? She felt stiff and cold. Where was Spence?

Had he gone home? She'd counted on spending the night with him and awakening next to his sleep-warmed body. Spooning naked next to his morning boner and making love, relaxed and unhurried.

Yawning, she spied a light shining in the adjoining room. Her uncle's office. She shook the wrinkles from the skirt of her cotton dress as she stood up and padded toward the glow.

Chapter Twenty-five

"What are you doing?" Mercy stood shadowed in the doorway of her uncle's office, her gaze disarming.

Spence froze, his hands full of papers from rifling through Parker's desk.

He wanted to talk to Mercy, but later, when he'd gathered enough information to pose the right questions. After he searched the place and was armed with proof to substantiate his suspicions about her and Parker's deception.

Caught like a whore in a police cruiser's flashing lights, Spence had no choice but to come clean. "I'm looking for evidence." His voice sounded scratchy and defensive as he met her solemn blue eyes. Eyes that could fire his libido and melt his heart. Under other circumstances.

"Evidence?" Mercy's blonde brows crooked into a small, imperfect vee. Her pretty face had gone pale.

Spence dropped the papers he'd been going through back into the file folder and slammed the drawer shut.

"Why was this hidden from sight, face down?" He turned over the framed photo of Parker and a nameless man, the driver of the Caddy who'd knocked Spence and Mark down before punching Mark into kingdom come. Spence's fingers smudged the glass as he tightened his hold on the picture of the men who were responsible for spinning his life out of control. "Both of these bastards were responsible for sending me to jail." He trained his unblinking eyes on Mercy, gauging her reaction.

"I—I don't believe you." Her faint lips quavered.

She shook her head back and forth. She was visibly upset and a part of him wanted to comfort her, even now. "There must be a mistake of some kind," she uttered, barely audible. "One of those men is my uncle."

"Parker." The perjurer's name tasted bitter in his mouth.

She nodded, her blonde hair bobbing against her colorless cheeks. "How do you know his name?"

"He testified against me," Spence spat out, his tone grim. I'll never forget his name, or his face, or the sound of his lying voice."

"Don't let one mistake lead to another." She quoted some philosopher, but in a mindless monotone. The usual pleasure at finding the proper adage for the given situation didn't gleam in her eyes. She leaned her shoulder against the doorjamb as if for support.

Spence wanted to go to her, touch her, soothe her, but he stopped himself, remaining cautious while her motives were still in question.

He hardened his demeanor. His voice became rough and tight in his throat. "I saw Parker in court everyday, but I swear I never saw him that night." A loud tap, tap broke the silence in the still room as he drummed the callused pad of his finger against the pleased grin of the other man in the photo. "This was the man who drove Parker's car and knocked Mark and me down. He killed Mark."

"I don't know who he is." She lifted her hands in a sign of appeal. "But I can tell you my uncle's a fine, upstanding person. Ask my mother."

She reached for the phone. Her hand shook. Spence felt the tremble of her slender fingers when he stopped her from picking up the receiver.

"I don't want to talk to your mother," he said, slow and emphatic.

As if her mother wouldn't lie for her brother. As

if the niece wouldn't for her uncle. If she was his niece. Spence's chest heaved with hurt at being used by Mercy for Parker's benefit.

He continued holding her hand as she gripped the phone. Her skin felt satiny soft beneath his work-hardened palm. He exhaled a long breath in an effort to keep his mind on his goal of getting Parker and away from Mercy's treachery or her attributes. She smelled sweet like orange blossoms, even in the stale quarters of the closed-up office. He fought off the temptation to take her, here on the floor or the desk.

"Wh—why not?" she stammered. "My mother knows her brother better than anyone."

"Does she know the other man in the photo? Will she tell me who he is and where the two of them are hiding?" Spence felt himself losing his cool. His grip tightened. The delicate bones in her fingers stacked against each other.

Letting go, he backed away before he squeezed too tight and had more regrets where Mercy was concerned.

"My uncle's not hiding." She dropped her hand to her side and flexed her fingers. "He's visiting a sick friend."

"Where does the sicko live?" Spence persisted, giving her every opportunity to redeem herself and put an end to his doubts. He wanted to believe she was a bystander in Parker's disappearance instead of his decoy. He wanted Mercy in his life, in his bed. Not just in his head.

"I don't know." She shrugged her creamy shoulders, bare in the pretty pink sundress she'd worn to lure him away from his prey and to who knows where. His gut knotted. And another pain twisted, higher in his chest around his heart. "I don't know my uncle well enough to know his friend's name or his address."

"How convenient." The sight of Mercy weakened him, even as it angered him. He glanced away toward the window where dark emptiness reflected his despair back at him.

Her voice was gentle as a bedtime whisper when she said, "But I do know he wouldn't deliberately hurt you or anyone."

He turned toward her, despite himself. Her blue eyes shone with sincerity and innocence. He didn't dare believe in either. Not without proof.

"Right," he bit out. "That's why I spent eighteen months in jail."

"If you truly believe he was responsible," her wan lips trembled again, "how do I know you haven't used me to get to my uncle?" She searched his face. "Are you planning to harm him?"

"Beat the truth out of him if I have to," Spence growled, hoping for the chance to do just that.

Mercy shivered. Covering her arms with her hands, she rubbed her flesh. "I don't know you at all. Do I?" She shrank away from the doorway, standing partway into the living room.

"Better than you should. I should've never let you get as close as I did." Swallowing hard, he kept his disappointment from surfacing.

"*Let me?*" Her laugh was tinged with irony. "You were pretty persistent as I recall." She stepped further away, and he stifled the urge to drag her back into the den and somehow force her to surrender her uncle to him. And then herself.

He eyed her stance. She was either a good actress or sincere. If he only knew which.

But he intended to be honest with her.

"Okay, we both enjoyed the sex. But I let you in. I shared my pain. You used me. How much is he paying you to report what I say and do back to him?" His hurt poured out. He threw the framed picture onto the desk. With an unexpected crunch, the glass cracked into several pieces.

"Don't you dare accuse me of selling myself." She marched back into the office with all the fury of a Texas hurricane and shook her finger in his face from across the desk. Her body was rigid, but her color had returned. "If my uncle lends me the money to start fresh it will be because he loves me not because I sold him any of your so-called secrets."

"Admit my doubts are well-founded. You search me out, have sex with me, and afterward turn out to be the niece of the man who set me up. If you even are his niece," he added, raising his eyebrow.

"If?" she sputtered. "Who in the heck do you think I am?" She leaned across the desk on braced arms, her pretty nose almost touching his. Her eyes were bright like blue flames. "I damn well know who you are. You're an ass." She pounded her small fist on the desk, the blotter muffling her thumps.

"I'll tell you who I think you are. I think you're his trick."

Silence stretched between them, taut like a rubber band about to snap.

"Get out." She pointed to the door, moving aside so as not to come into contact with any part of him when he rounded the desk.

"Gladly, lady." He thought the day Mark died had been the worst day of his life, and then he thought going to jail had been, but Mercy's betrayal rated right up there on the cusp.

"Don't act as if you're the injured party here." She tapped her chest. "I am."

Spence didn't move. He stood there, defiant. He couldn't go until he got what he came after. Parker, or her admission that she was guilty as sin.

"If you're the reason I haven't seen my uncle," she went on as apparent new thoughts formed. "And if he had to leave town and flee his home because of you, I should call the police." Her hand hovered over the phone, awaiting his reply.

"Yes, do that." He didn't stop her this time when she picked up the receiver. "Let the police catch the suckers for me. I have proof they conspired. Or at least knew each other."

When he snatched up the picture frame, pieces of shattered glass fell away, littering the leather desk pad. He nicked the side of his hand, a droplet of blood forming as he tore the photo from its frame and stashed it in the pocket of his jeans.

"Is your hand okay?" she asked, concerned even now.

Faked or honest, he couldn't help but wonder.

He made heated eye contact with her, daring her to come and take the picture back. He cocked his hip to make the sexual challenge more obvious.

She moistened her dry lips with the tip of her enticing, pink tongue, and with a clatter dropped the receiver back into its cradle.

"I'd better let my mother do the calling," she said. "I don't know my uncle well enough to answer many questions. What would I say?"

"That you're in it up to your tasty earlobes," he accused, swiping his bloody hand clean on the side of his jeans.

"How can you say such a thing when we've been so intimate?" Her voice steeled, her eyes narrowed. "You're an—"

"Ass," he finished for her. "That's what you called me a minute ago." He was surprised how much her accusations hurt him. He'd played her fair. Why should he care what the little liar thought?

"Just go home." She crossed her arms as if there wasn't anything else to be said.

He had plenty to say. A part of him wanted to stay and work it out, somehow. Argue it through until they came to terms and made up in a session of unbridled lovemaking. But her stance told him otherwise. He gave up. Sidling out from behind the desk, he sauntered toward the door but then stopped. He couldn't leave without one last try.

He turned and grabbed her in his arms and kissed her. Her lips gave beneath his, opening on a warm, breathy sigh. She responded with as much passion as he gave. Her honeyed mouth made him ache for want of her.

He'd promised himself not to fuck her out of revenge, but he was hard-pressed to stop from making love to her. Even now, when it was so obviously one-sided.

Leaning Mercy back, he swiped the surface of the desk behind them clean. The desk mat flew, along with pens, papers, and shards of glass from the frame. He lifted her bottom onto the wooden top.

"Spence," she murmured.

He kissed her hard, reveling in the feel of her before he released her mouth to nuzzle her neck, scrape his teeth along her skin, and taste her flesh. The scent, sound, taste, and feel of her enveloped him, surrounded him. He allowed himself to become completely lost in her sensuality for another second before he forced himself to gain control over his senses.

He hugged her to him as silence took over like regrets. With a groan of surrender, he pushed away.

Oh, yeah. He got what he came after. His last taste of Mercy. He'd paid a high price. He'd let her too close to his heart.

Her eyes widened, searching his. "Aren't you going to stab me in the back now?"

The movie scene flashed between them. Betrayal by a lover. Was she admitting her guilt? Or blaming him? Her accusing eyes answered the unasked question.

He held his hands up to show his innocence as he backed from the room. "I'm not the backstabber."

She'd plunged the knife. Now how the fuck did he pull it out without bleeding to death?

She was right. There wasn't anymore to be said. Without another word, he left her alone in the den.

He headed for the door and whatever Mercy and her Uncle Parker had waiting for him.

Chapter Twenty-six

Once Mercy heard the front door slam, she knew Spence was gone for good. She felt hollow on the inside. Did he actually believe she'd used their sexual intimacies to spy on him for her uncle?

He could've just as easily been using her to gain inside knowledge about her relative.

Why had she thought the passionate kiss they shared would change his mind, remind him of their closeness. She should've shaken off the unrealistic idea sooner. She knew him better than that. Had seen his resolve in his piercing eyes. He wouldn't put anyone ahead of his goal to uncover Mark's real killer.

She straightened her shoulders and shook out the hem of her dress. The spicy hint of aftershave and man lingered on her skin. Sex between her and Spence had been phenomenal each and every time, but there was more involved between them than sheer animal satisfaction.

When they were engaged physically, nothing and no one else seemed to matter. She'd given away pieces of her heart each time. She wouldn't feel so devastated right now if she weren't so in love with him.

Cindy was right all along.

Forcing herself to move, Mercy skirted the desk to kneel and sift through the mess on the floor. After tossing the pieces of the broken frame into the wastebasket, she scooped up the desk blotter and her uncle's scattered pens and papers. Once she had his desk righted, she reached for the phone.

Her hand went limp on the receiver. She wasn't ready to speak to her mother, or Cindy. Plopping onto the leather chair behind the desk, she looked around the den where she and Spence had argued, indulged in their last flicker of desire, and then parted. She touched her tongue to her lips. The tantalizing taste of his hot mouth still remained.

She loved the heat and feel of him, and not just in bed, but when they walked down the street or danced together. The way he moved, teasing and arousing her. His unexpected humor and candor when he let his guard down.

All their laughter and passion had now turned into pain.

How could she have been so wrong about him?

Closing her eyes, she massaged her forehead while she worried about Spence and her missing uncle and her mother's reaction to the news and what was to become of them all.

With a loud, unexpected *brr-ring*, the phone rang. Spence. A nerve in her forehead jumped when she blinked her eyes open.

Picking up the receiver, she heard, "Mercy." Cindy's voice was hushed. "I'm sorry if I interrupted anything." She paused, waiting for Mercy's reply.

"It's okay," Mercy croaked, then cleared her throat. "Is Jay still there?" She wanted to talk about something pleasant, having wrung more than enough misery from her own situation.

"Jay left early. Another excuse about a meeting. As soon as we shut the computer down, which he promised we weren't supposed to use during off hours, he brushed me off." Silence.

"I'm sorry, Cindy. Maybe he did have to meet someone."

"My intuition tells me no." Cindy sounded needy.

"Things didn't go well on this end either." Mercy

gave the misery-loves-company Doriaism a shot for her friend's sake. Even though she didn't want to think or talk about Spence again tonight, she was willing to listen and console Cindy about Jay.

"Does ice cream cure sexual frustration?" Cindy asked.

"Ice cream cures everything." She hoped foolish hearts were included.

"Are you coming home soon?"

"As soon as I can get a cab."

"I have a half-gallon of gourmet ice cream in the freezer. When you get here, we'll kill it."

****

After a lot of ice cream and little sleep, Mercy dialed her mother once Cindy left for work.

"Don't worry about Parker, he's a big boy and can take care of himself as well as everyone else. Always has," her mother assured her when Mercy related most of the details from the night before. She left out the intimate, steamy ones about her and Spence. "My main worry has been that he wouldn't return to float your loan before you had to leave."

"Then I shouldn't call the police and report him missing?" Mercy wanted to make sure she understood her mother perfectly. She didn't want her uncle's welfare hanging on a misunderstanding.

"He isn't missing. Parker told Cindy he was visiting a sick friend. I think we should take your uncle at his word and not some stranger with a gripe."

"His name is Spence." He wasn't a stranger, not to Mercy. She knew every inch of his magnificent body by taste and touch.

"Maybe you should check at the club if the manager or bartenders have heard from Parker yet."

"I will," Mercy promised, although she was sure Lenny, the bartender, would've notified her if her uncle had called.

212

After their good-byes, she felt better about her mother and her uncle.

Until later when Cindy came home from the office.

"Suppose your ex, the *killer,* did send your uncle packing and he never shows his face in Texas again. It'll be that awful man's fault." Cindy paced, her platform shoes making stomping noises even through the heavy padded carpet of the living room.

"He isn't that awful, and he didn't kill anyone." Mercy felt the need to defend Spence to Cindy, and her uncle to Spence. Her loyalties were so confused. "Besides, Mom assured me—"

"Not only has the man messed with your Uncle Parker's life, but your mother's and yours as well. If your uncle's worried about phone taps, he may *never* call anyone again."

Mercy sank down onto the sofa while Cindy circled her. "He hasn't called Mom since any of this happened," she conceded.

"There goes the loan for your future. No uncle, no call, no money." Cindy stopped on her wedged soles and threw her hands up in hopelessness.

"I didn't think about any of that." Mercy had been too busy soothing her aching heart with frozen chocolate and brooding over her uncle's safety to delve any deeper. Hugging the sofa cushion to her chest like a stuffed security toy, she said, "I'll just have to stay in Lily Pond for a few years longer than I cared to."

"Dating duds," Cindy added.

"More than likely it will turn out to be a celibate few years." Mercy's womb clenched in protest. "But I'll save my money." Along with the memories of the sensational orgasms she'd enjoyed with Spence.

"And continue to live with your mother, so there goes her sewing room." And Cindy as she took off at a parade ground pace.

"Can't you try to think of something good to add?" All Mercy's positive energy after talking to her mother was quickly dissipating.

"I can't think of a thing."

"I can always sell my vacations back for the extra money."

"What?" Cindy shrieked. "If you stop taking vacations, I'll never get to see you."

"Maybe you could visit me."

"In Lily Pond?" Cindy heaved a loud sigh of exasperation to show what she thought of that idea. "You know what I think?"

"What?" She was almost afraid to ask.

"We need more ice cream. Lucky for us, I stopped at the market on the way home."

****

By the time they arrived at the *Starry Night Club*, Cindy's harping during the taxi ride had undone the pleasant brain freeze Mercy had going from the ice cream.

Added to that, through the smoke and the band's fake fog and the dim lighting, Mercy managed to make out Spence's tall, shadowy figure, leaning against the wall of the outdoor patio near the dance floor.

But he wasn't hers to care about. Would never be again.

She and Cindy elbowed their way to the crowded bar. "Jay's not here," Cindy said, scanning the room. "He didn't talk to me at work today either. He's definitely avoiding me."

"Not necessarily. There doesn't seem to be anyone here from your office yet." As Mercy surveyed the place, her eyes met Spence's sullen ones. She would've glanced away, but he didn't, and she'd be damned to be the first one to shake her tail and run.

His expression remained grim, but his eyes were

smoky and alluring. They pulled her in the same way they had the first time, nearly two weeks ago. But now the pull felt different, more intense. It tugged at her pounding heart as well as her pussy.

"Don't look at him. He's trouble."

"I was watching for Jay." She turned her head and scanned the dance floor. "There he is with Rita."

"No." Cindy snapped her head around so fast her barstool swiveled with the momentum. After a few seconds she whirled in reverse. "What do you suppose that's all about?"

"Maybe he's passing the time while waiting for you," Mercy offered her friend hope.

"If he had the hots for me, he wouldn't be dancing with her. We thought Killer had the hots for you, and look how that wound up. He was spying on Parker."

"Speaking of which..." Mercy caught sight of Lenny from the corner of her eye and signaled to him.

While he popped the caps on icy longnecks for two men further down the bar, Cindy drooled. "That man is the best eye candy in all of San Antonio. Too bad he's only a bartender. They all play around."

"Meaning bartenders aren't as reliable as Jay?" Mercy raised her eyebrows. Her words were harsh, but Cindy needed to be more open-minded.

She'd never approved of Spence, and aside from Mercy's conflict of interest with him over her uncle, he was the most steadfast man she'd ever dated. Or slept with.

He might not always be tactful or sociable, but he was loyal to a fault. He was loyal to Mark and his parents and himself, despite jail. Too bad his loyalty included getting back at her uncle.

Cindy didn't reply but grinned instead as Lenny moseyed over, leaned on the bar, and hit her with a hundred-watt smile. "Haven't seen you ladies in a while. What can I get you?"

"Have you missed me, er, us?" Cindy tapped her foot to a beat far faster than the one the band was playing.

"You're my favorite patrons." Lenny leaned in closer. He smelled like an upscale department store cosmetic counter.

"I'll have sex on the beach," Cindy said, staring longingly into Lenny's eyes.

Mercy cleared her throat. "I was wondering if anyone has heard from my uncle lately."

Lenny shook his handsome face, shaved to a perfect shadow. "Not since he stopped in that last time."

"Thanks." Mercy would phone her mother in the morning and pass along the disappointing news. "Just give me a glass of water with lime."

As he sauntered away, Cindy drooled, "What a butt."

"You seem awfully interested for a woman who claims he isn't her type," Mercy teased.

"Hold that thought." Cindy held up her finger. "The band finished their number. I'm signaling Jay and Rita over. We're going to fish around for what's going on or not going on between my coworkers." Before Mercy could inquire about what method of fishing they were to use, Cindy spun on her stool, and yelled, "Over here."

By the time Jay and Rita threaded their way over to the bar, the band struck up another tune. Cindy shouted, loudly, over the music, "I thought you had a meeting."

Mercy shook her head. Nothing subtle about her friend. Lenny served their drinks, and Mercy tipped him while listening to Jay's response.

He twisted his finger in a circle. "Care to dance?"

And away strolled Cindy, hand-in-hand with

Jay, leaving Mercy with Rita and the opportunity to dig into Jay's on-again, off-again interest in Cindy.

"They seem to get along well." Mercy smiled toward the couple, who were already swaying to the slow, romantic song before they'd reached the dance floor.

"Jay gets along with everyone," Rita clipped.

Mercy sipped her water and tried again, using Cindy's terminology this time. "He seems to have the *hots* for my friend."

Rita's laugh sounded faked. "Yes, he does seem to kick the charm up a notch for her, but—"

Just then, a tall figure shadowed over Mercy. She smelled his particular scent of outdoors and man before she heard his rumbling voice.

"Dance?" he rasped, low and commanding.

"Why?" Mercy looked up and met his all-consuming eyes.

"I'll dance with you, cowboy," Rita offered, grasping his bicep and snapping her shoulders back to show off her bust.

"No thanks." Spence flicked her polished nails from his arm.

"Dance," he repeated, standing firm at Mercy's side.

Lenny came over, wiped down the bar in front of Mercy, where it didn't need polishing, and gave her a questioning eye. Did she need the bouncer?

She shook her head no, not wanting to make Spence's life any more difficult than it already was. She'd be gone in a few days, and he'd be left with Lenny and the bouncers to deal with until Parker contacted his family and learned of the situation. Then she was sure her uncle would set right the terrible misconception Spence lived with.

Standing up, Mercy brushed against Spence's familiar hard body. Her pulse thrummed and her heartbeat quickened. She hid her yearnings behind a forced smile. Grabbing his hand, she moved with him toward the dance floor. She'd let him have his say so they could both move on.

As soon as he took her in his bold embrace, she melted into the intimate feel of him. Cradling her crotch up against his groin, she savored the hot rush of adrenaline only Spence could elicit from her body.

Along with the heated emotions only he could provoke. With a sigh, she asked again, "Why? I thought we said it all last night."

"I'm not asking you for anything." His breath was warm and close to her ear, sending waves of desire crashing through her.

"We can't just pick up where we left off as if nothing earth-shaking has come between us." Like her falling in love with him. She studied his handsome face. "You said some awful things about me and my family."

"I wish it could've been different between us." He held her tighter, closer. Her face nestled near his throat, and she struggled not to indulge in his nearness.

"If that's an apology," she mumbled, "it's a pretty weak one." She wished he'd take back his ridiculous assumptions about her and her uncle so she could forgive him and they could work out a solution.

Instead, he said, "Your uncle wronged both me and Mark and has to come clean about it. I want you to tell him that."

She stopped moving her feet and stood still within the circle of his arms. They were so near she felt him breathe, yet they were worlds apart. "I told you, I don't know where my uncle is. I can't tell him anything."

"That was yesterday. I figured you'd contacted him by now."

With a jerk of her hand, she slapped him.

Chapter Twenty-seven

Spence didn't flinch but held Mercy tight so she wouldn't storm off the dance floor. Her slap stung, but he'd been hit a lot harder.

"I don't know where my uncle is. Do I have to shout it out?" Her voice rose, but the drumming beat of the music drowned her out to everyone but him.

"No." He searched the depth of her hot blue eyes for honesty. "Would you tell me if you knew?"

"What do you want from me?" Her wispy breath sounded resigned. As her body sighed, he felt her lush breasts tease his chest.

He knew what he wanted from her. He wanted her to go to hell and back for him. He needed it. He couldn't rely on anyone since his parents' and Mark's deaths. The girlfriend who'd professed to love him didn't last through the trial. He felt alone and floundering.

"The truth," he murmured, burying his face into the crook of her neck, seeking closer physical contact with her before she kicked him to the curb.

When she hesitated, he knew he wasn't going to like her answer. Why couldn't she love him, and love him enough to help him.

He held her close and let her softness and warmth flood through him before he let go of her slim waist and slight shoulders. He stepped away from the mesmerizing fragrance of her body.

"No, I wouldn't tell you where my uncle was even if I knew," she said as she slipped from his arms. "I'm afraid you'd hurt him. But I'll give him your warning if I ever get the chance."

Spence's heartbeat dulled. He should've expected as much. What he didn't foresee was that it would hurt this bad.

"And I'm sure you will." He clenched his jaw. Cold disappointment flooded through him. Flattening his hand against her spine, he nudged her toward the exit. "Go home. To Pennsylvania."

With a sassy pivot of her hips, she turned and walked away in the other direction. The sexy sway of her behind made him hard, even now when he knew her lust had been faked.

Her husky moans in the sack when she was ready to come. Her tart remarks that made him laugh. The tenderness of her feathery touch on his body. It was all a sham.

Mercy returned to the bar that was crowded with her friends and Parker's employees. The bartenders and bouncers hired to watch the owner's back. Her back. The corrupt Jay cozying up to Cindy. The club's flunkies catering to Mercy. Why hadn't he put them all together sooner? Suddenly, it made sense.

They were all Parker's allies.

Spence strode out onto the patio and sucked in a whiff of the damp, breezy river air as he took up his post against the wall, watching, waiting. Time dragged on, endless. He only moved from the spot when he spied Mercy and her noisy, laughing friend leave the building.

He flexed his muscles, stiff from lack of movement. The shout of last call reached him. For the most part the place had emptied out, except for a table of four and Jay and his companion, the brassy lady who'd tried to horn in on Spence's dance with Mercy. He approached them. What the hell. Worming his way into the enemy camp was worth the price of a few shots.

"Buy you a drink?" Spence straddled the

barstool next to Jay. "Owe you one for giving me a thumbs-up that night with Mercy."

"Thanks aren't necessary." Jay closed one eye, giving him a macho wink.

"Guess not, seeing as you took off with Cindy." Spence chuckled, acted impressed, trying to sucker the guy in with some good-ole-boy camaraderie.

"Jay's involvement with that *kook* is strictly business," the woman butted in, her jealousy obvious in her bold tone, her enhanced breasts heaving.

"Didn't catch your name," Spence said, wondering if he could play her green-eyed envy to his advantage.

"Rita." She smiled wide, showing her gums. "I'm Jay's *very close* friend." She shifted on her stool, leaning her over-blown breasts against Jay's arm to stress her point.

He appeared indifferent to her.

"Bad rap you took," Jay said, and she went back to sipping her fancy martini. When Spence didn't reply right away, he added, "People talk."

"Yeah, they do. I hear you've got something going." Spence lowered his voice to a conspiratorial tone, pretending he wanted in on a piece of the action.

"I guarantee you it isn't Cindy," Rita said, snidely, intruding on the conversation she was still obviously following.

Jay elbowed her. "He didn't mean that kind of action." She snooted her nose in the air and pulled out her day planner in a blatant gesture of ignoring the men. Turning back to Spence, Jay said, "I do all right. Ten K here and there adds up. I pull down an extra hundred grand a year."

Spence whistled. "I didn't know selling corporate secrets was so lucrative." If Jay replied, Spence figured he had a good chance at winning the guy over.

Jay laughed, then downed the last of his whiskey-gold drink. "Who knew?"

"Guess it depends on how many ways you have to split the take." If Jay bit again, Spence was going after the names of his partners next.

With any luck, Parker would be one of them. When Parker caught word of Spence's interest, he'd figure Spence could be bought off, and that might bring the weasel out of hiding.

"I work alone." Jay leaned in to hiss. "Although the *bitch* wants a piece of my action. That's why she's always hanging around."

Bingo. Cindy was corrupt, and who knew what Parker was into beside perjury. Which made the odds against Mercy being honest nil.

Triumph didn't wash over Spence at the discovery. Instead, a gloom settled over him, making his chest feel as heavy as a sack of feed grain.

"I thought you worked for Parker." When Jay jerked his head, puzzled his brows, Spence shrugged. "Everyone else here seems to."

"Not me." Jay puffed up his narrow chest, showing off his designer shirt along with his independence. "I never met the man. From what I hear, I'm not about to any time soon."

Spence grabbed at the sliver of information and hoped for more. "Why's that?"

"Heard his sick friend is on his last leg but lingering." Jay pushed his empty glass to the edge of the bar and tossed some bills next to it. "That was last call. See you around."

"You bet," Spence said.

If Jay didn't know Parker, personally, he sure as hell knew of him. And he didn't seem to mind sharing whatever he heard. Every bit of information helped. Seemed Google was right in his assumption that Parker's friend was dying.

****

Spence didn't bother haunting the club the next night. He'd taken a final crack at Mercy, and she'd let him down. Besides, from what Jay had said it wasn't likely Parker was going to show up any time soon.

Mercy would be leaving the state soon to fly back home. Spence decided to wait her out. Seeing her was too painful. She made him ache, physically. His gut clenched, along with his balls at the sight of her. She made him long for would-have-beens when there was only room in his life for right now.

He tried to sleep but tossed most of the night, remembering her luscious body. Velvety and touchable, not distant, with Parker between them, like now.

Giving up, he brewed a pot of coffee around four a.m. and sat drinking, waiting for the sun to come up, waiting for Parker to show up, waiting for closure so he could begin his life anew.

He was getting fed up with waiting.

He heard the vehicle drive up and then the knock. Flicking the porch light on, he glanced through the filmy sidelight window before cracking the front door open.

"What do you want?" he asked none too sociably.

"To help you."

Spence jammed his hands into his pockets, glanced down at his bare feet, before sizing up Lenny, the muscle-toned bartender, with suspicion. "How?"

"I know someone who knows where Parker docks his boat."

Spence figured he'd hear the man out. Hell, he had nothing to lose but time.

"Come on in." He held the door open, nodding his head toward the kitchen, signaling Lenny to go on back. "Coffee's on." He clicked the lock on the door, in case Lenny wasn't alone, before he followed

223

the man down the dim hallway toward the fluorescent-lighted kitchen.

Lenny took a vinyl-seated chair at the chipped Formica table while Spence poured mugs of coffee. After handing him one, Spence held out the milk carton.

He shook his head. "Black's fine."

Spence remained standing, leaning against the nicked porcelain sink, his coffee cup cooling beside him. "What's on your mind?"

"You're down on your luck, and I'm feeling generous." He blew on the hot coffee, the aromatic steam waning into a thin vapor.

"Parker wouldn't be backing your generosity, would he?" Spence asked outright. He was too exhausted for mind games and no amount of coffee was going to perk him up.

"Nope. He hightailed when you showed up so I figure he's guilty of something. His signature on my paycheck doesn't buy my loyalty. I can bartend anywhere along the river."

Spence scratched at his stubble, two days worth. Mourning over a woman sure took its toll on a man's appearance.

Lenny, on the other hand, looked well groomed.

"Ever been in love, Lenny?"

"Don't believe in the percentages." He sipped from his mug.

Spence nodded. "There aren't any."

Lenny chuckled. "Sounds as if love's made you a cynic."

He didn't answer. Discussing his love life, or lack of one, with Lenny wasn't part of his agenda. Finding out if Lenny was setting him up for Parker was though.

"The whole situation with Parker's a bummer." Lenny shook his head. "Mercy's a nice lady. So's her friend, Cindy. Hate to see everyone fucked over by some old fart and his dying friend."

"You sound like a smart man, and I'm a desperate one. So I'm inclined to take your charity. Where's the boat?"

"One of our bouncers noticed the address on an envelope when the bookkeeper sent him to the post office. Hugo was instructed to make sure the bill for the docking fee got mailed *pronto,* before it became past due."

"Your bookkeeper is a talkative man. Isn't there some kind of accountant/client privilege he should honor?"

"Guess not. Anyway, Hugo mentioned the incident to me. Everybody spills their guts to their bartender."

"And loose lips sink ships. That's a Doriaism. Ever heard of her?" he asked. "She's a philosopher."

Lenny tugged at his ear, thinking. "Can't say that I have. She some kind of female Confucius?"

"Exactly." Spence wished Mercy was here to share the conversation. She loved a good platitude. She'd grin, her lips pink and lively and kissable. He swallowed a groan, set his mind back on Lenny's deal. "The boat you're talking about is the *Mermaid,* right?"

"Yes." Lenny nodded. "That's her name. Hugo has a friend works in the marina. He's going to call him, see what he knows."

"How do I repay you for your kindness?" Spence asked, with a touch of sarcasm. He still wasn't sure how trustworthy Lenny was.

"Tip big. Hugo needs the money. Has a sick kid." Lenny stood up to go and dropped his cup in the sink. "Stop in at the club around ten-thirty tonight. That's when he takes his break. I'll hook you up."

"I'll be there."

Lenny stretched and yawned. "I need my zzz's." He started down the hall to leave.

Spence didn't stop him. The only way to find out if he was walking into a trap was to meet Lenny and Hugo tonight. It sure as hell beat sitting around waiting.

"Lock up when you leave," Spence called after him.

"Got you covered, man."

Spence dumped his coffee down the drain. His stomach revolted at the idea of drinking any more of the strong, black brew. Or maybe his gut was sending him a reflexive warning.

On a second thought, he strode toward the hallway, figuring it wouldn't hurt to deadbolt the door after Lenny.

Chapter Twenty-eight

After a spritz of a spicy cologne, which happened to be one of Spence's favorites, Mercy dressed to go out for the evening. But she had no intention of spicing up her life with him again.

Go home, he'd told her two nights ago, and it still stung.

She'd show him. She couldn't leave Texas fast enough, even if sex with him had been the greatest event in her life to date. Even if his savory attention to every inch of her naked flesh made her feel special, glorious, desirable.

With a purring moan, she admitted to herself how much she missed him.

She'd missed his smoldering presence at the club last night, too, which at least assured her that he was nearby and okay. Could his absence mean he finally believed in her and had given up hunting down her uncle?

Her heartbeat surged. Abandoning his search for her sake meant he had feelings for her, deep ones. A thrill throbbed her pulse. She wanted to shout out the news, but Cindy hadn't arrived home from the office yet.

Needing to talk, she settled for dialing Pennsylvania to inquire about her uncle, expecting her mom's happy voice to say she'd finally heard from him and he was fine.

By the time she finished her conversation, a dullness replaced her joy.

"No," her mother had said, "Parker hasn't gotten in touch with me yet."

Looked like love wasn't Spence's motive for not showing up at the club. After hanging up, she crossed her fingers that he hadn't caught up to her uncle.

Her trouble-free spirit had crashed, fast. Where was Cindy?

She glanced at her watch. It was almost ten o'clock. Cindy had left word on the answering machine that she was working late, but this went beyond her usual sense of duty. Mercy pushed the speed dial on her cell, but Cindy didn't answer. She left a voice message and called a cab. The quiet in the condo was driving her wild. She needed to do something, go somewhere, talk to someone, and soon.

When she arrived at the *Starry Night* there was no Spence, no uncle, no Cindy, no Jay. No one she knew at all, only Lenny.

"Where's your pretty friend tonight?" the good-looking bartender asked, serving her a sparkling water with lime, and busying himself wiping down the bar elsewhere once she replied, "I don't know."

Only the lingering smell of Lenny's expensive aftershave kept her company while she sat with nothing to do but stress out.

She kept watch in the smoke-stained mirror behind the bar, wondering what was keeping Cindy. After many glances, she spied the tall, hunky, familiar physique of Spence as his shadow darkened the entrance. Her breath caught. Dressed in black, her fantasy man incarnate looked sexy and hot. Her heart thumped, hungering for his love, while her pussy quivered, aching to be satisfied.

A glimmer of emotion sparked in his eyes when he first caught sight of her. But he averted his head and sauntered toward the other end of the bar.

What had she seen in his dark eyes? Anger. Doubt. Did he still insist she'd betrayed him?

At a loss to work things out with him, she tapped her nails against her water glass and went back to worrying. Mercy didn't know where her uncle was, and obviously neither did Spence or he wouldn't be here. If she did know, she wouldn't tell him. Not in his state of mind. Her uncle's safety and her own peace of mind were both at stake.

Down the bar from her, Spence leaned his magnificent body against the railing. Heck, even his elbow was sexy. One look at his large hands and long fingers stirred her sensual longings. She chewed on the ice chips in her glass to cool her ardor.

Spence said something to Lenny and shook his hand. She hadn't known the two men were friendly aside from a bartender/patron association, which didn't require handshaking.

Lenny motioned Spence into the backroom and closed the door behind him. The bartender went about his duties, avoiding Mercy and her curious looks. From the corner of her eye, she continued to scrutinize the backroom door. She couldn't fathom what was going on in there.

She shifted on her seat and strained her ear toward the room. No ruckus that she could hear. She relaxed, confident that Spence's brain and brawn would protect him if a need arose.

About fifteen minutes later, he emerged with Hugo, the bouncer. Neither looked worse for the wear. No bruises, no apparent punches thrown.

She scanned the room, wishing Cindy would hurry up and get here. Cindy always had an insight, however offbeat, into unusual situations.

Lenny handed Spence an icy longneck and asked, "Everything okay?"

Spence nodded and straddled a vacant stool within easier hearing distance. "Corpus Christi. At one a.m."

"That's a two-hour drive." Lenny gave him a

thumbs up. "You have just enough time."

"Want to go for a ride?"

A ride? They were much better acquainted than she suspected.

"My shift doesn't end until closing." Lenny busied himself collecting empty glasses from the bar.

"I thought as much." Spence tipped back his beer bottle and drank a thirsty mouthful.

She moistened her lips. She knew all too well the taste of his lusty mouth, warm, moist, and giving. As he tossed his head back further and exposed his throat, she craved to nip his flesh and make him groan with want for her.

Just to teach him a lesson, she assured herself.

"Don't want to drink and drive." Spence handed Lenny the almost-full bottle when the bartender looked up. "I have to talk to someone on my way out."

Mercy crossed her legs and adjusted the neckline of her low-cut blouse. She was ready to hear him out this one last time.

As Spence vacated his seat, Lenny said, "Take care."

"If I don't see you again—" Spence never finished his sentence, just strode away, out toward the patio.

She uncrossed her legs and slumped her shoulders, wondering who he'd gone to talk to. But before she could puzzle over the odd goings-on she was smacked on the back.

"Hey, there." Cindy had arrived at last, with Jay, Rita, and Bob, who she hadn't seen since he'd taken her sightseeing.

"A late meeting?" Mercy asked as Cindy slipped alongside of her, her coworkers in tow.

"A big meeting," Cindy said. "Heads are going to roll tomorrow. Someone accessed the computer file for next year's brand new bath line. Tubs, sinks, toilets. The works."

"Probably some hacker." Jay waved to Lenny and set drinks up for all of them.

"We're months ahead of schedule," Bob said once Lenny took their orders. "How would a hacker know our newest line of bath fixtures was available already?"

"I wonder," Rita purred, squeezing next to Jay, sliver-eyed and grinning.

Cindy crossed her eyes and made a face when Rita scrunched in closer to Jay. Mercy choked back a groan at the woman's obvious tactics.

"The company's going to enter and search everyone's computer system and files," Cindy explained to Mercy. "That will exonerate all of us honest employees."

"Look." Jay pointed across the room. "A table's available."

Everyone bustled off, except Cindy. "I'll see you later," she called to her coworkers then turned to Mercy. "How are you doing tonight?"

"Never mind me. Are you okay? The crisis at the office sounds serious."

"Not to worry." Cindy waved her hand. "I haven't used my computer for any unauthorized reasons."

Mercy stilled her hand. "What about the file you and Jay worked with?"

"I'm authorized to access that file."

"Good." Mercy smiled, relieved, leaning in nearer to Cindy. "You missed some strange happenings in here tonight. Have you ever noticed that Lenny and Spence are friends?"

"No. Can't say that I have."

"Something went on between Spence, Lenny, and Hugo, the bouncer. Spence's driving to Corpus Christi for one a.m. Lenny couldn't go with him."

"Spence with your uncle's employees? Do you

think it concerns your Uncle Parker's whereabouts? Should we tail him to Corpus Christi?" Cindy clunked one of her red platforms onto the bar's brass foot rail.

Mercy shrugged. "A cab to Corpus Christi would probably cost a fortune, and suppose Spence loses us."

"Jay wouldn't trust us with his Jag, but I could ask Bob to lend us his car." They swiveled around on their barstools to check the table where Cindy's coworkers sat. Bob was still there.

That's when Mercy spied Spence in the shadows of the outdoor patio. He was head-to-head with a pudgy guy wearing baggy pants and thick glasses.

Spence glanced her way but kept nodding to whatever the guy was saying. Then in a flash, the man scurried off by way of the outside stairs leading to the river. Spence rambled toward Mercy.

Her throat went dry. Cindy nudged her in the side. "Here comes trouble."

Yes. His long, jean-encased legs were coming right at her. Her gaze strayed to his fly. A quiver pulsed between her thighs. Despite their differences—his ambition to ruin her uncle's life and upset her mother's, not to mention a possibly long delay to her own plans for the future—she couldn't stop her body from clenching with wet want for Spence. To have him deep inside her, throbbing, driving them to orgasm. Desire welled up, hot and fast. Her heart pounded.

But he passed her by for Lenny, again. After the two exchanged words, the bartender winked, and Spence exited by way of the front door. Where in the heck was he off to now? Had there been a change in plans about Corpus Christi? He was a torment, mentally as well as physically.

"You look worried," Cindy said.

"I still want him, Cindy. After the threats to my

uncle and the false claims he made about me." She stared into her friend's stunned, rounded eyes. "And not just my body. My heart wants him, too. With sputtering beats, every time I see him."

"Sheesh," Cindy said. "Talk about lovesick." She pushed her glass of scotch and water into Mercy's free hand. "Try to hold yourself together till Saturday's flight. Okay?"

Mercy closed her eyes and swallowed a healthy swig of the strong alcohol. She smelled Lenny's expensive cologne before she saw him. Flicking her eyes open, she said, "I've been trying to talk to you all night."

He leaned across the bar, shifting his eyes between both her and Cindy. "Meet Spence outside. Take the metal steps down to the Riverwalk. It's important."

"I don't know." Cindy drawled. When Lenny rested his manicured fingers on top of hers, Cindy's mouth stopped whining and started drooling.

"It's okay. Trust me. It concerns your company's computer glitch." He met Cindy's gaping gaze. "Don't even breathe in your coworkers' direction. Just go out through the front door and circle around. Now."

But Cindy didn't move. She let Lenny hold her hand and coax her a few more times, basking in the glow of his handsome, masculine attentions.

Until he finally caught on and released her hand. Even then, she still sat there, watching his tight ass walk away, whistling under her breath.

"I told you it was strange around here tonight," Mercy said.

"Let's see what this is all about. I might end up with a monetary reward from the company if I come away with a valid tip on the computer crime." Hopping down from her stool, she scurried toward the front exit as deftly as a woman in four-inch platforms could, while still avoiding detection by her coworkers on the other side of the room. Mercy trailed after her, watching the threesome from the corner of her eye.

Near the exit, Cindy pointed toward the restroom. "I have to pee." Slipping through the restroom door, she disappeared while Mercy ducked behind a four-foot signboard of the night's food and drink specials.

When Cindy finally emerged, she hissed, "What took so long?"

"I had to comb my hair and freshen up my makeup, and then my cell rang. Jay wanted to know where I was, so I told him you were feeling ill and I was taking you home."

She grabbed Cindy's arm. "If we don't get out there soon, Spence might leave and we'll never find out what's going on."

Outside, they turned the corner of the building toward the unlit metal steps spiraling down to a section of the Riverwalk that had pretty much shut down for the night. Mercy blinked into the blackness.

"Let's wait for our eyes to adjust," Cindy said, skidding to a stop.

"But only for a moment. We've wasted a lot of time already. It has to be after eleven. Spence may have given up on us."

"Lenny sounded like he was concerned about me," Cindy said into the darkness. "And about my problem at the office. A viable lead could get me a bonus and Lenny a big tip, which I'll deliver in person."

Mercy wondered where Spence fit into the scenario. "I can see a little now. How about you?"

Cindy was already picking her way down the spiraling steps.

Mercy gripped the metal railing and groped her way along behind Cindy, slow and single file.

"Down here." Mercy recognized Spence's low, rumbling voice. Her stomach flinched, sending wish-you-were-here contractions to her pussy and her heart.

Spence and the man she'd seen him with earlier were waiting beneath the shadowy, large branches of a sprawling tree alongside a deserted stretch of the river where the darkness was thickest. Mercy followed Cindy's wobbly footsteps to the bottom of the stairs.

Suddenly, a man wearing a ski mask dashed out of the murky night, jostled Mercy, and grabbed her handbag, small as it was. The key to her uncle's house and her ID to get on the plane for Pennsylvania were inside. Mercy gripped the leather straps with both hands and held on tight.

The masked man yanked and ran. With a jolt strong enough to jar her shoulders, he dragged Mercy along with him toward the river but in the opposite direction of Spence, his friend, and Cindy. The muscles in her arms strained and pain shot from her elbows to her wrists. The straps cut into the palms of her hands, and two of her fingers went numb.

"Help," she screeched as she tried pulling backward to stagger the purse snatcher's momentum.

He slowed, momentarily, but picked up speed again. A lamppost glowed up ahead of them, and she whipped her body to the opposite side of the pole than the thief took. The straps tangled and halted them. In the gleam of the lamplight, a knife glinted.

Mercy tasted fear in her mouth, and it tasted rusty like blood. When she felt warm liquid on her lip, she realized she'd bitten her tongue in the struggle.

"Help," she managed to shout, while squirming around the post, ducking and weaving until her feet tripped beneath her and one knee grazed the stony walkway. Dirt and stones scraped her skin, and she grappled back up onto her feet.

The man began sawing at the strip of leather with the knife, too close to Mercy's hand. He grunted with each hack, and his labored breath smelled sour. Panicked, she glanced behind her. Wasn't anyone coming to her rescue?

Cindy trotted up the pathway on her tottering platforms, giving new meaning to the old adage 'to hit bottom' when she crumpled and bounced onto her rear end.

Mercy grimaced and felt the leather strap loosen. She wrapped her end around her wrist as she looked back again.

Spence was sprinting up the path, attempting to pass Cindy, who had gotten to her feet and had a tight grip on his shirttail. Twisting his body a few times, he shook her loose, and gestured to his friend to help her as he yelled, "Mercy, let go of the damn purse."

The mugger sawed faster, the knife blade coming nearer with each slash. Mercy rotated her wrist to shield her radial artery. Her skin burned. Beads of perspiration broke out across her forehead.

Another glance back. Spence's powerful legs seemed to be eating up the ground fast, so she concentrated on holding onto her handbag. The brute must've suspected his time was running out fast. He tossed the knife and wrestled her for the purse. With all the strength she could muster, she clung on, bracing her legs against the lamppost.

Spence caught up to them and dove into the man with such force that he knocked him to the ground. By some kind of balancing act, Mercy was able to hang on and stay upright.

Until the purse strap slipped through the fingers of her attacker, and with a whomp, Mercy landed flat on her back.

The fall knocked the breath out of her. For a moment, she lay dazed, trying to kick-start her lungs by gulping in air.

She heard a fist sink into muscle and the scuffle of feet. Her eyelids fluttered open, briefly. Spence held the man by the collar of his shirt with his knuckles aimed at his chin. He stopped mid-punch and looked down at her. Still gasping, she was too exhausted to keep her eyes open.

"Get the hell out of here before I call the cops," Spence threatened.

She flickered her eyes open and began inhaling a shallow breath in an unsteady rhythm just as Spence bent over her. She coughed.

"I was getting ready to give you mouth-to-mouth and work on your chest," he said, cocking his dark, handsome eyebrow.

"Can I have an IOU?"

He chuckled. She coughed again and struggled to sit up. He supported her spine with his broad hand until she was steady enough to stand. In that moment, she felt safe and secure, and lonely, knowing he'd be gone soon.

"Are you all right?" He checked her limbs for broken bones. She stood still and let his capable fingers examine her. As he gently prodded up and down her arms, her skin tingled beneath his expert touch. When he knelt down in front of her, testing her ankles, shins, and working his way upward, her wanton thighs opened with anticipation. But his fingers stopped short at a tender spot above her knee.

"No bruising or swelling. Only a road rash." He got to his feet.

She bit back her disappointment and regrouped her defenses. He was the enemy until her uncle turned up and could fend for himself.

Cindy arrived, limping and leaning heavily on the arm of Spence's friend. "I think I sprained my ankle." She pouted her bottom lip.

Mercy put a pitying arm around Cindy's shoulder. "Are you in a lot of pain?"

"It hurt at first," Cindy said, "but now it seems to have stopped."

Bending on her uninjured knee, she unbuckled Cindy's red platform shoes. "Your ankle's sure to feel better once these are off."

Cindy propped her elbow on the man's shoulder, lifting one foot and then the other while Mercy rid her of her shoes. "Oh," Cindy called down to Mercy, "I forgot to introduce you. This is Google."

Mercy nodded up at him. "Hi." Her fingers twitched with the impulse to toss the heavy-soled shoes into the river, so she quickly handed them off to Cindy.

"If everyone's all right, Google has some inside information on who hacked into the computer network at your office," Spence said. "He'll explain in detail, but I have to shove off."

"How do we know what he says is true," Cindy protested.

"Why do I bother?" Spence shook his head. "Just hear him out. I've got to go. What time is it?"

Mercy strained to read her watch, holding her wrist under the lamplight. Google flipped his cell open. "We've got a half hour until my friend, the network administrator, does the scheduled inspection on the office system." Google shook his head and looked at Spence. "It's eleven-thirty."

"Damn," Spence groaned, briefly closing his eyes and his fist. "Mercy, why didn't you let go of the purse?"

Chapter Twenty-nine

"I'll never make it now," Spence muttered, the realization striking him like a fist.

His hopes of reaching Corpus Christi and getting his hands on Parker before his boat sailed from the marina ended when he'd stuck around to help Mercy.

Nice guys did finish last. He shook his head at the idea of the proverb applying to him. He'd come out of jail dead set against doing things the nice or right way again. He'd sworn to do whatever it took to reach his goal, avenge Mark's death, clear his own name. He'd let it slip through his fingers because of Mercy.

Why didn't she just let go of the damn purse?

What took so long for them to leave the club in the first place?

His eyes burned with a grittiness. The smell along the river, stale from unsold flower and food from the stands closed for the night, choked at his throat.

"Sorry," Google said, the first one to speak. "I know how important getting to Corpus Christi on time was to you."

Spence stared at Mercy, haloed beneath the lamplight. Was her assault orchestrated to delay him? There had been women involved the night of his and Mark's attack, too. Were they also so-called relatives of Parker?

"I—I need my drivers license for an ID to board the plane for home," she said weakly. "The key to my uncle's house is in my bag, too. I'd feel responsible if

239

his house was broken into."

Fact or excuse? He wasn't sure which, but he wanted to believe she was telling the truth.

"What took so long for you two to meet us?" he barked, flexing his shoulders to toss off his anger and disappointment. He needed to keep a cool head.

"I had to pee," Cindy said, her voice small and meek for the first time since he'd met her.

Spence didn't say anything. He'd analyze their reasons later, when he'd slept and his mind was sharper.

"We've got to hurry. My friend in administration starts the inspection at midnight." Google pulled his cell phone from his roomy pocket, punching in numbers while he informed the women, "My car died recently. I'll get us a cab."

Spence saw no sense in pissing away the rest of the damned night. "I'll drive you," he said.

In no time, Google was hunched into the tight back seat of the extended cab while Mercy and Cindy huddled up front with Spence.

In spite of everything, Spence liked the feel of Mercy's lithe body next to his again.

Her sweet scent and silky shoulder had him shifting on his seat, wishing she'd slip her hand between his legs, like after the movie, and arouse his cock to within an inch of its life.

Her closeness played with his mind and heart. But she'd probably leave him for dead for her sleazy relative, who didn't deserve caring about, just like the other women had that fatal night.

Once at the condo, Cindy and Google went straight to her computer to contact Google's computer-geek friend in administration. Spence sat on the edge of the sofa, waiting for him. Seemed all he ever did was wait.

When Mercy sat down on the sofa cushion next to him, he had to fight off an instant boner to boot.

"You can relax." Mercy propped her long, silky leg up on the glass coffee table to elevate her injured knee. "You don't have to look like you're going to bolt for the door. I won't jump your bones, unless you ask me to."

"I won't be asking." The words squeezed at his throat.

He sat back against the leather cushion and crossed his foot over his knee, trying to show his disinterest in her enticing offer, when in reality it enveloped him, searing his mind and balls.

She smiled, smug with herself. "Want coffee?" She swung her leg down from the table, brushing his knee as she did and arousing him further. He was hopeless to the mere touch of her body. "Coffee?" she called into the computer office.

"Yes," a chorus of two answered.

She stood in front of Spence, hands on her seductive hips, tilting her pretty face toward him for a reply. Her blouse with its fuck-me neckline flaunted her creamy breasts, which begged to be manhandled. Desire blazed through his body like lightning.

"Yes." He nodded when coffee was the last thing he wanted. After his sleepless night, he didn't need caffeine keeping him up again. What he needed was Mercy's soft, warm body grinding beneath his—with no deception between them.

Mercy left to clatter around the kitchen and return with a tray of steaming mugs. He took one and watched her remarkable ass swivel as she walked away toward the office. The woman made walking a primetime event.

He plopped the untouched cup on the table in front of him and leaned back. Propping his elbow on the leathery arm of the sofa and his head on his hand, he closed his eyes.

Next thing he knew, he heard her wispy voice

tickle his ear and penetrate his dreams. "Wake up, Spence." His first reaction was contentment. How much he'd like to hear her each morning of his life. But he gave up the dream, opened his eyes, and closed off his heart.

Google and Cindy were standing in front of him, grinning. "I guess you were successful," he said.

"Yes." Google puffed out his grunge T-shirted chest.

Cindy's grin widened. "It was a toss up whether to leave a computer trail to both Jay and Rita's passwords or just his. But as Google pointed out, Jay was the one who profited."

Spence nodded. "He mentioned to me how she wanted a piece of his action. He wouldn't cut her in though." Spence didn't say he'd thought Jay was referring to Cindy at the time, or how he believed they were all in on the shady deal. Parker and Mercy included.

"Ha," Cindy said. "Not only was he using me, but Rita knew it and didn't warn me."

"So much for sisterhood," Mercy said, always loyal to family and friends.

Spence envied them.

With a yawn, he hiked himself up from the sofa. "Ready?"

Google nodded.

Spence clapped him on the back. "I know how much revenue this cost you with the loss of a paying customer."

"I've been thinking about going legit anyway. I like helping people. Maybe lost and found, missing persons. Like that." Google grinned. "I'll make the cash back when Jay has to sell his sports car at a loss to pay his legal fees. I've been dying to own a Jag."

****

"What a night." Cindy sighed, her foot propped

up on the coffee table next to Mercy's.

Her ice bag dribbled water onto the glass top, puddling and chilling Mercy's heel. But Mercy was too exhausted from her struggle with the assailant to lift her foot. "Yeah, Jay turned out to be quite a parasite," she said.

"He wasn't the safe ticket I thought. Even Rita knew better." Cindy slumped onto her cushion and scowled. "Can you believe he was only dating me to get to my password?"

"No, I can't," Mercy said to soften the blow to her friend's ego. "Can you believe Spence thought I only dated him for information to pass along to my uncle?"

"Aw," Cindy purred. "Don't let what he thinks get to you. We know different."

"I wish he knew better." With the edge of her foot, Mercy nudged the sliding ice bag back onto Cindy's ankle. "I miss his dry sense of humor and his close-mouthed comments. Even his silences." She looked to Cindy for understanding. "I sense his loneliness and his despair, and he touches those hidden parts in me."

Cindy sniffed. "Mercy, you're going to make me cry. I don't like thinking of you as lonely or abandoned. I'm the orphan." She grabbed a tissue from the box on the end table and blew her nose.

"A person can be alone in a crowd, Cin. Being an orphan doesn't corner the market on loneliness. Aside from my family, people—men—aren't exactly clamoring to spend time with me."

"Don't say that," Cindy clucked.

"Don't go pitying me. My life's about to change soon, if I secure a loan from my uncle. Or later if I'm forced to save up on my own." Mercy reached down and removed the ice bag from Cindy's frozen ankle and away from her own cold heel. "I never told you," she said, smiling at her friend, "but I'm very proud of you, living on your own. Independent. No mother to rely on, like me."

"Independence isn't all that," Cindy quipped. "I wouldn't mind finding a man to lean on." She wriggled her brows. "And make love with, and exchange vows with."

"Wouldn't we both." Except Mercy wanted only one man. The one she couldn't have.

****

Spence had fucked it all up. Parker, the woman, the rest of his life. He'd taken his eye off the prize and lost. Now he had to start all over, waiting for Parker and more leads.

He couldn't even look at Mark's picture the next morning when he strode down the hallway, grabbing his Stetson from a peg near the door.

With a squeak, squeak, the screen door snapped open and shut. He needed some physical exhaustion so he could sleep. The past two nights of tossing were hell. Laboring in the hot sun would take his mind off the infernal waiting.

Taking the three porch steps in one leap, he landed with a crunch on the gravel. As he was about to step up into his truck to drive out to the far pasture and dig postholes, he caught sight of a vehicle coming up the dusty lane.

As the car came closer, he saw the bar atop with the red and blue lights. The police. This ought to be good. He thumbed his hat back and shoved his hands into his pockets.

When the squad car pulled up next to him, the driver rolled his window down and shut off the engine.

"Morning, officer," Spence drawled. Whatever the cop was here to defend or protect, from his past experience with the law, Spence knew it wasn't him.

Spence ducked his head toward the open window. He peered down at the short, thin man with a bad haircut. The cop hadn't bothered to put his hat on so Spence figured this wasn't an official visit.

"Howdy," the policeman said, sounding polite and friendly. Spence wasn't falling for his phony good-humor. "Name's Officer Harmon." The man rested his blue-sleeved arm on the car door.

"Nice day for a ride, Officer Harmon," Spence said, equally polite.

"Yep, but I'm here for more than a social call."

As the sun beat down on the windshield, heat built inside the car and beads of sweat popped up on Officer Harmon's forehead, rolling down the side of his face. He cranked up the engine again and the air conditioner started up with a whoosh.

"What can I do for you?" Spence asked, eager to end the suspense.

"Unofficially, I'm here to ask you to stay away from the *Starry Night Club*." The officer looked up at him, met his eyes to show the seriousness of his intent.

Spence broke eye contact and backed up a step. Fuck this shit. "Isn't the club a public place?"

"Do yourself a favor before harassment or stalking charges are filed against you. I'm asking nice." But he wasn't asking, he was warning Spence. There was an unspoken 'or else' in his authoritative tone.

Damn that weasel, Parker. Why didn't he climb out of his hole and do his own dirty work?

"Who complained?" Spence asked.

"The employees of the establishment."

Employer was more likely. Parker had used the legal system before.

Or had Mercy complained to protect Parker, using the strong-arm of the law against Spence?

Spence pulled his Stetson low on his brow so the cop couldn't see the fire in his eyes. He nodded from beneath the shadow of the brim. "Consider me duly advised."

Chapter Thirty

"Looks like the early bird catches the worm," Cindy said the next morning, eyes shining, wearing a gray, pinstriped business suit.

The office had phoned earlier with an offer of a promotion. With the unexpected arrest of Jay, and Rita's demotion for not reporting her suspicions, a couple of higher-paying, junior-executive positions had opened in the department.

"Good luck," Mercy said.

"Thanks," Cindy said, rushing by. "Where are you off to today?"

"I'm going out to Spence's ranch."

Cindy skated to a stop on the marble foyer floor, short of the door. Luckily, with her ankle still sore from last night's mishap, she was wearing a pair of Mercy's flats.

She cocked her head, her hair flopping to one side. "What for?"

"To thank him for rescuing me from the purse snatcher. With everything going on last night, I didn't get a chance."

"We also never got the chance to find out why he was so desperate to get to Corpus Christi. If it had anything to do with your uncle, we may have saved him from Spence's clutches." Cindy shook her head. "So don't go thanking him just yet."

"I considered all that until the wee hours this morning. I barely fell asleep when the phone rang."

Cindy nodded. "I really think you should sleep on your decision a while longer."

Mercy's head felt groggy and her judgment

fuzzy, but she shook her head, not up to rehashing the issue.

"I can see determination gleaming in your eyes so I'm going to bite my tongue and leave." With that, Cindy grabbed for the brass door handle. "Thank him for me while you're at it," she called out, slamming the door.

Mercy went back to bed and tried to curl under the covers and snooze as Cindy had advised. But she couldn't. Giving up, she showered and tossed on a pair of jeans and a T-shirt. What she wore wasn't important. Her plan included a stop at the lingerie shop.

After brushing her teeth, she applied her makeup carefully, then hopped a cab ride to the mall.

After an extensive search of the shops, she found the perfect thong teddy in scarlet red. With any luck, Spence might snip it from her body, or better yet, snake it off with his teeth, inch by tantalizing inch.

She stopped for a late lunch, mostly for energy and stamina. After her sleepless night, she was feeling lethargic when her hormones should've been zinging at the prospect of the sexy tryst. She ordered a second cup of coffee just for the caffeine jolt.

On the long taxi ride out to Spence's ranch, she dozed off. After paying her fare, she stood in the dusty lane in front of the house. Spence's truck was gone. She shrugged, undeterred. He had to come home eventually, and she planned on being here when he did.

Mercy was prepared to break one of the forlorn windows, but both the screen door and the wooden one were unlatched. She entered the cool dimness of the entryway, taking herself and her lingerie package directly upstairs in case Spence arrived soon.

In his bedroom she stripped off her jeans and

the rest of her clothes. Standing in front of the scarred glass of an antique Cheval mirror, she dressed in the red teddy, which looked as *extremely se-xxx-y* as the banner in the store promised.

Perched on the chenille bedspread at the foot of Spence's bed, she crossed her naked legs and waited while studying his room. His black jeans were slung over the back of a slatted chair with his black boots kicked off alongside the spindled, wooden legs.

A low dresser in blonde wood was cluttered with a pocket watch, a bottle of aftershave, a comb, loose coins, and a wad of dollar bills. He must not have gone far.

His closet was open so she got up, flicked the door wider with her index finger and peeked inside. On hangers were denim work shirts, a white shirt, a black shirt with snaps on the placket and cuffs, pants, mostly jeans, and a vest. Leather.

A cowboy vest. She withdrew it from the closet and tried it on. Looking in the mirror, she grinned, finding the leather as naughty as her new lingerie. She shed both garments and donned the buttery soft vest alone.

Another glimpse reflected a scantily clad cowgirl. The vest hung open, exposing a lot of cleavage, yet covered her nipples. Through the sides of the armholes, an enticing peek of her breasts was visible. The leather garment was long enough that she didn't need panties, yet exposed a tempting slash of pubic hair.

Turning around, she tossed a glance over her shoulder. The vest was shorter in the back and her butt peeked out, pink and inviting against the tanned, grained cowhide. Returning to his closet, she found a cowboy hat on the shelf and a faded, blue kerchief. Putting them on, she checked her image in the mirror again. She fitted the hat at different angles until she settled on a casual, thumbed-back look.

She looked like a seductive cowgirl from a centerfold spread. Thinking back, she remembered Lenny saying, "Cowboys like cowgirls."

So she stuffed the fishnet teddy back into her satchel and decided Spence deserved a cowgirl.

She didn't have too long to wait. She heard his truck drive up and watched from behind the lacy curtain panel as he strode up to the house. Rangy and tall, he was wearing a Stetson hat but was shirtless. He made her mouth water.

His dark T-shirt was tossed over one shoulder. She could see his bare torso, glistening with a sheen of sweat from the hot sun. His muscles were defined, and they rippled with each flex of movement.

Her body scorched with a familiar heat as he neared the house. The leather vest felt bulky and restricting, and she couldn't wait to strip it from her and feel Spence's toned arms around her.

He stopped, removed his hat, tamped the dust from the brim against his leg. His jeans were worn and torn and fit his body like a glove. He raked his fingers through his dark, damp hair and then he ambled out of sight.

She heard his booted footsteps enter the hall downstairs. His keys jangled and clunked onto the wooden table at the foot of the newel post. Then his thudded steps began taking the stairs fast, two at time.

He didn't enter the bedroom but went into the bathroom. Doubt flooded her, and Mercy questioned if this had been a smart move.

She chewed her lip, listening as the rush of water from the shower washed over him. Listened as he hummed a low, sad melody.

She fidgeted her fingers, trying to decide whether to stay put or grab her clothes and run. But where? She'd have to hide out in the bushes and call a taxi from her cell phone, and tell the cabby what? To pick her up at the third tree on the left-hand side of the road? Dumb idea. She was full of them today.

The water stopped running, and a final gurgle of the drain told her she didn't have time for second thoughts. She threw back her shoulders, struck a sensual pose, and smiled just as Spence walked into the room.

With no towel.

One look at his hunky body and his ample endowments and she was glad she wasn't out in the brush phoning some cab driver.

He was wet, his hair toweled carelessly, his dark eyes wide and glinting with surprise.

She propped her hands on her hips and gave him her come-hither stare, the one where she narrowed her eyes and he got hard, fast.

Spence couldn't find his voice. The sight of her had tied his vocal chords like a lariat knot.

"What are you doing here?" he choked out at last.

"I came to thank you for saving me from the thief," she said, slow and husky, and his dick got hard.

Despite the boner he sported, his first reaction was to tell her to take off Mark's vest and leave the way she came, which he supposed had been by an expensive taxi ride.

Mark had worn the vest on many Saturday nights to pick up many women. One too many. But he brushed that fateful night from his head with a shake.

Cruel as it sounded in his mind, Mark was dead and he was alive. Very alive. And naked, and Mercy was too damn desirable and too willing to pass up.

He opened his mouth to say, *Come here*, when she stepped forward and put her finger to his lips to shush him.

"No talking," she whispered against her finger. Her breath was warm and luring, taunting him to take her mouth and kiss the breath from her until she was wet with desire and panting for him to hurry.

But he went along with her game. Stilled his urges. Let her take the lead. Slowly, seductively, she untied the bandana from around her neck and dangled it in front of him.

"They'll be no talking tonight, not a word. I don't want you saying I'm here to wheedle secrets from you for my uncle."

Spence flinched at the mention of the man.

Mercy lowered her voice to an even more syrupy tone, one he remembered and liked. One she used when she was dreaming up raunchy things to say and do. "I'm here strictly to repay you for saving me."

He nodded. He had no intention of breaking the lusty spell she was weaving. She took the kerchief and tied it around his mouth. He could have easily slipped it down, but he let her have her way.

No talking could be damn exciting. She took his hand in her soft one and led him over to the bed, patting the spot where she wanted him. She arched her slender neck, her silky blonde hair swaying while she waited for him to oblige her.

Before she could blink, he plopped onto the middle of the bed, arms and legs spread and ready. She tossed the cowboy hat, which also had belonged to Mark, onto the dresser and then straddled Spence's lap.

She was a very seductive and nearly-naked bronco rider, but he intended to last longer than the eight-second countdown. Mercy was in charge, and he wasn't about to shorten any pleasure she fancied.

She stroked her fingers over his bare chest with feathery flicks, and his skin reacted with shivers of goose flesh. Putting her index finger into her mouth first, she teased the delicate pad over his nipple. When his nub was wet and hard, she plucked it and kissed it. His groan got lost deep in his throat, muffled by the bandana.

She must've detected the sound, nipping the very spot on his neck that hummed with his hunger for her body. Her teeth were gentle and the tug enflaming. Heat jolted his hips, tightened his balls, and engorged his cock.

But she wasn't interested in his cock just yet. He knew Mercy. She'd get to it sooner or later, depending on her surging appetite.

She said no talking, but touching was allowed so he dug his hands into her silky hair, massaging her scalp while he stretched his neck and let her kiss him mindless.

She nipped and licked at his chin, his jaw, his earlobe. He was tempted to tear the kerchief from his mouth and give her access to his lips and tongue, but he restrained himself, knowing whatever she did would prove to be sizzling and satisfying.

All the while she caressed him, her wet, hot folds notched and wriggled over his shaft. Sleek and slick, she shifted from the head of his dick to the base, gliding up and down in slow, sensuous motions.

A moan gurgled in his throat. He gripped her hips and stilled her moves. He wouldn't last if she continued at her present pace.

She flattened her body against his, nestling her smooth legs over the length of his, her toes brushing his ankles, her arms resting alongside his head. Her breasts were a pleasing crush against his chest, her nipples stiff as they teased and tormented him.

He slipped his hand between their bodies, and she spread her legs. He toyed with her clit, the kernel swelling beneath his playful fingers, and

253

Mercy moaned. But it wasn't good enough. He wanted more from her. He tweaked and pinched until she moaned again, this time, calling his name.

"Spence," she pleaded yet again, and he slid his finger inside her. She braced herself on her arms, giving him more access. Spreading her lips wider, he slipped another finger in and then drew both of them out and in again until he felt her melt, becoming wetter, slicker, hotter.

Her muscles closed around his fingers, and a spasm contracted in her womb. He moved his fingers faster, harder, steadier until she tossed her head back and orgasmed, whimpering with satisfaction.

He'd like to tell her that no thanks were necessary for that service. Not that any had been for rescuing her from the robber either. But he kept the gag in place and her rules enforced. For the time being.

Mercy panted against his chest. Her warm puffs of breath tickled his hairs and his cock jerked, demanding attention.

Once her breathing steadied, she kissed her way down his chest and belly and went down on him.

The leather from the vest caressed his flesh while she fitted her mouth onto the head of his cock. She moistened the tip with her hot tongue, swirling and dipping and riling his juices to a boil. Her tongue stroked and taunted his scrotum and the length of his shaft until he mumbled pleading commands from beneath his kerchief.

She chuckled at his garbled coaxing and continued to torture him by taking him fully into her mouth and pumping until he was ready to come.

Abruptly, she quit. Kneeling back on her heels, she stripped off the vest and exposed all of her glorious naked flesh to his eyes. Mercy. He wanted her with his every fiber.

He reached out and stroked her slender neck,

her supple breasts, her firm stomach. He teased around her belly button and felt her quiver.

Come closer. He crooked his finger to lure her in.

She straddled him again, fitting herself over his rigid erection, her sex lips stretching to give him entrance. He jerked his hips away, embedding his butt into the mattress. She stared down at him, puzzled.

When he gestured with his eyes and hand toward the dresser drawer, she understood and hopped from the bed. Rooting through his drawer, she hurriedly found the condoms and bounced back onto the mattress with her hands full and a greedy grin.

He laughed, the gag sucking in and out with his chuckles.

She winked, tossing the rest and ripping one of the foil packets open. He took the rubber from her and rolled it onto his hard length. He didn't have the willpower for her to play around. He'd waited enough, for everyone and everything.

Mercy didn't make him wait. Soon as he was sheathed, she resumed her position over his stiff cock and lowered her hips until he was inside of her to the hilt. He kneaded her breasts, swollen and pliable in his hands, making her moan, urging her to a rocking rhythm.

She threw her head back and closed her eyes, losing herself in the sensations of her body and the thrill of the ride. She was fluid ecstasy to watch. Graceful and wanton.

He slid his hands around her waist to help her maintain her balance and the tempo she'd set. He closed his own eyes and let himself drift.

Their motions became one rolling, pumping action. He felt himself begin to spasm, release. He clenched his fingers into her lower back where he gripped her, trying to stop his orgasm, hoping he didn't leave marks. He wanted to hold onto the feeling of being inside of her, a part of her, for as long as he could.

But her bucking became wilder and more frantic. She gasped for air. When she dug her nails into his shoulders, he opened his eyes and met her intense blue ones. She held him there, suspended in time, between heaven and hell, between climaxing and denying himself the pleasure.

Mercy moaned, contracted, spasmed, and then came in a flood of hot moisture. He let go. He had no will but hers at the moment.

She collapsed onto his chest, straightening her legs, groaning at the stiffness in her muscles from the workout.

Stroking her hair away from her face, he cradled her head against his neck. He breathed heavy, the cloth of the bandana sucking the moisture from his mouth. His tongue felt dry.

When she calmed and looked up, he cocked his eyebrow. With a smile, she yanked the bandana from his mouth, flinging it away, replacing it with her burning lips and a welcoming kiss.

He swept his tongue into her mouth, enjoying the taste of her passion. Her tongue greeted his with equal enthusiasm. Their lips remained planted to one another's for a long time, inhaling and exhaling each other's breaths.

When she dragged her mouth from his, he didn't say anything. He didn't want to force reality into the moment. Anything he said would only lead back to the chasm that separated them. For now, he wanted to forget about Parker, her connection to him, and Mercy ever leaving.

"Shower," she whispered.

He nodded.

When she stood, she dug her cell phone from her handbag and called for a taxi. Looked like they only had enough time to wash their lovemaking from their bodies, and she'd be gone.

He indulged himself with the soap, lathering her skin, luxuriating in the beauty and the satiny feel of her and her intoxicating fragrance. Her sweet, tart scent mingled with the antiseptic suds, the steam, and the musky smell of sex they'd enjoyed.

"I have to go," she said after they rinsed and the water had run clear a long while. He twisted the spigots off and handed her a clean, dry towel.

Back in his bedroom, he watched her dress, preparing to leave him. She pulled on her jeans and T-shirt, re-tucked a red nightie in her bag, and looked around for anything she may have forgotten.

Without warning, the cab honked its horn. The blare startled both of them, breaking the comfortable silence that had built between them.

As she stood in the doorway ready to go, he couldn't bear not speaking any longer.

Wondering if he'd see her again before her flight, he asked, "Was that a thank-you-fuck or a good-bye-fuck?"

She reached over and picked the damp kerchief off the bed, stuffing it gently into his mouth. He didn't fight her.

"That was an I-love-you fuck." She dropped a kiss onto his stunned cheek and fled.

Chapter Thirty-one

Mercy left Spence speechless. She had a knack for captivating his attention with her sexual antics, but this went way beyond. Every nerve in his body hummed with the impact of her words. *I love you.*

He'd longed to hear those words from her, and now he was forced to deal with them. He tugged on his jeans and shirt and jammed his feet into his boots. After shoving his money from the bureau into his pocket, he strode for the door. He turned back to snatch Mark's vest from the bed where Mercy had flung it.

Spence gunned the engine on the truck and headed for the cemetery at the edge of the property line. Trudging through the iron gate, he wove his way around grave markers and tombstones, checking names. He'd never attended Mark's funeral. He'd been behind bars.

He found the gray granite stone easily in the small graveyard. *Mark Rendell.*

He draped the vest on the corner of the headstone, shucked his hands into his pockets, and stood there, feeling sad and awkward. Sad because Mark was dead. Awkward because he wasn't.

He listened to the wind whisper through the leaves of the oak near the entrance. A crow squawked from its perch on the rusted fence before flying off. The sun lowered, glowing orange on the blue horizon.

Spence dropped to one knee, the grass cool and plush beneath his weight. The air smelled fresh from green growth. Odd for land littered with the dead.

He reached out and rested his hand on the etched letters of Mark's name.

"Well, buddy," he murmured. "If you've been following, you know I've been in jail and have tried to make things right. For both of us. Clear my name and catch your killer."

Spence's voice caught. He coughed. "I've been trying real hard to keep my eye on the prize, like you said, but..."

He fell silent. Dropping his hand to the ground, he flattened his palm on the grass as if to feel the energy of his friend through the casket lying beneath the earth.

Mark had been like the brother he'd never had. Spence had tried to always respect that loyalty.

"I fell in love, and Mercy claims she loves me. I may have to abandon my search for justice to keep the woman. I just wanted to tell you myself."

He stood to go, then reached out at the last minute for the vest, deciding to hold on to it as a keepsake of Mark. And Mercy, if he should lose her. But he intended to try like hell to keep her.

****

"Your mother called. She said it was important," Cindy yelled from the living room as soon as Mercy walked through the marble foyer of the condo after leaving the ranch and Spence.

Mercy hadn't meant to open her heart and tell him she loved him. It had just spilled out when she was faced with parting from him for the last time. Not only were they at odds about her uncle but headed in different directions when her flight left tomorrow evening. Revealing the truth of her feelings didn't help the situation any.

Flopping onto the sofa next to Cindy, Mercy dropped her satchel onto the floor near her feet. "How did Mom sound?" she asked. "Did she hear from Uncle Parker?"

Her spirits lifted at the faint hope, despite knowing full well her mother would've told Cindy if she had, and Cindy would've blurted it out without Mercy having to ask.

"No, but she's figured out who his dying friend is. Soon as you locate him, you locate your uncle." Cindy shrugged, clearly not sold on the outside chance.

"If it were only that simple." Mercy reached for the phone beside the sofa and dialed, anxious to hear what her mother had to say. A name could well be the key to locating her missing uncle.

Her mother sounded emphatic and pleased with herself for recalling her brother's friend from Mercy's description. Sort of. On Cindy's hobbit-shaped pad near the phone, Mercy scribbled down the different pronunciations her mother gave for the man's name. Before hanging up, Mercy promised to call her as soon as she heard anything positive.

"Grant *Murray, Merray, Morrey*." She spelled out the various forms of the name for Cindy.

Cindy listened and snapped her fingers. "I know who can help us. Google. He called a half-hour ago to ask how everything worked out with corporate. He left his number in case I hear any news about Jay needing a buyer for his Jag. Undervalued, of course." She nodded.

"How did you make out with corporate?" Mercy brushed a stray hair from her face, ashamed that she was so caught up in her own situation with Spence and her uncle that she hadn't thought to inquire about Cindy's promotion.

"I'm the new assistant vice-president in charge of sales." Cindy sat up straighter and fussed with the collar of her tailored blouse. "With a modest raise in pay to go along with the duties."

"I'm so happy for you." Mercy squeezed off a quick hug before Cindy brushed her off.

"Let's see about producing more good results. Let's both check our ready cash to see how much we can come up with to pay for Google's services." Cindy snatched her purse from the sleek, glass coffee table where it lay alongside her high-polished leather briefcase.

Mercy dug her wallet from the tote at her feet and counted out her twenties while Cindy tossed a handful of crumpled bills onto Mercy's lap, a fifty among them.

"We have a couple hundred here. Is that enough to hire him?" Mercy asked, grateful to her generous friend.

"I'm sure it is." Cindy leaned in. "You know what else Google told me?"

"No. I couldn't begin to guess." Mercy unfolded and piled the bills into a neat stack on the coffee table in front of them.

"Spence's trip to Corpus Christi last night was to catch Parker before his boat sailed. Someone at the club—Google wouldn't give me a name—got a tip from a friend who works in the bait shop at the marina and passed it along to Spence."

Mercy's mouth gaped. A rush of air fluttered the bills before she had time to sink back against the firm leather cushion of the sofa.

"You know the rest. He missed leaving on time," Cindy explained, "because he lingered to set us up with Google and then had to save you from the knife-wielding thief."

"Do you know what that means, Cindy?" Mercy stammered.

"Aside from his saving both our butts and losing his chance to get his hands on your uncle, no."

"Spence loves me. He chose me over my Uncle Parker."

"And let me guess. You love him, too." Cindy ruffled her fingers through her hair, sending the strands flying. "After all my warnings."

"Yes."

"Yes, you love him or yes about my warnings," Cindy asked, forcing Mercy to say the words aloud.

"Yes, I love Spence."

Cindy sighed. "Sister Doria believed when someone showed you who they were, you should believe them." She paused. "Looks like I misjudged Spence. And Jay? Safe, my ass." She crinkled her nose. "I wonder. If I was so off base about both men, maybe I should change my viewpoint on Lenny. Underneath his playboy exterior could beat the heart of my true love." She chuckled at the notion.

"It's not so laughable. Lenny *did* help Spence and Google by passing along the message to us," Mercy rationalized.

Cindy reached around Mercy and grabbed the phone. "One problem at a time." She checked Google's number on her notepad, dialed, and handed the receiver to Mercy.

After Mercy explained the situation and gave Google the various spellings of the man's name, she called Spence's number. There was no answer.

But within the hour, unexpected, Spence showed up at their door. Cindy let him in and yawned. "All this late-night and early-morning activity has me exhausted. I don't know about you two, but I need a nap." She winked and sashayed down the hall, safely, in Mercy's flat-soled shoes.

Once they were alone, Mercy watched Spence's rangy body reflected in the mirrored wall of the foyer. He hadn't come into the living room to sit by her and she considered going to him. For the moment, she contented herself admiring his potent physique. Both front and back, in the mirrors. Hard muscles, bulging fly, tight butt, strong hands, powerful legs. She exhaled, readying herself to stand up and go after him.

Before she could, with his unique style of manly grace and flexing sexuality, he moved toward her. He shoved his hands into his pockets. His dark, dreamy eyes met hers. Her pulse quickened.

Before she got sidetracked by his smoky eyes and the wanton flickers of heat between her thighs, she decided to get straight to the matter. "I have the name of my uncle's friend. Google's searching for his address as we speak."

He nodded. "If I'm allowed to speak. I have a question." His husky voice alluded to the steamy romp they'd recently enjoyed with the bandana as a gag, and that surprised her. She'd expected him to jump right for the information.

"Please, speak," she said, his sensuality stirring her interest to a full-bodied burn. With Cindy retreated to her bedroom to give them privacy, Mercy's body yearned to give itself over to his evocative presence without preamble or, in this case, foreplay.

He sat down alongside her on the dark blue leather sofa. His thigh brushed hers and need shot through her like white-hot lightning. "Are you going to tell me where Parker's friend is when you find out?"

Not the question she'd expected. She'd anticipated something lurid to go with the sexuality radiating between them.

"Yes," she replied, simply, while holding back her hunger to strip him naked and show him how much she wanted him, trusted him, loved him.

Spence's dark eyes reflected her love. "Why the change of heart?"

"I want this situation cleared up as much as you do. I know you'll do the right thing by my uncle." Spence's mouth was temptingly close.

"How do you know?" His breath teased her lips. Her mouth parted eager to devour his.

"Because you lost your chance at Corpus Christi to rescue me. You chose me over my uncle."

"I didn't know how late it was," he said in a teasing tone, kissing the corner of her mouth, the mere touch of his lips hot and firm and stirring.

"You didn't care when you saw I was in trouble. You didn't pull out your pocket watch to see if you had enough time." She snuggled onto his lap, reveling in the feel of his strong arms at her back, while her bottom settled onto his firm thighs and hardening dick.

"I didn't have my watch with me. When I'm around you, I forget a lot of things."

"You do?" A thrill ran through her. As she squirmed for a better position on his lap, he balanced her by wrapping his arm around her waist.

"I'm inclined to forget about your uncle, Mark's killer, and my vindication." His eyes met hers. They blazed with more than desire.

"You don't have to," she insisted. "Once we locate my uncle, he'll make everything right. I'm sure."

"Suppose he can't." He stroked her spine to ease the realization that her uncle might be guilty of some underhanded involvement. "Your offer was enough. You don't have to deliver."

She tangled her arms around his neck, pulling his mouth to hers. His mood seemed mellower, more caring, loving. This softer side of him added to her sexual curiosity. A loving and sexy Spence was something she couldn't wait to experience.

"I intend to deliver." She slipped her hand between his thighs and tugged at his zipper.

"You always do, babe." With a growl, he undid the fly on her jeans. The leather of the sofa squooshed beneath the weight of their shifting bodies as she shimmied her jeans down below her knees and he knelt over her, tugging his fly open wider.

He held her eyes with the intensity of his dark, gleaming ones while he dug a foil packet from his pocket and protected himself.

The exquisite contact of his deep concentration swept hot lust through her limbs. Her pulse throbbed wild with expectation.

With both of his broad, work-roughened hands, he grasped her around the hips and dragged her slowly beneath him. The coarseness of his jeans stroked her tender inner thighs as he positioned her where he wanted her, pinning her in place with the weight of his slim hips. She strained her hips up to meet the rock-hard, swollen head of his penis.

She was drenched with lust for him. Nudging his erection into her folds, he spread her hot moisture around.

Remembering Cindy down the hall, Mercy stifled her moan of torturous anticipation, letting it die in her throat. Then he entered her with a swift plunge that took her breath away for a second. She attempted to open her thighs wider but her jeans and the sofa back wouldn't allow it.

With his arms at either side of her neck, Spence braced himself above her. His breath was heated and tinged with the heavy scent of coffee drunk black.

"You don't mind if I deliver something of my own, do you?" he asked, his voice lusty and hoarse.

"I was counting on it," she whispered. Wrapping her arms around his neck, she pulled him closer and arched her hips.

He needed no other urging. He withdrew and plunged, deep and swift, filling her with heated muscle and pulsing veins. He became a palpable part of her, the intimacy profound. Again, she tried to spread her legs, to give him wider entrance, but her jeans wouldn't allow it.

Although, as she wriggled, she realized the tight

width of her thighs was making for a more erotic sensation. When he withdrew, fully, and lunged again, the size and length of him stretched her, possessed her, defying the restricted entrance of her narrowed spread. She felt closer, deeper, more connected to him than ever before.

Awareness of him, them, and their immersed emotions spiraled through her with every highly charged stroke. Her body reacted by clenching his thick shaft, milking him, surrounding him with the fiery pull of her body. Her love.

She clutched the back of his head. His hair was damp from the exertion of their lovemaking. He nipped biting kisses along her throat as her grip tightened and her senses heightened with the incredible, entirely new, bond forming between them.

He pumped faster, harder, higher, titillating her clit with each fierce thrust. As she bucked her hips, she began to tremble and shatter. He wrapped his strong arms around her shuddering body as she rode the spasms of her orgasm. His lips met hers in a demanding kiss, swallowing their cries of satisfaction as they reached their orgasms.

Her insides melted like butter, hot and dripping. Exhausting himself, he contracted, let out a soft groan, and lifted himself up on his arms. She fell limp.

Closing his eyes for a second, he rested his forehead on hers. The warm pants of their breaths mingled.

Once steady, he opened his beautiful dark eyes and smiled at her. "Babe, that was a thank-you and I-love-you fuck."

Before she could reply, all hell broke loose. The doorbell chimed, the phone rang, and mere seconds after they yanked their jeans up, Cindy skidded down the hallway toward the front door.

Spence sprinted toward the bathroom to dispose of the condom, while Mercy finger-combed her hair and straightened her T-shirt.

Cindy jarred the door open. "Hello, Google."

"Hello," Mercy said, picking up the phone. "How are you, Jay?"

The women looked at one another. Then they switched.

Chapter Thirty-two

By the time Spence returned, Mercy was standing in the living room, chattering away with Google and clutching a tattered piece of paper in her hand while Cindy sat on the sofa, on the very spot where Spence had just professed his love to Mercy. From Cindy's end of the conversation, it sounded as if Jay was whining about his financial problems.

"Hey," Google said with a nod to Spence.

Spence nodded back and raked his fingers through his hair. He eyeballed Mercy. Her lips were pink and swollen from his kisses. He supposed both sets of her lips were still inflamed from his recent ministrations.

Mercy acknowledged him with a smile as if nothing earth-shattering had recently occurred. Like him making love to her and telling her he loved her.

Women. He'd never understand them.

"It didn't take me long at all," Google bragged, folding and tucking the money Mercy gave him into his deep pants pocket. "There were four Grant Morreys, but only one was sixty and ailing." He grinned, rocking back on the rubber heels of his high-tech leather sneakers, inches from where Mercy's bare toes peeked out from beneath the hem of her jeans.

She had sexy feet, Spence thought when his mind should be on the business at hand and his dick should be satisfied. But hell, any noticeable bare flesh of hers turned him on.

Love. With a muffled groan, he accepted his fate and strolled over to join her.

"Thank goodness we were so lucky," Mercy said, reaching out her arm to capture Spence's when he approached. She handed him the torn scrap of paper.

Spence shook his head. With all the money Google took in, you'd think he could afford whole pieces of paper. He read the address.

"It's about a six hour ride to the Louisiana border," he told Mercy, glancing up from the note to her eager eyes.

"We should go tonight," she said.

He nodded. "We shouldn't waste any time, what with your flight taking off tomorrow night."

As soon as he agreed, she grabbed up her tote from the side of the sofa and hurried off toward her bedroom. "I'll freshen up and get my sneakers."

"I guess I'll get going." Google shook Spence's hand.

But before he even reached for the doorknob, Cindy began waving frantically at Google not to go yet. Muffling the phone to her chest, she mouthed, "I may have a bargain Jaguar for you."

With a wide grin, he ambled toward the sofa, plopping his large frame down next to her, the firm leather making a whooshing sound as he settled in.

By the time Spence wrangled his truck keys out of his pocket, Mercy was back. "Ready," she said, tucking her T-shirt into her waistband.

She looked ready. Her blue eyes shone bright and her cheeks were rosy with her lust for life. She stood there, eager and receptive. His heart thumped. Mercy was always up for adventure of any kind.

"Yeah, I'm primed," he said, taking her elbow, keeping her at arm's length to stop himself from kissing her inviting mouth. He wasn't making any public claims on her until this thing with Parker came to a head.

"Take care of Mercy and don't do anything you'll regret about her uncle," Cindy said.

"I'll walk on eggs," he muttered to Mercy's ever-interfering friend.

"Good one." Cindy laughed, approving of the adage.

Once out of town and away from the dense traffic, Spence wanted to discuss the possibility of a future with Mercy before things started happening, before misunderstandings could get in the way of feelings.

But she nodded off, and he didn't wake her. It was going to be a long night and day. She'd need her strength to deal with whatever went down between him and Parker.

As he tooled the truck down the highway toward the border, he cracked the window open for fresh air. The night was warm and smelled sweet like fresh-cut hay. He fidgeted with the radio, tuning in a lively country-music station and tapping along on the steering wheel to stay awake and alert.

Before dawn, he felt stiff and tired. He stretched and yawned and headed for the nearest off-ramp to get a coffee. When he parked beneath the brightly-lit canopy of the service plaza, Mercy fluttered her eyelids open.

"Are we there?" she asked in a throaty, sleepy voice that made him ache to have her wake beside him every morning after a long night of sweaty lovemaking.

"Not yet. Want coffee?" He leaned over her to shadow the neon light from her eyes and toyed with a tempting lock of hair that teased the delicate shoulder he longed to bite.

He resisted. Taking her here in the truck stop wasn't his style. Besides, they didn't have the time. He quit touching her, moved away, got out of his pickup.

When he opened her door, she dropped down in front of him with a full body hug, giving him an instant boner in spite of his best intentions. Her soft breasts pressed against his chest and her crotch cradled his fly in an enticing way. As he reconsidered his decision about screwing in the cab of the truck, she pecked his cheek and sidled away, saying, "I wonder if they have donuts?"

"Sugar and caffeine are a great high." And so was sex with Mercy. He trailed after her tantalizing ass.

The smell of brewed coffee buzzed his head as soon as they entered the building. After they filled their paper cups with coffee from the various-flavored urns and snapped on the plastic lids, he leaned back against the counter, taking her hand.

"We're about an hour away. Are you sure you're up for this? Your uncle is the key to clearing up the unanswered questions surrounding Mark's death and my incarceration." He studied her eyes for signs of stress. They looked clear and bright, but a crinkle of uncertainty touched the corners.

"Do you think your, our, showing up so unexpectedly will make him disappear, only for good this time?" she asked.

He shrugged. "I honestly can't say what will happen."

"My mother will be heart-broken if she never hears from him again. Even though he doesn't visit Mom and me often, he does stay in touch and we do love him." Her eyes welled with unshed tears.

"I understand sorrow," he said. He certainly didn't want to inflict any into Mercy's life.

Her suddenly cold fingers tightened their grip on his hand. "I know I said I trusted you to do the right thing. But if he tries to run, you won't lose control and harm him, will you?"

"No." He lowered his eyes from hers. Her doubt in him was too painful to watch.

Hadn't she heard him when he'd said *I love you*?

271

Sylvie Kaye

Did she think he took the words lightly? He'd never hurt her, and harming her uncle was part of her.

She ducked her head to meet his eyes and regain his attention. Her voice sounded soft and sweet when she spoke next. "Thank you."

He nodded but gritted his back teeth. A thank you for loving her wasn't what he wanted. He wanted her undying love and loyalty. Needed it, actually.

He'd never felt so alone. Not in jail and not while with Mercy—until now.

"We better get on the road." He moved toward the checkout counter, digging a bill from his pocket to pay for the coffees. "And two donuts," he told the clerk, winking at Mercy and tilting his chin toward a lighted, glass case filled with pastry, bagels, and donuts.

Her eyes lit up, and she tapped her sneakered foot while she studied the showcase. He came over to stand beside her, just to feel her body heat and nearness. He took her coffee cup to free up her hands while she stuffed two powdered rings of pastry into a bag.

Once she ate her sweets—licking the powdered sugar from her lips and wiping her hands on her jeans—he let her drive for a stretch to keep her occupied. He didn't want to speculate over the day's outcome or argue over it with her. He wanted to cement a future with her regardless of what happened.

He watched her in the dancing lights of the oncoming traffic. Mercy behind the steering wheel of his truck. She looked adorable and capable. She'd bucked the clutch once pulling away from the service plaza, but after that she drove the vehicle like she'd been born to it. He hoped she was. He liked the idea of her being a part of his destiny. He'd drive with her anywhere. Live with her anywhere.

272

Miles later she broke the silence. "The Louisiana line." Gripping the wheel with both hands, she glanced over at him.

"Pull over, and I'll take it from here." He pointed to a place where the berm along the roadway was the widest.

He lifted her by the waist to help her out of the truck. She felt so light and supple as she slipped away and around to the passenger door. His heart ached along with his dick for want of her. He sucked in a deep breath and hopped into the driver's seat, gunning the engine toward Port Lou and the address Google had given them.

Once they hit in town, a station attendant gave them directions to the street. She scouted the street signs and directed while he steered.

"We're here," she said, thumbing toward a brick home bordered by a high green hedge, with large, visible house numbers staggered down the side of the door in a horizontal line.

"Place looks locked up tighter than a bull chute before the bell," Spence said, parking alongside the street. "Let's knock and see if we can stir up any action."

He got out of the truck and stretched the kinks out of his neck before hoofing around to open the door for Mercy. She stumbled out but with a jerk, snapped to attention.

Spence eyed the long walkway and the inset door. Now that he was here with his two-year journey at an end, he felt hesitant. Not scared, apprehensive. A lot hinged on the outcome of this meeting with her uncle and his friend.

Mercy grabbed hold of his hand, and they strode up the cemented sidewalk together.

It was a cool, quiet predawn. The sun had just started to rise in a hazy, mellow light. They rang the bell. Waited. Rang again. Nothing. Spence hammered with his knuckles a few times in a wasted effort. The place felt deserted. The shades were drawn. The porch bare of chairs or a doormat. Everything was still. Not even a blade of grass stirred.

As they walked back toward the truck, he felt defeated, and by the slump of her shoulders, he could tell she felt the same. Their gloom was interrupted by the *brr-ing, brr-ing* of a bell. A newspaper deliveryman with a bulging, canvas sack attached to the handlebars of his bicycle came pedaling toward them, tossing a paper into the driveway of a nearby house before waving to them.

"Morning," the man of about forty with a gap-toothed smile said. He stopped next to them, hopped down from his seat, and straddled the red bike to keep it upright.

"Howdy," Spence said. "This your regular route?" If it was, the man probably knew more about the neighbors than what edition of the paper they read.

"I've been the carrier in this neighborhood for the last five years. Are you looking for Grant?" He jerked his chin toward the walkway they'd just abandoned.

"Yes, we are," Mercy chimed in. "Do you know him?"

"Are you a close friend or relative?" he asked, repositioning his feet to keep the bike's front wheel from wobbling beneath the weight of his newspaper sack.

"A friend of a friend," Spence half-fibbed.

Mercy was friendly with her uncle.

"So I can speak freely without upsetting anyone's sympathies."

Spence and Mercy both nodded.

"If you've come to pay your respects to the deceased, you're too late. He's down in the Gulf."

Spence felt Mercy's intake of breath. He missed a beat himself.

"Grant's dead then." Spence closed his eyes, briefly, to gain control of his emotions. Damn. He was too late. He'd have killed to hear what Grant had to say for himself. He'd come so far, been so close, and now what?

He didn't have a clue. He looked at Mercy. Her eyes were soft and understanding.

"Grant passed away several days ago," the paper carrier said. "They scattered his ashes at sea. Somewhere out in the Gulf. A favorite fishing spot, I think."

Spence couldn't say anything. He felt burned out like the dying embers of a campfire.

"My Uncle Parker was a fishing crony of Grant's." Mercy kept the chat going. "I'm visiting from the East and trying to catch up with my uncle. I keep missing him."

"He's probably onboard." The man scratched his head. "Let me think on it for a moment." Then he flashed a grin. "I remember now. The boat's supposed to dock in Corpus Christi around noon for a wharf-side memorial service. That's what Mrs. Miller, the next-door neighbor, told me yesterday when she was up early with an attack of indigestion." He thumbed behind him to the driveway where he'd tossed a newspaper. "Nobody from this neck of the woods is attending the service except for the Bartons. They have family down that way."

"You've been a great help." Mercy climbed back into the truck with Spence close on her heels.

"We can make it in time," he assured Mercy with a pat to her knee.

He wished he could guarantee her properly. But the cab of the truck was tight, and the bed of the truck was dirty, and they didn't have a moment to

275

spare. Even for a quickie.

Somewhere in his gut, a knot tightened. His fear wasn't over *not* catching Parker but over *not* having Mercy much longer. Suppose he'd already made love to her for the last time.

On the road again, he said, "Let's talk about something other than this crummy situation." For nearly two years, he'd dwelled on Parker and his friend. Now the whole thing had snowballed with Mercy's involvement. He needed to get his mind around something positive.

"What would you like to talk about?"

He looked across the seat at her beautiful face and decided to take the future on. Her bright future, possibly without him.

"Colleges. Where are the most prestigious ones for finance?"

"I did a search on Cindy's computer one morning. Depends on what you want to pursue, banking, business finance, investment management, insurance, Wall Street."

"I see. And what's important to you?"

"I'm still undecided."

He nodded, smiled. He was glad. If her plans were up in the air, he still had a chance.

The rest of the ride to Corpus Christi was loud with music, quiet with talk, and heavy with monotony, after having just traveled part of the same route previously. When Mercy insisted on taking another turn at the wheel, Spence dosed off.

She woke him outside of the city. "I'm not sure where the marina is."

The motor idled in a soft hum along with the sound of her voice. The muscles in his legs felt cramped from sleeping in a seated position. He stretched as much as the cab permitted before scrubbing his hand over his face to shake off his grogginess and adjust to the sunlight.

"Is it noon?" His voice sounded scratchy from sleep.

"Yes." Mercy nodded, slowly. She looked pretty but tired. Her blue eyes were red-rimmed, and her usually rosy lips pale.

"The memorial service has probably started. We'd better get moving."

When they arrived at the wharf, the service was in full swing, solemn music and all.

Spence spied the over-bleached blonde and her long-toothed friend from the bar that night. They were dressed in black. One dabbed her eyes with a hankie, grief-stricken, while the other consoled her.

Mercy spotted her uncle first, before Spence did. Pointing, she took his hand and pulled him along. Despite all his promises to her, Spence was hard-pressed not to grab the man by his collar. As they got closer to the group, he heard someone call the sobbing blonde Mrs. Morrey.

That put a whole new light on the incident.

Spence slowed down. "Mercy, regardless how this turns out, I want you in my life. But not at the expense of the future and career you planned for yourself. If your loyalty to me jeopardizes the chance of your uncle lending you the money, I'll walk way."

"It won't," she said, her reply naïve in his eyes.

As they closed in on the mourners, she broke into a run, eager to see her uncle at last.

True to his word, Spence didn't stand in her way. He let go of her hand and slipped away as she disappeared among the people and flowers and music.

Chapter Thirty-three

"Uncle Parker." Mercy threw herself into her uncle's hug. "Mom and I have been so worried."

"Wha—at are you doing here?" Before she could reply he squeezed her tighter. "I'm so glad to see you. There's nothing for you or your mother to worry over. Nothing anybody could do for Grant." He wiped at his crinkled, gray-browed eyes. "It's difficult watching an old friend die."

"I'm sorry for your loss," she said, snuggling even closer to his warm, round chest, trying to comfort him.

"Grant was like a brother to me. Thick and thin, we went through a lot together. We were both career marines. Served together in Vietnam," he said proudly. "Watched each others' backs from time to time after that." He broke down and sobbed.

"I know it hurts." At a loss as to what to say to console him, Mercy held him at the waist and stroked his back. After a few moments, when the funeral guitarist stopped playing and the minister asked everyone to gather, her uncle heaved his chest and dried his eyes with a white handkerchief he took from his khaki suit jacket.

"How did you get here?" He chucked her under the chin.

"Spence brought me." She looked around to pull Spence and his predicament into the conversation, but he was gone. Her heart thudded. Where was he? "I—I guess he didn't want to intrude."

A sad, lost feeling weighed her down as she searched each face. Why had Spence deserted her?

They had important things to discuss after meeting with her uncle. Love things. She hadn't wanted to pin him down about their loving emotions until after his turmoil with her uncle was satisfied.

She chewed her bottom lip. Before she'd lost contact with him in her zeal to reach her uncle, he'd said, "I want you in my life but not at the expense of your future."

He'd been mistaken in his belief that loving him would cause her uncle to reject her loan. Even if it had, she wouldn't have chosen a life without him in it. Her heart jarred as her sadness was replaced with a warm flood of love. He'd walked away because he loved her.

Spence loved her that much.

"How well do you know this man?" her uncle asked.

"More to the question," she said to her uncle, "how well do you?"

He took her elbow and moved closer toward the gathering. "Now's not the time. After the memorial service."

The salty, fishy smell of the wharf mingled with the overwhelming bouquet of the floral sprays the mourners tossed upon the water while the minister eulogized Grant Morrey.

If he was the man who was responsible for running Mark down, it was a shame Spence hadn't stayed until the end. As closure.

After the ceremony, Mercy and her uncle called her mother to tell her the good news about Parker and the bad news about his friend, Grant, who her mother had never met but heard about sporadically over the years and had seen in snapshots.

On the long ride home in the infamous red Cadillac, Mercy and her uncle caught up on family news, discussed her career opportunities, and danced around the subject of Spence.

"I see no reason not to invest in your future. You look like an up-and-comer to me." Uncle Parker flashed a pleased smile at her. "San Antonio has several excellent universities, and Baylor's right nearby in Waco. If you remain in the San Antonio area you can stay at the house and work at the club for extra spending money. The tips are good." He winked.

"Or only work at the club," she said, quirking her eyebrow. "After living with my mother this long, I was hoping to step out on my own again."

"Understandable." He nodded, loosening his tie.

"Thank you for your generosity. That's a huge weight lifted from my mind." And an appropriate Doriasm. She wished Spence were here to hear and appreciate it.

"That's what family's for." Her uncle reached out and patted her shoulder. "Taking care of each other in a pinch."

She remained silent for a few miles, but with her plane taking off this evening, she didn't have time to ease into the subject of Spence. "Spence seems to think there was a misunderstanding with your testimony at his trial."

Her uncle slumped his shoulders, seeming to shrink in his seat. "I'm going to make it up to the boy."

Mercy's stomach flinched. Her nerves were frazzled from days spent defending her uncle to Spence only to hear that her uncle did have something to make up for. "Why?"

He tightened his grip on the steering wheel, his knuckles turning white. "I lied under oath."

She gasped. Poor Spence.

Trying to remain calm, she kept her voice even when she said, "He lost two years of his life and his best friend. You said good-bye to your friend today so I'm sure you know the depth of his grief."

Her uncle heaved a sigh.

"What am I going to tell Spence?" The blood chilled in her veins. "What am I going to tell my mother?"

"I intended to handle the situation discretely. I didn't want to tell either you or your mother. When my accountant mentioned you had been seen in Spence's company, I was afraid he'd involve you so I sent the police out to his ranch to warn him away."

"He never mentioned it," she said with a shake of her head, glad he'd ignored the police's warning.

"I don't plan on telling your mother about this." He glanced at her, and Mercy nodded back. It wasn't her secret to tell. "Although, if she finds out, she's family, and she'll stand by me." He tapped his fingers on the steering wheel in a nervous gesture. "Spence will be informed of the truth and recompense will be made by both Grant and me. Grant provided for it in his last will and testament."

Hope warmed her veins. Money wouldn't make up for Spence's losses, but an admission of guilt from her Uncle Parker and Grant Morrey would go a long way toward healing his raw emotions.

She pursued more details. "Why would Grant pay for your crime?"

"Grant and Iris, his much younger wife, had a fight that fateful day. They'd all been drinking, Grant, Iris, and her sister, Rose. When Iris hooked up with the good-looking rodeo rider, Grant became enraged. He was afraid she'd leave him for the young stud. He took my car and chased after them."

"You weren't there?"

"I followed minutes later on foot. The confrontation happened two blocks from the club. Grant and the women were drunk and hell-bent on leaving the scene of the incident. He told me the two drunken men had been fighting and knocked each other down. I was the only sober person in the group so I stayed while they fled. I called 911. When the police and medics arrived, I repeated the story Grant told me. Only I said I had witnessed the scene. The rest you know."

"Grant body-slammed Mark as he got to his feet and you covered for him," she said numbly.

"I thought Spence had done it. Grant never told me differently. Until he was on his deathbed. Only time he ever lied to me." Uncle Parker's eyes misted with regret. He pulled the car over to the side of the road and hung his head. Interstate traffic whizzed by. The only other sound was a choking sniffle before he picked his head up. "Grant knew he was dying, even back then. He didn't want to die in jail or without Iris by his side." He swiped at a tear. "He died in his own bed."

Mercy patted his shoulder before she got out of the car and went around to the driver's side and opened the door. "I've always wanted to drive a Cadillac convertible."

They both knew her uncle needed time to compose himself, and he accepted her offer. He eased his heavy-spirited body from the seat and hugged her. "I'm sorry you were dragged into this."

"I wasn't dragged. I came willingly. For your sake as well as Spence's."

"So that's how it is." His eyes crinkled with understanding. "Looks like I sent the cops too late."

****

Spence stood on the porch the following morning, barefooted and sleep-weary. Leaning against the paint-faded post, he speculated on the rundown ranch and the work needed to get it up and going. He felt restless instead of exhilarated.

He and Mark had discussed all kinds of plans for painting, planting ryegrass for haying, and breeding horses. While Spence was in jail, his enthusiasm to get outside and work in the fresh air and sunlight had grown even stronger.

Now, all he could think about was Mercy. Her flight took off last night. Staring out at the empty blue sky, he imagined her plane had already landed in Pennsylvania.

On the horizon, a swirl of dust barreled up the road. Who in the hell could be coming to visit him at such top speed? Had Parker sent the cops again?

He stood his ground, squinting to determine the trouble in the distance before it arrived. As the vehicle closed in on the ranch, he saw red.

Parker's Caddy. The man himself had finally come out of hiding. He braced himself against the post and crossed one bare foot over the other, faking a casual stance he didn't feel.

The car sped up the lane, not slowing for potholes or bumps. Dust engulfed the vehicle. If Spence had any sense, he'd duck inside because the crazy driver was heading for the porch at an improbable speed for stopping short of crashing.

But Spence toughed it out. Seemed he had more guts than brains, and both were likely to be splattered across the porch at any moment.

In a whirlwind of dirt and grit, the car braked and lurched to a halt mere yards from the steps leading to where Spence stood.

Refusing to choke on the cloud of dirt, he swigged on his coffee and eyeballed the Caddy over the rim of his mug.

As the dust settled back to the ground, the convertible top lowered. The moment of retribution had arrived.

Paybacks were hell. This was one adage Mercy wouldn't enjoy, and he was glad she wasn't here to witness it. He flexed the fist at his side and waited, for the last time.

A film of dirt covered the windshield, blocked his view of the culprit, and tried his patience. Finally, the red door flung open and a slim figure emerged.

Coming around to the front of the car, Mercy hopped up on the hood, rested her booted feet on the bumper, and smiled at him.

She was wearing cowboy boots.

He smiled back but didn't move, mostly because he couldn't. He was stunned. His heart leaped in his chest, happy to see her again.

"I gather you missed your plane, and you're in your uncle's good graces." He pointed his coffee mug toward the car.

Mercy couldn't stop smiling. He was so darn handsome and rugged and hers.

"I have a message for you from my uncle."

He nodded, barely. "Let's hear it."

"You were right. Uncle Parker perjured himself at your trial. He believed Grant when he said you had fought with Mark. Grant's lawyers have signed documents admitting their guilt and a check for restitution. It's a substantial amount."

She held up her hand, wanting to finish before she let Spence have his say. "My uncle and Grant were best friends, like you and Mark were. Like brothers. I know it doesn't excuse what Uncle Parker did, but I think it might help you to understand." She paused. His eyes were still, and he didn't say anything. "I know the money doesn't make up for what happened, but their sworn statements are contingent on you accepting compensation for your pain and suffering. They felt strongly...guilty about it."

"How much is it?"

The question surprised her. She didn't think the amount would interest him. "Enough to get your ranch up and running. Enough for a fresh start."

He nodded, putting his coffee mug on the porch railing. "Enough to turn down because I love you. Do you think I could accept the offer on the outside chance of implicating your uncle of perjury? I couldn't put your uncle in jail anymore than I could you."

Her heart pounded. She didn't argue, sure her uncle would convince him otherwise, talk him into accepting the money he deserved. She was here for another reason, to cement a future with the man she loved and who loved her.

"Oh, Spence." She slid from the hood of the car and pounced up the wooden steps and into his arms. "I know how important family and loyalty are to you. I'm privileged to be a part of that." She took his face in her hands and met his intense eyes. "I love you, too."

Their lips touched. His mouth, sensual and searching, fired her heart and her body. She tasted his profound need to love and be loved and returned his heartfelt feeling with her own. Softly, gently, giving and taking with her mouth. By the time he lifted his head away, they were both breathless and eager.

His serious eyes met hers. "When will you be leaving?"

"I'm not." When he blinked in surprise, she explained, "I'm applying to the University of Texas at San Antonio. The temp who's covering for me is glad to stay on at the medical office. My mother's going to ship my things and both my uncle and Cindy have offered me a place to stay until I get an apartment of my own."

"Stay with me." When she didn't answer right away, he added, "Or if you'd rather we take it slow and easy, stay with either of them."

"I'm partial to slow and easy," she slid her hands around his neck. "If I stay with Cindy or Uncle Parker, I'm sure to get more studying done, but you have that certain touch a hard-working student needs to relax."

"Like when I touch you here." He slid his hand between her thighs and cupped her. Even through the thickness of her jeans the heat built fast.

"Uh-huh," she moaned, swaying into him, widening her stance.

"And like this." He shifted his hand back and forth.

"Oh, yes." She coaxed him on by rocking her hips.

"And this." He swung her up in his arms and headed toward the screen door and into the house.

"And exactly why you're my dream guy." She hugged his neck tighter.

Heading toward the screen door and into the house, he said in a voice husky with promise, "Let's see about making all of our dreams come true."

About the author...

Sylvie Kaye was born and raised in Pennsylvania in the shadows of the Pocono Mountains and its honeymoon havens where she breathes the air of romance daily. After getting one short story published in 1994, she went from hooked on reading romances to hooked on writing them. Her years of work experience in varied jobs from manufacturing to retail and banking, to name a few, lend itself to writing contemporary romances. Road trips to exciting locations in our beautiful country inspire the settings for her stories.

Contact Sylvie at sylviekaye@sylviekaye.com
or visit www.sylviekaye.com

Printed in the United States
134240LV00007B/72/P

9 781601 543936